THUNDEROUS

W9-BCG-553

by
M.L. SMOKER &
NATALIE PEETERSE

cover by
Oriol Vidal

interior illustrations by
Dale Deforest

color by
Adriano Augusto,
Wendy Broome,
Lisa Moore,
and
Omi Remalante Jr.

Curiosity Ink Media

CURIOSITY BOOKS   LOS ANGELES

This is a work of fiction. Names, characters, places, and incidents either are the product of the authors' imagination or are used fictitiously. Any resemblance to actual persons, living or dead, events, or locales is entirely coincidental.

ISBN: 978-1-948206-46-4

Printed in Canada

April 2022

10 9 8 7 6 5 4 3 2

Second U.S. Edition

CURIOSITY BOOKS
An Imprint of Curiosity Ink Media, LLC
15301 Ventura Boulevard, Suite 340
Sherman Oaks, California 91403 USA
www.curiosityinkmedia.com

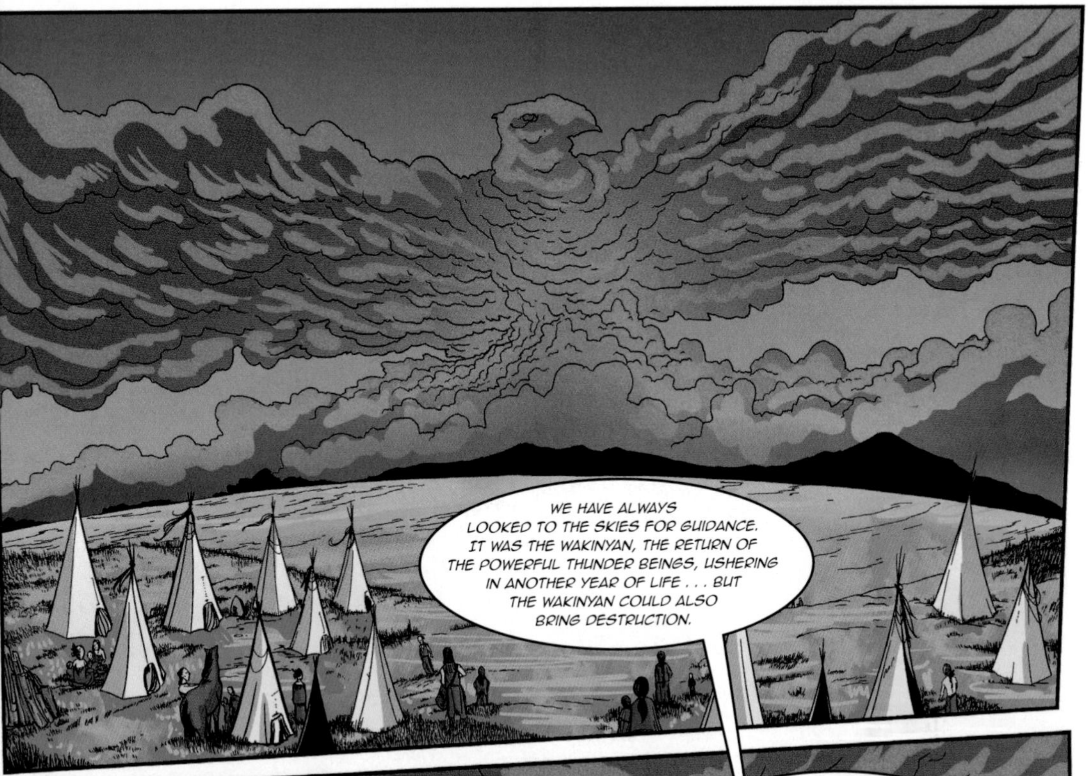
WE HAVE ALWAYS LOOKED TO THE SKIES FOR GUIDANCE. IT WAS THE WAKINYAN, THE RETURN OF THE POWERFUL THUNDER BEINGS, USHERING IN ANOTHER YEAR OF LIFE . . . BUT THE WAKINYAN COULD ALSO BRING DESTRUCTION.

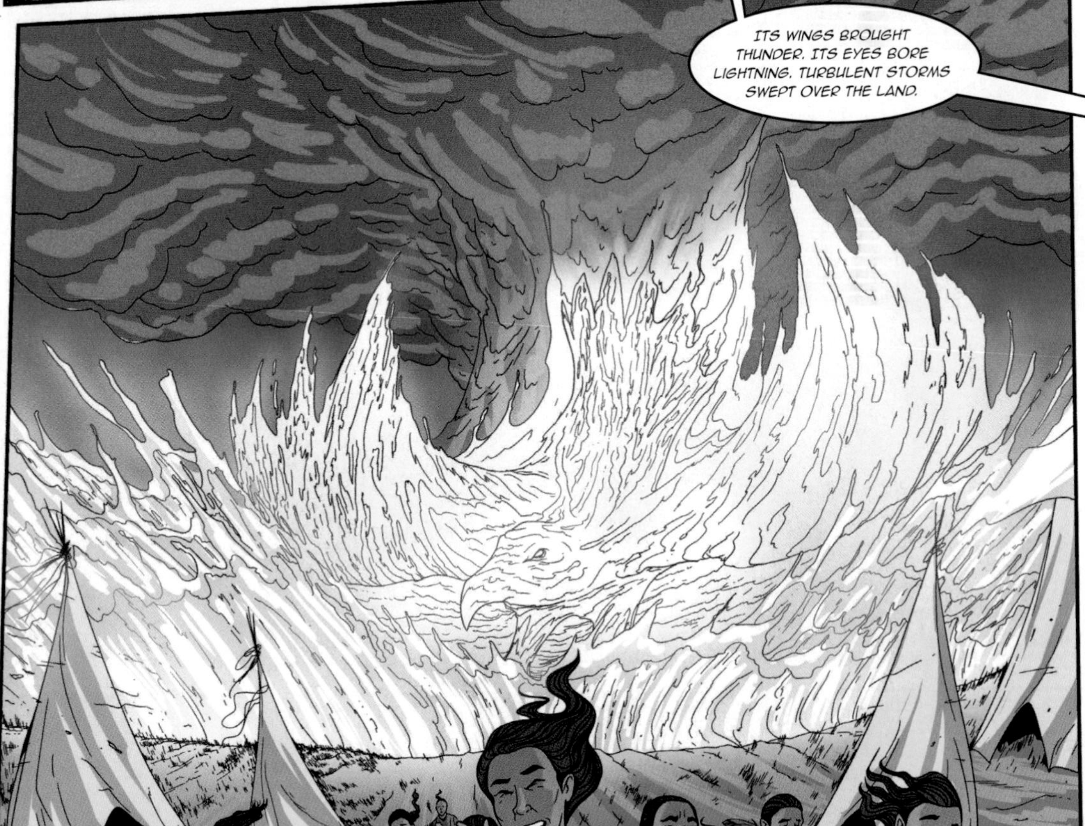
ITS WINGS BROUGHT THUNDER. ITS EYES BORE LIGHTNING. TURBULENT STORMS SWEPT OVER THE LAND.

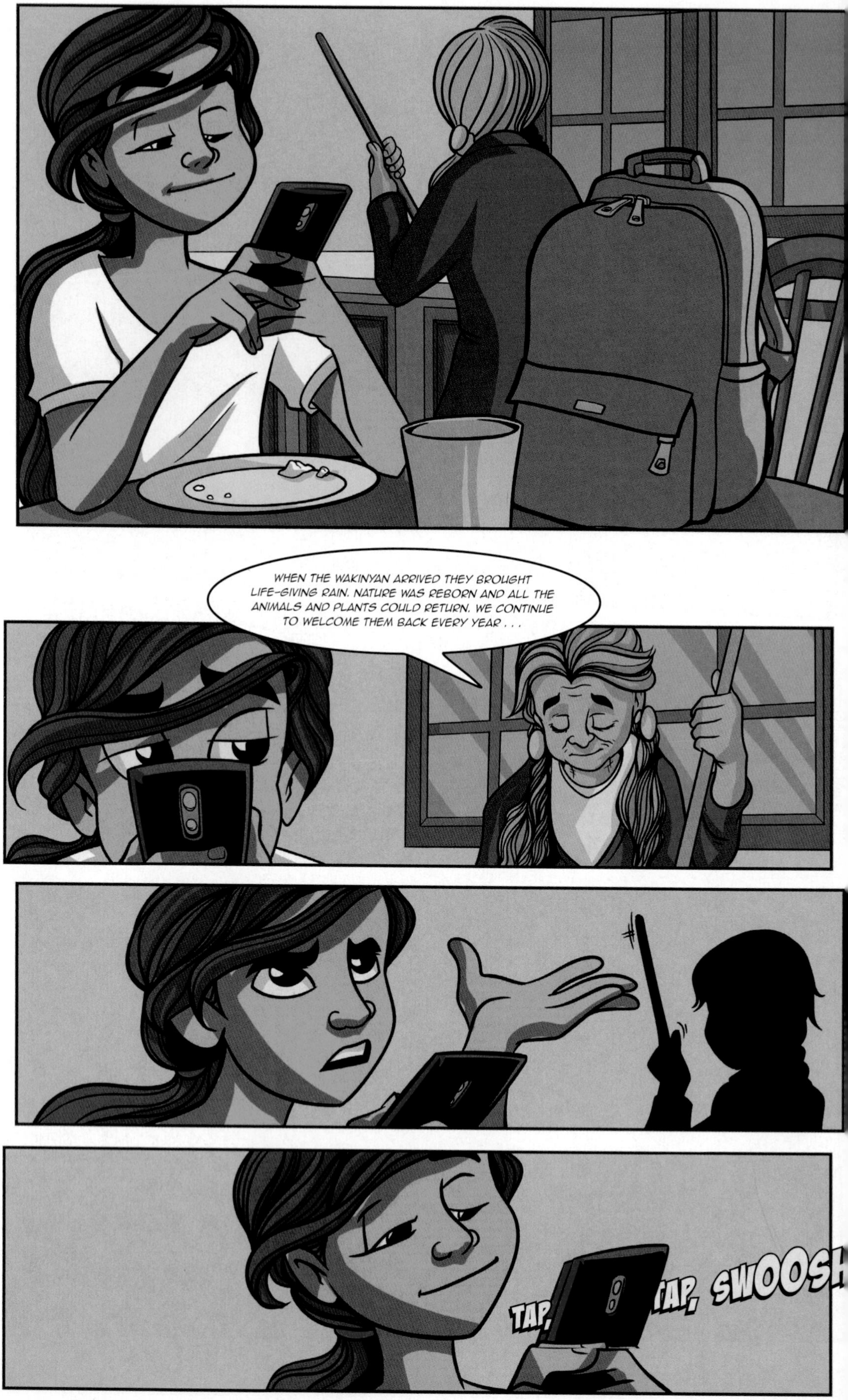
WHEN THE WAKINYAN ARRIVED THEY BROUGHT LIFE-GIVING RAIN. NATURE WAS REBORN AND ALL THE ANIMALS AND PLANTS COULD RETURN. WE CONTINUE TO WELCOME THEM BACK EVERY YEAR . . .
TAP, TAP, SWOOSH

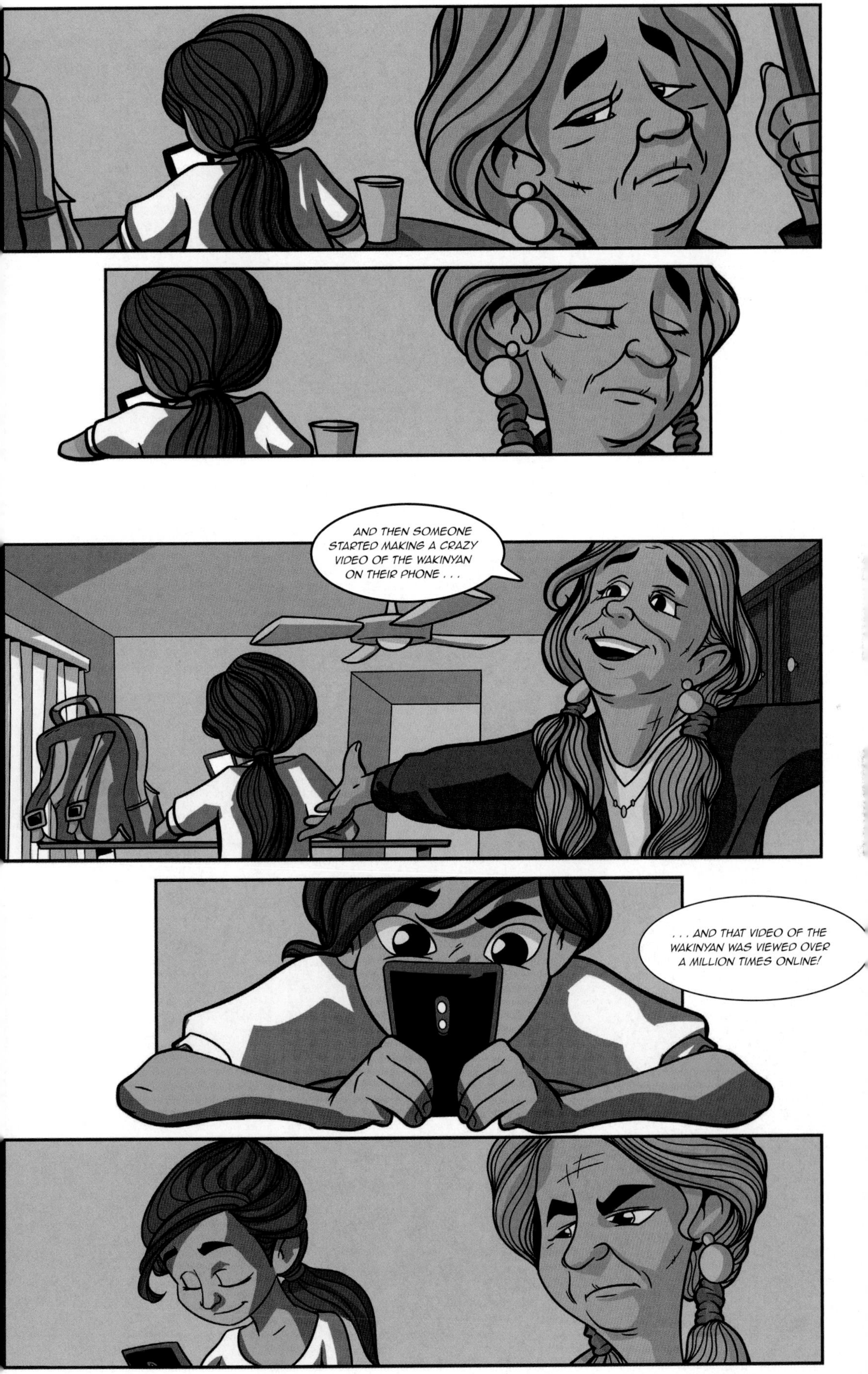
AND THEN SOMEONE STARTED MAKING A CRAZY VIDEO OF THE WAKINYAN ON THEIR PHONE . . .
. . . AND THAT VIDEO OF THE WAKINYAN WAS VIEWED OVER A MILLION TIMES ONLINE!

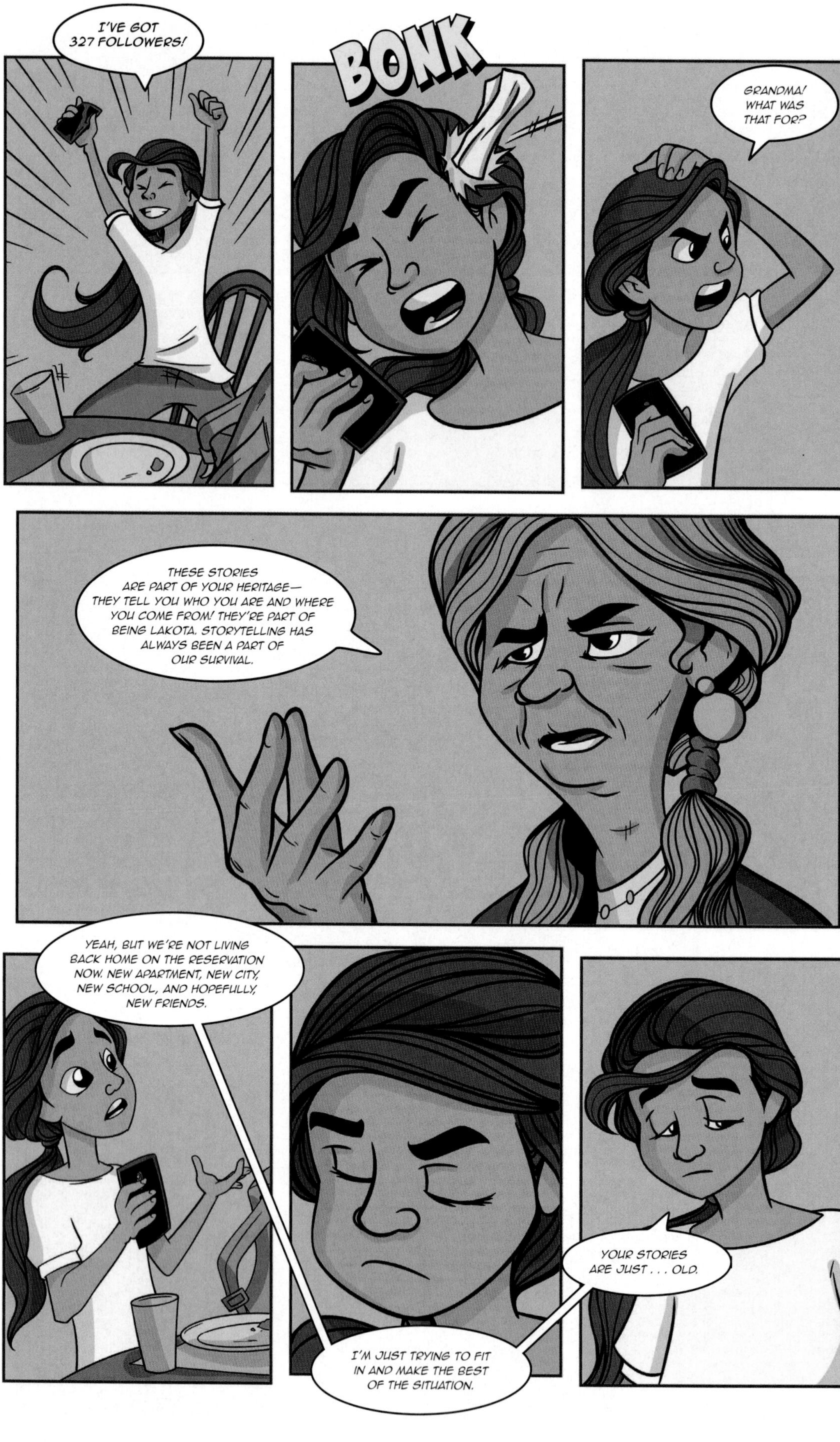
I'VE GOT 327 FOLLOWERS!
BONK
GRANDMA! WHAT WAS THAT FOR?
THESE STORIES ARE PART OF YOUR HERITAGE— THEY TELL YOU WHO YOU ARE AND WHERE YOU COME FROM! THEY'RE PART OF BEING LAKOTA. STORYTELLING HAS ALWAYS BEEN A PART OF OUR SURVIVAL.
YEAH, BUT WE'RE NOT LIVING BACK HOME ON THE RESERVATION NOW. NEW APARTMENT, NEW CITY, NEW SCHOOL, AND HOPEFULLY, NEW FRIENDS.
I'M JUST TRYING TO FIT IN AND MAKE THE BEST OF THE SITUATION.
YOUR STORIES ARE JUST . . . OLD.

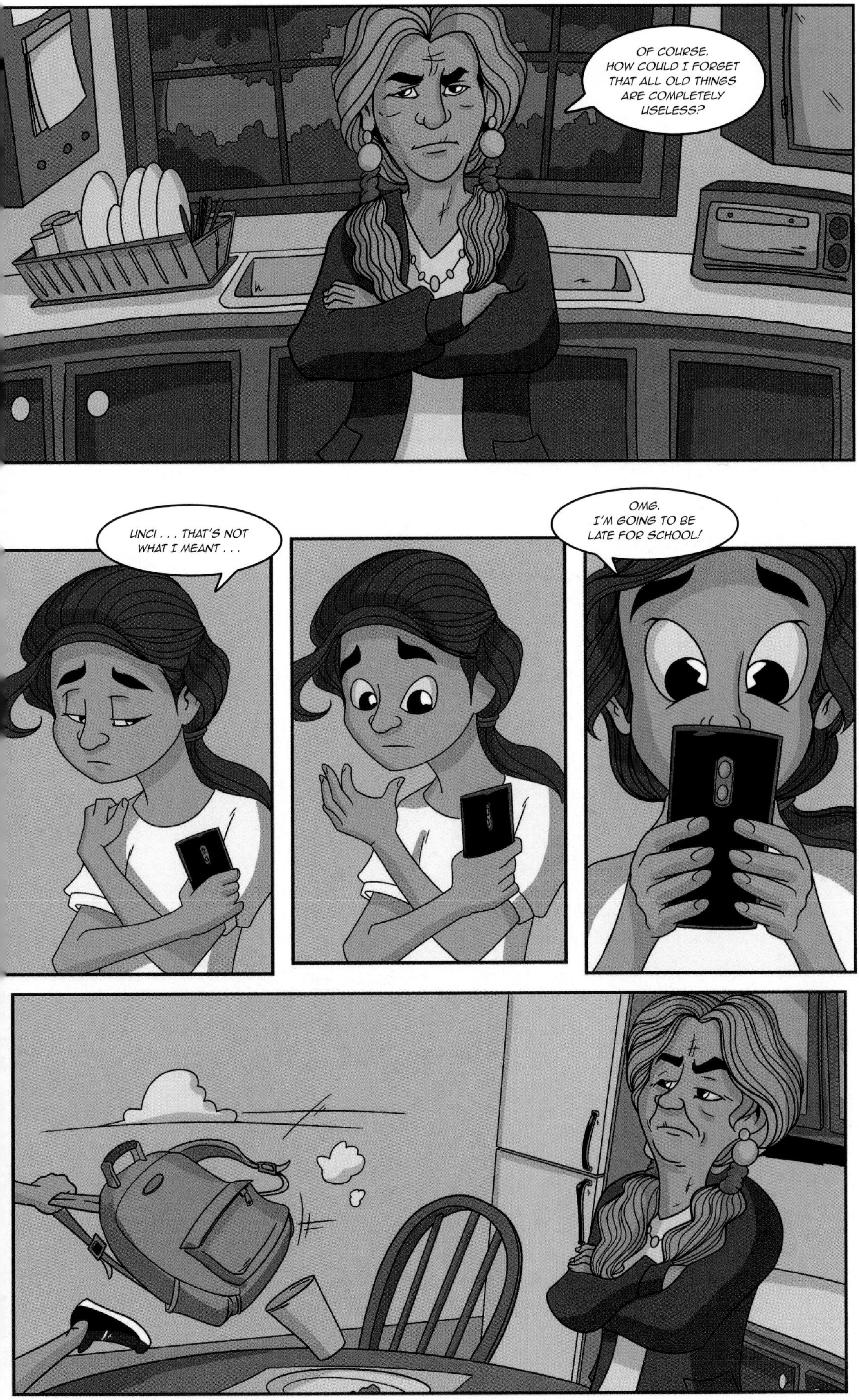
OF COURSE.
HOW COULD I FORGET
THAT ALL OLD THINGS
ARE COMPLETELY
USELESS?
UNCI . . . THAT'S NOT
WHAT I MEANT . . .
OMG.
I'M GOING TO BE
LATE FOR SCHOOL!

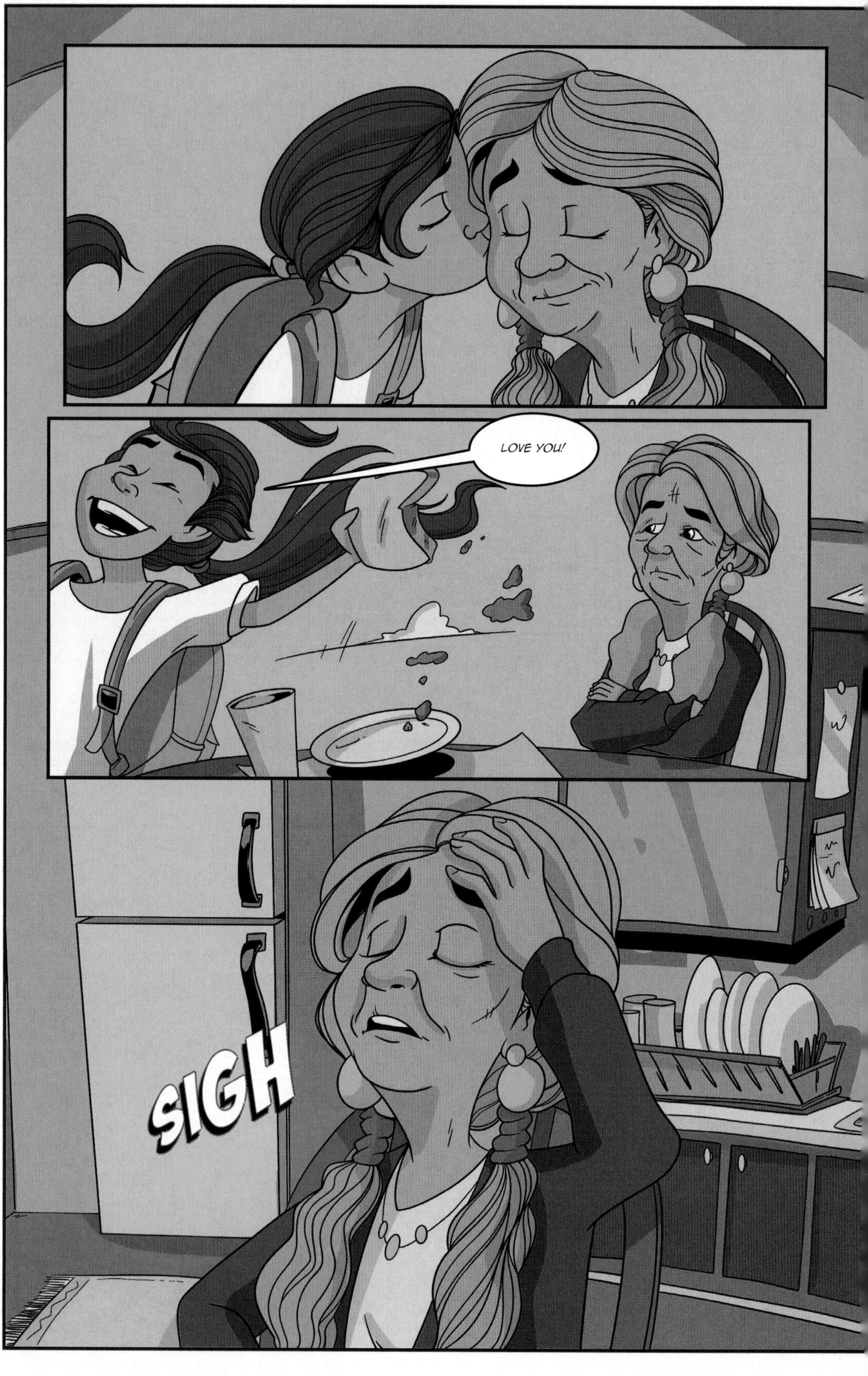
LOVE YOU!
SIGH

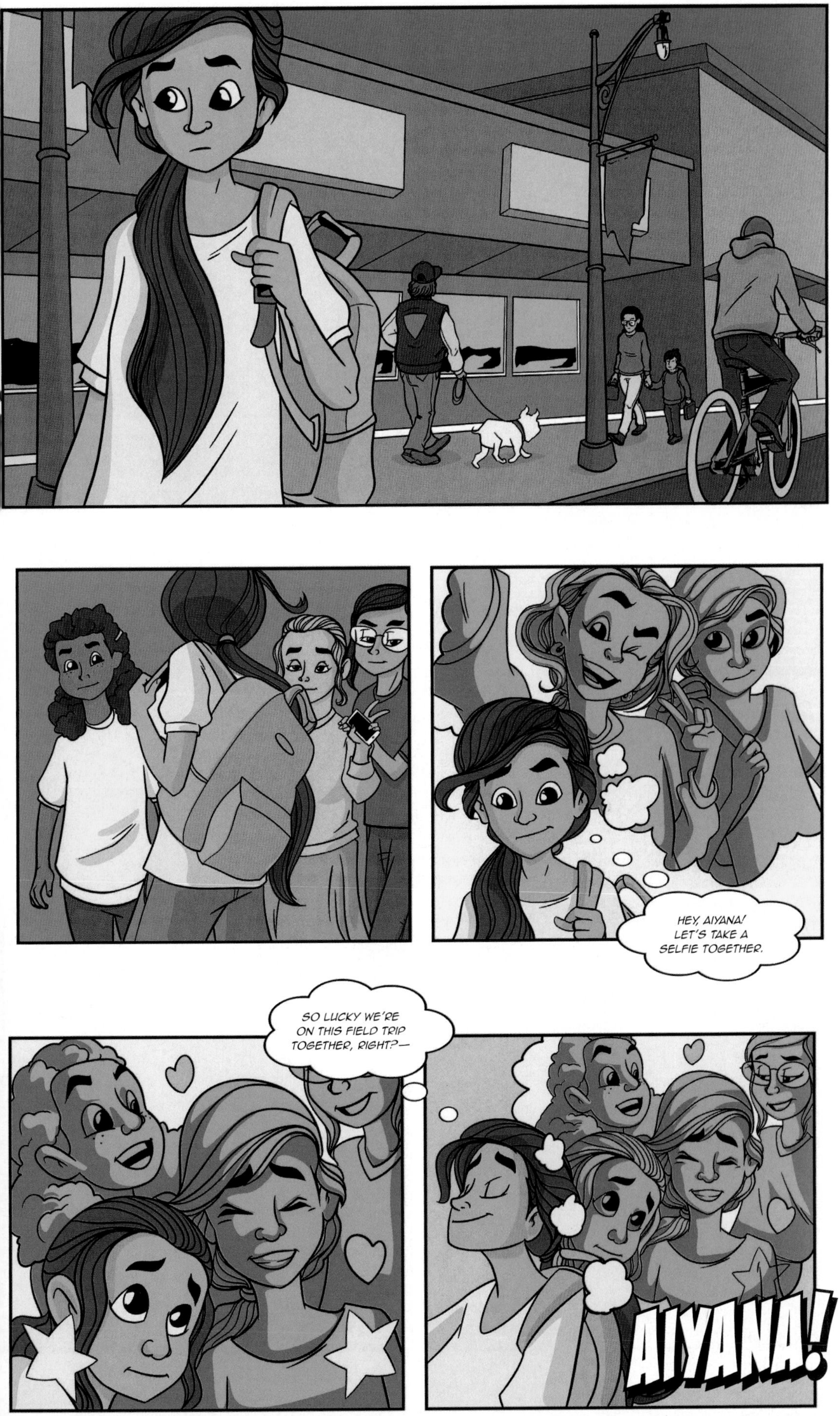
HEY, AIYANA!
LET'S TAKE A
SELFIE TOGETHER.
SO LUCKY WE'RE
ON THIS FIELD TRIP
TOGETHER, RIGHT?—
AIYANA!

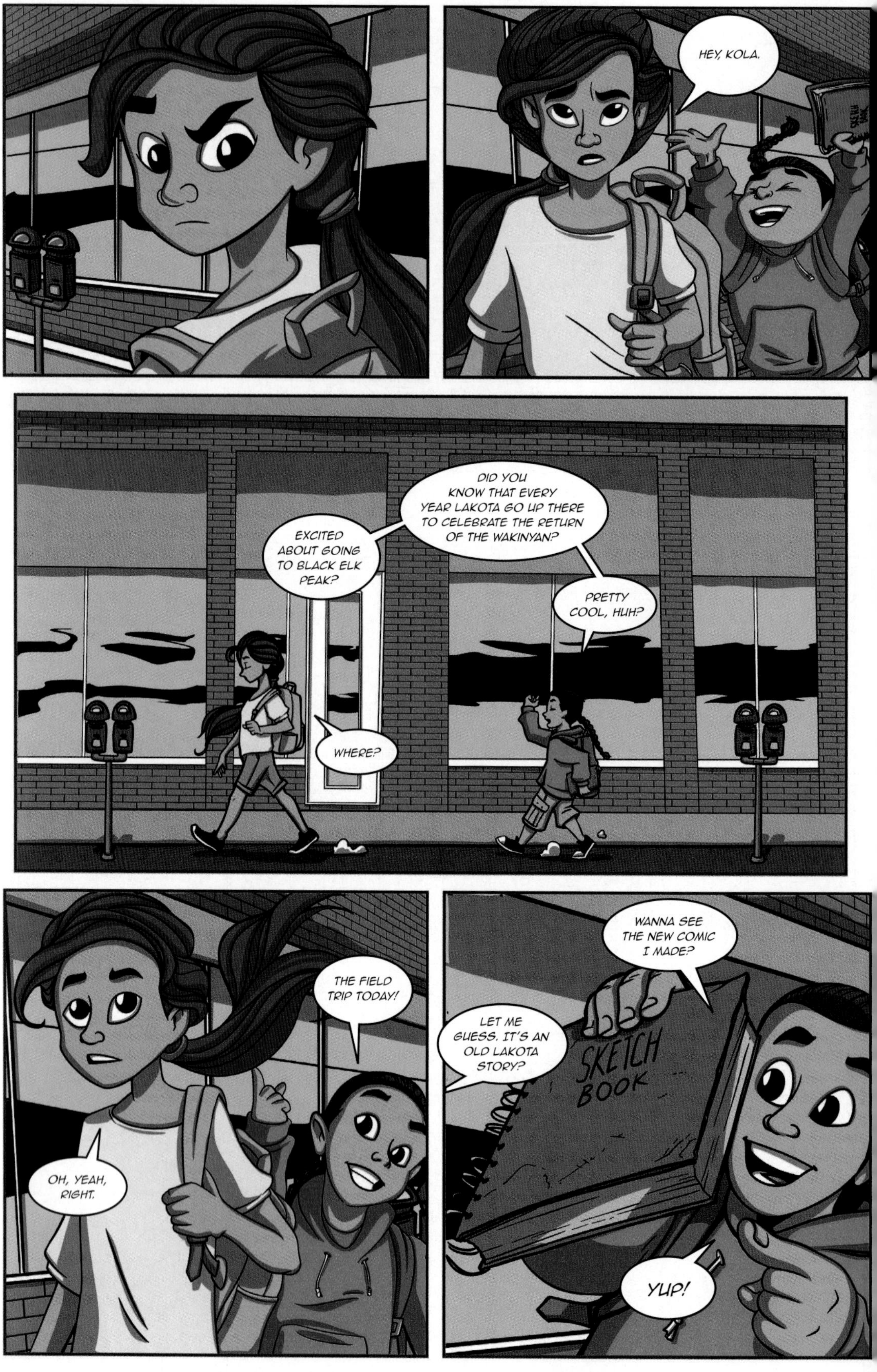
HEY, KOLA.
SKETCH BOOK
EXCITED ABOUT GOING TO BLACK ELK PEAK?
DID YOU KNOW THAT EVERY YEAR LAKOTA GO UP THERE TO CELEBRATE THE RETURN OF THE WAKINYAN?
PRETTY COOL, HUH?
WHERE?
THE FIELD TRIP TODAY!
OH, YEAH, RIGHT.
WANNA SEE THE NEW COMIC I MADE?
LET ME GUESS. IT'S AN OLD LAKOTA STORY?
SKETCH BOOK
YUP!

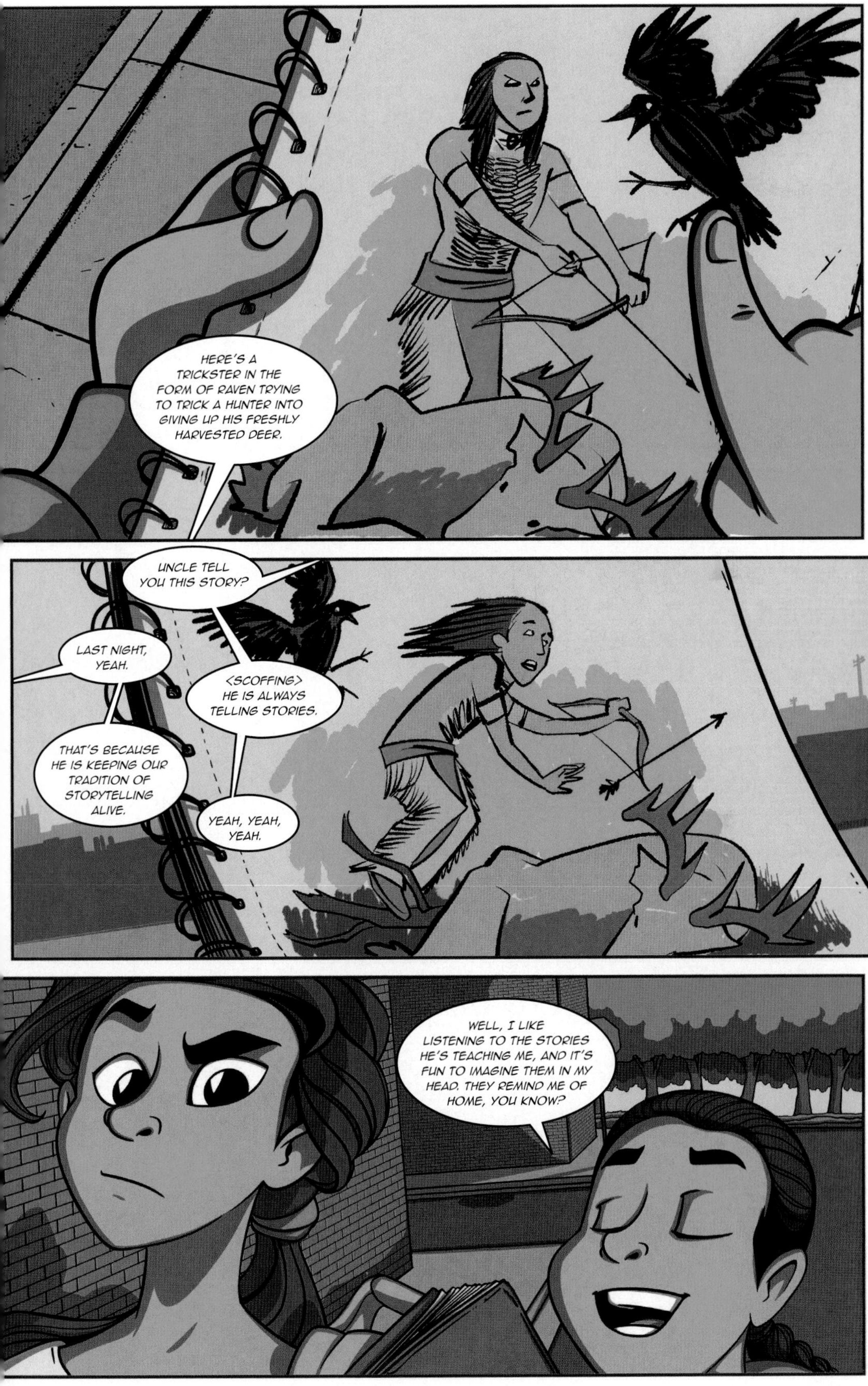
HERE'S A TRICKSTER IN THE FORM OF RAVEN TRYING TO TRICK A HUNTER INTO GIVING UP HIS FRESHLY HARVESTED DEER.
UNCLE TELL YOU THIS STORY?
LAST NIGHT, YEAH.
<SCOFFING> HE IS ALWAYS TELLING STORIES.
THAT'S BECAUSE HE IS KEEPING OUR TRADITION OF STORYTELLING ALIVE.
YEAH, YEAH, YEAH.
WELL, I LIKE LISTENING TO THE STORIES HE'S TEACHING ME, AND IT'S FUN TO IMAGINE THEM IN MY HEAD. THEY REMIND ME OF HOME, YOU KNOW?

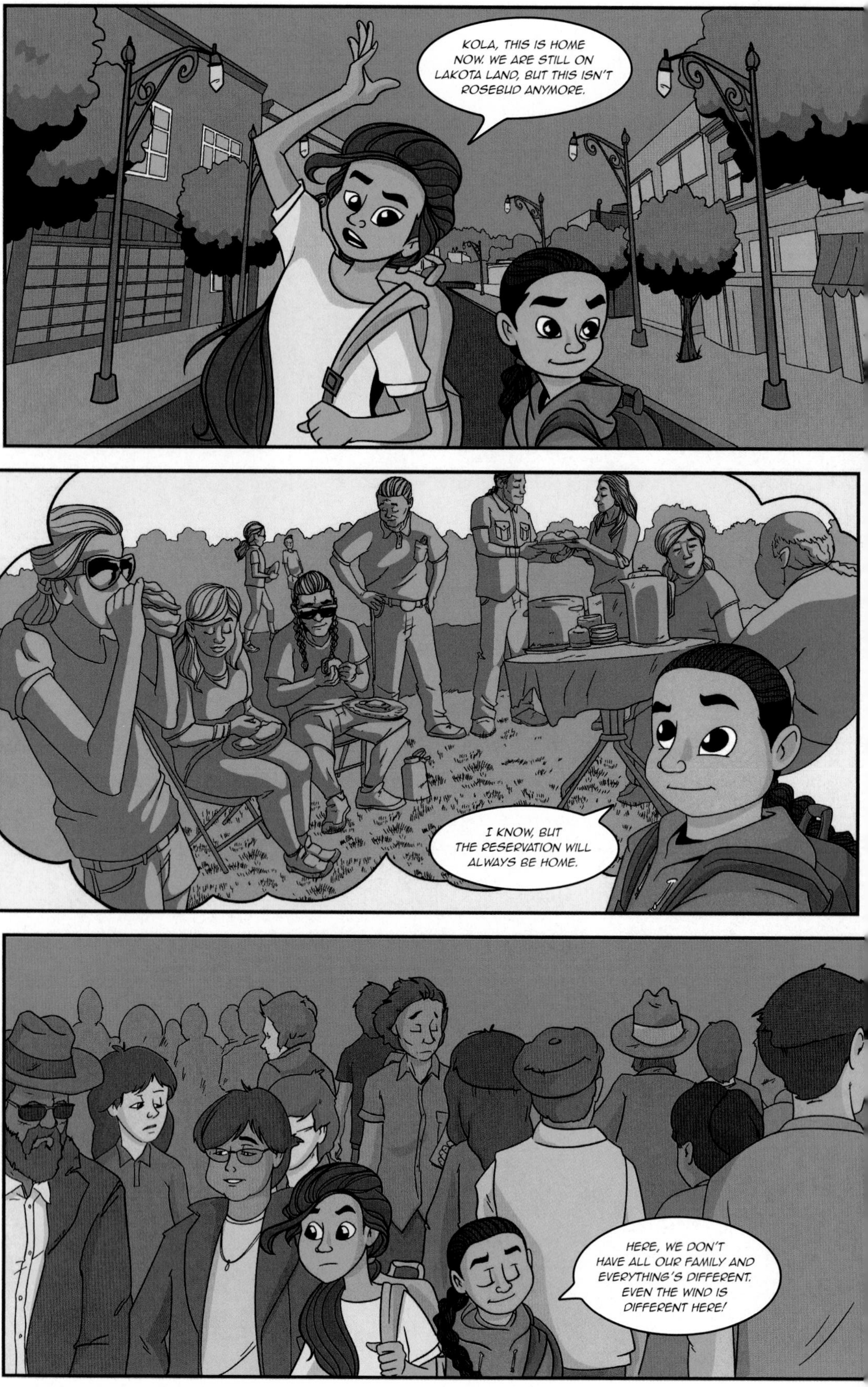
KOLA, THIS IS HOME NOW. WE ARE STILL ON LAKOTA LAND, BUT THIS ISN'T ROSEBUD ANYMORE.
I KNOW, BUT THE RESERVATION WILL ALWAYS BE HOME.
HERE, WE DON'T HAVE ALL OUR FAMILY AND EVERYTHING'S DIFFERENT. EVEN THE WIND IS DIFFERENT HERE!

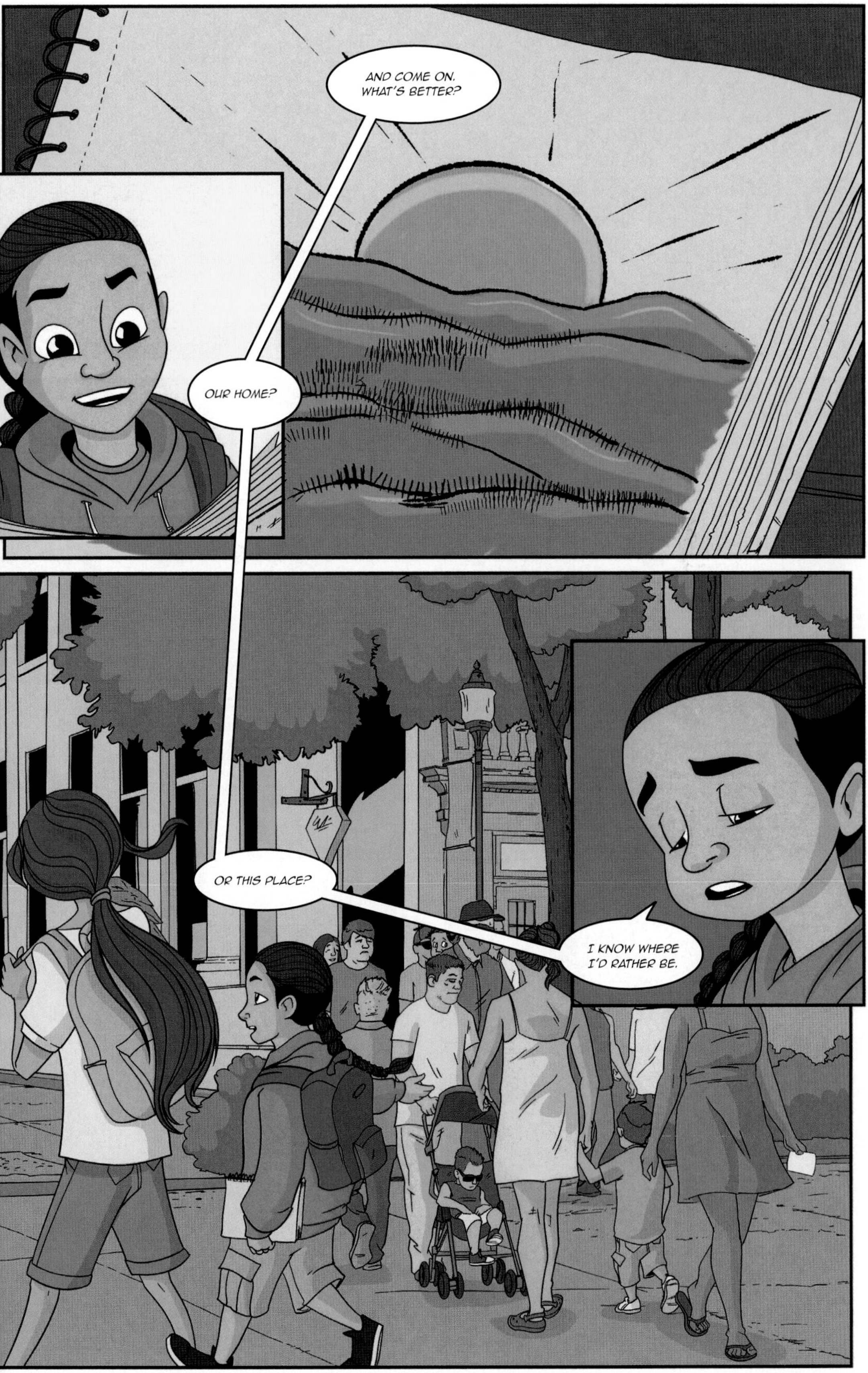
AND COME ON. WHAT'S BETTER?
OUR HOME?
OR THIS PLACE?
I KNOW WHERE I'D RATHER BE.

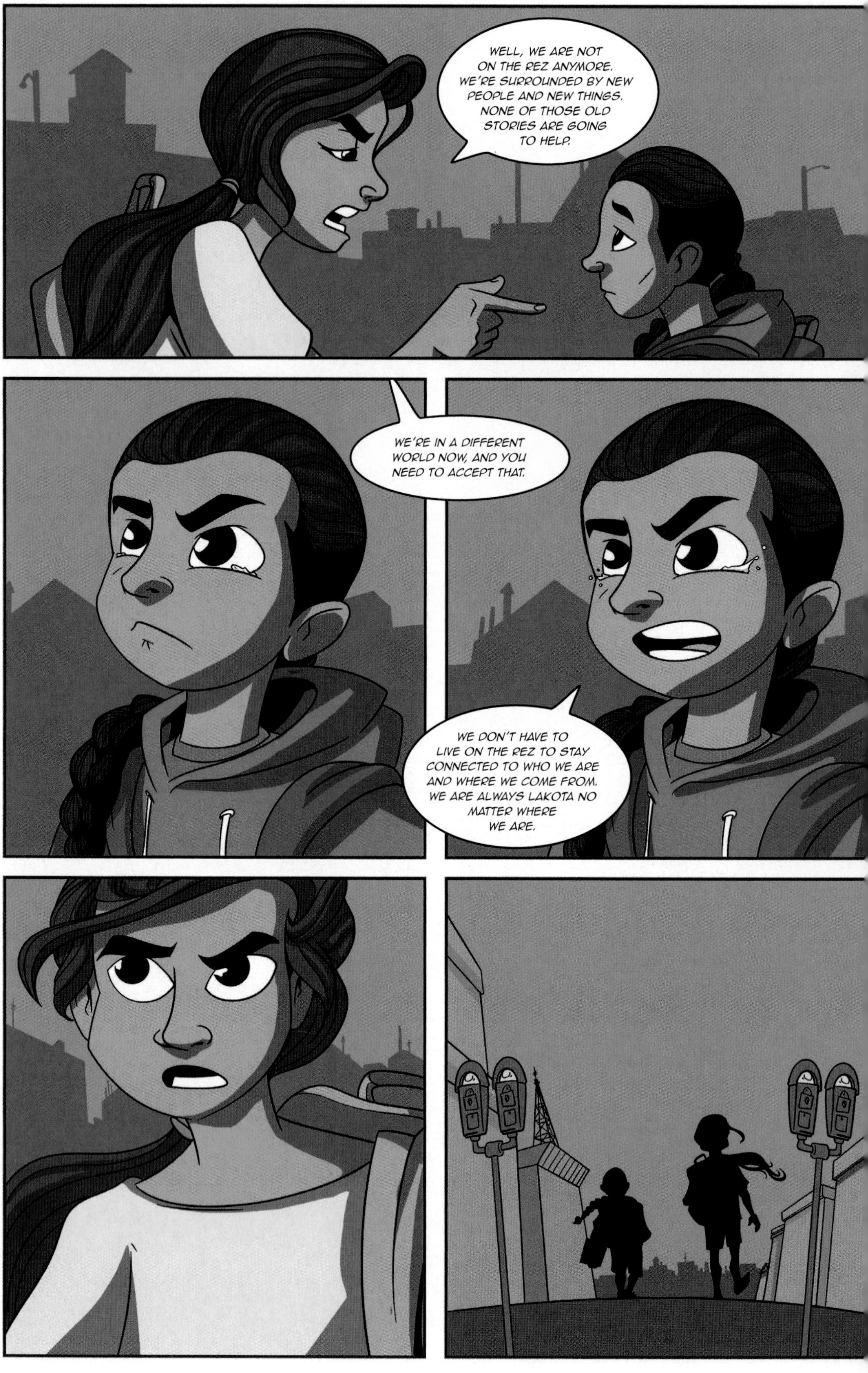
WELL, WE ARE NOT ON THE REZ ANYMORE. WE'RE SURROUNDED BY NEW PEOPLE AND NEW THINGS. NONE OF THOSE OLD STORIES ARE GOING TO HELP.
WE'RE IN A DIFFERENT WORLD NOW, AND YOU NEED TO ACCEPT THAT.
WE DON'T HAVE TO LIVE ON THE REZ TO STAY CONNECTED TO WHO WE ARE AND WHERE WE COME FROM. WE ARE ALWAYS LAKOTA NO MATTER WHERE WE ARE.

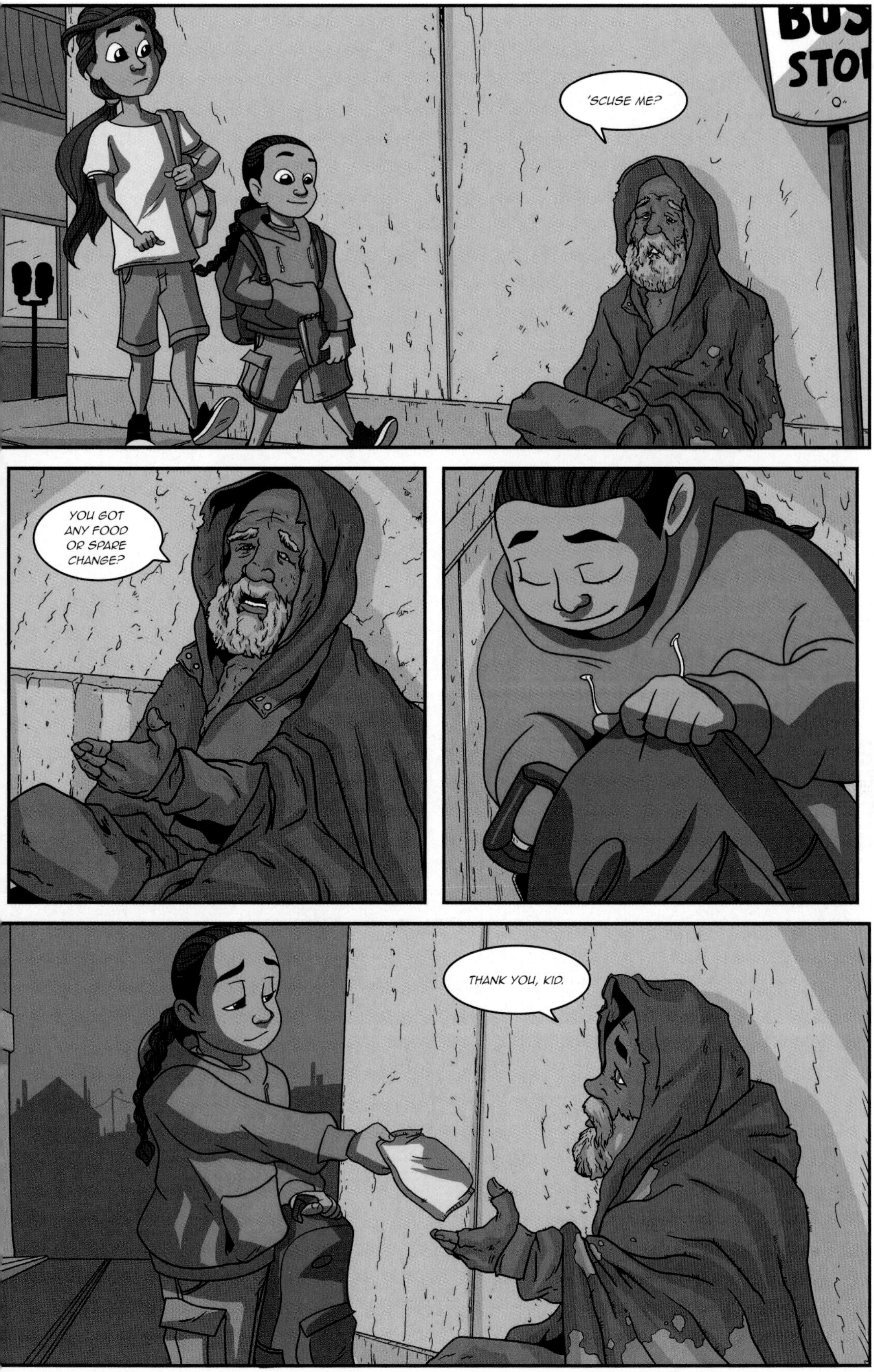
BUS STO
'SCUSE ME?
YOU GOT ANY FOOD OR SPARE CHANGE?
THANK YOU, KID.

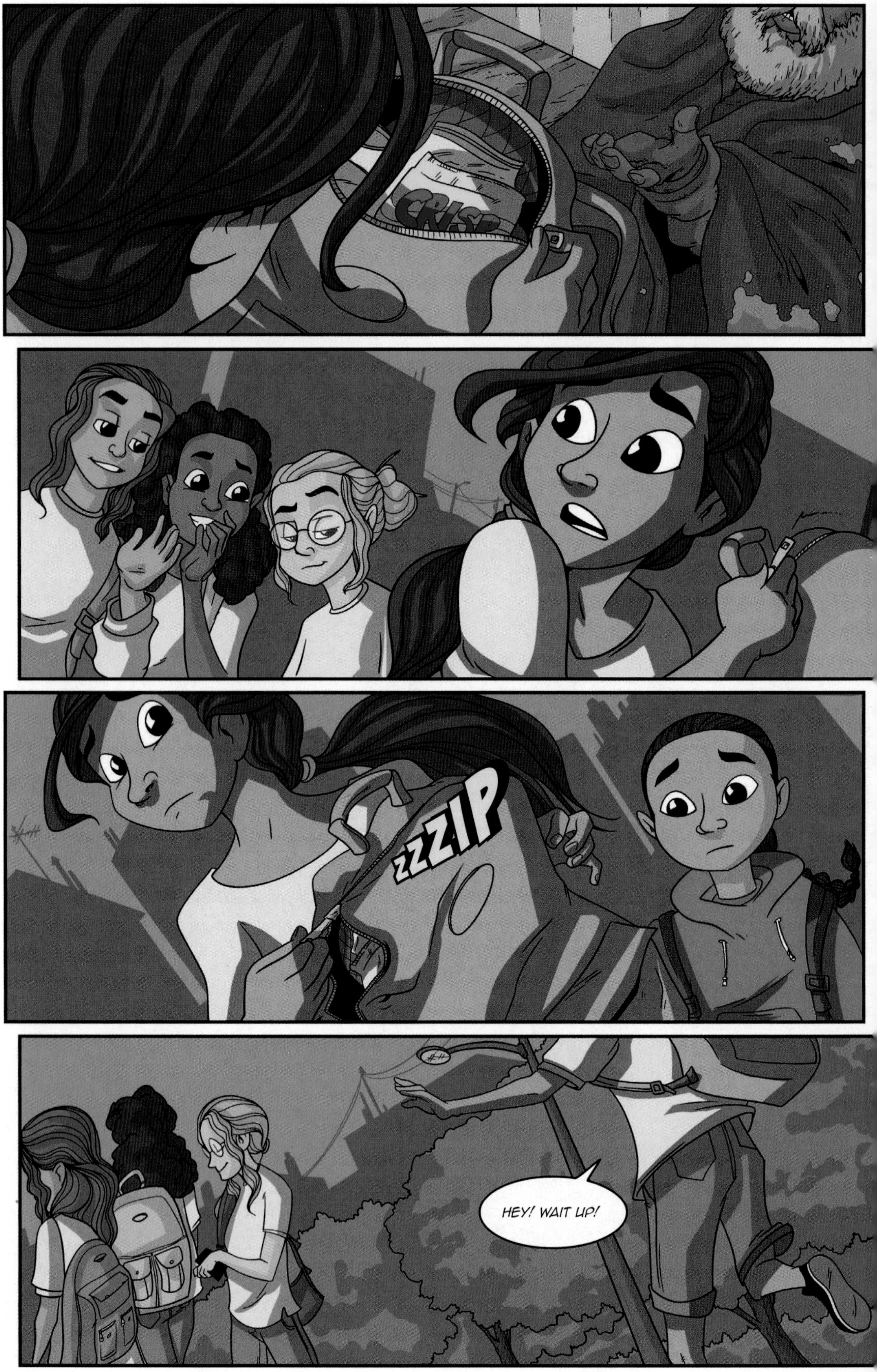
CRISP
ZZZIP
HEY! WAIT UP!

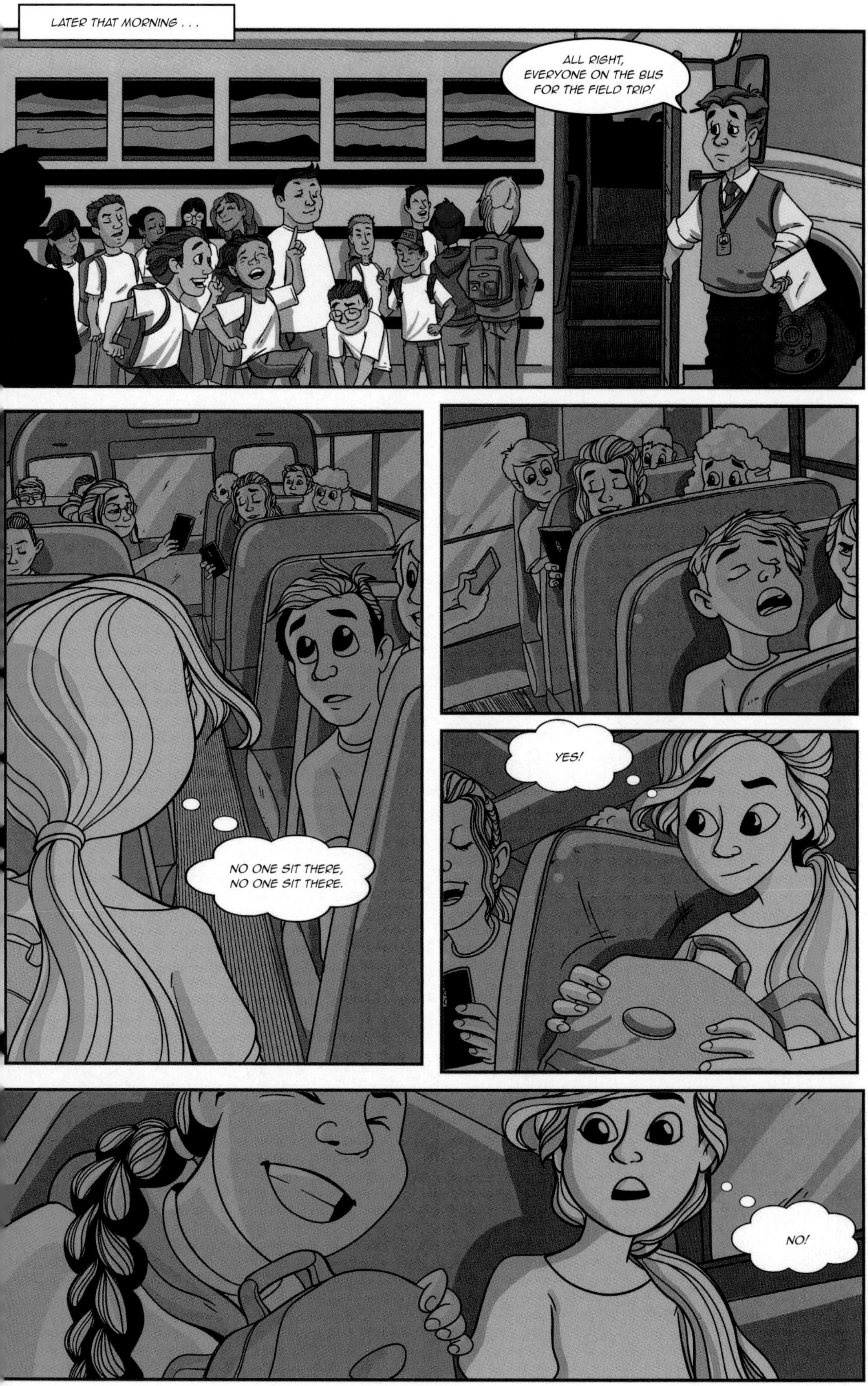
LATER THAT MORNING . . .
ALL RIGHT, EVERYONE ON THE BUS FOR THE FIELD TRIP!
NO ONE SIT THERE, NO ONE SIT THERE.
YES!
NO!

I CAN'T WAIT TO GET TO BLACK ELK PEAK.

WHY? IT'S A ROCK.

WHAT ARE YOU TALKING ABOUT? IT IS A SACRED PLACE.

THE PEAK IS NAMED AFTER BLACK ELK. HE WAS AN IMPORTANT LAKOTA FIGURE WHO HAD A VISION WHEN HE WAS YOUNG, WHERE HE JOURNEYED INTO A CLOUD WORLD WHERE HE MET THE SIX GRANDFATHERS.

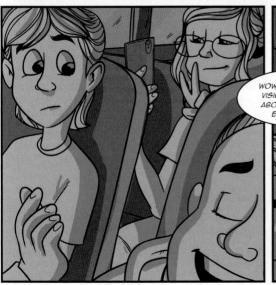

WOW, WHAT A SUPER VISION. LET'S TALK ABOUT SOMETHING ELSE, OKAY?

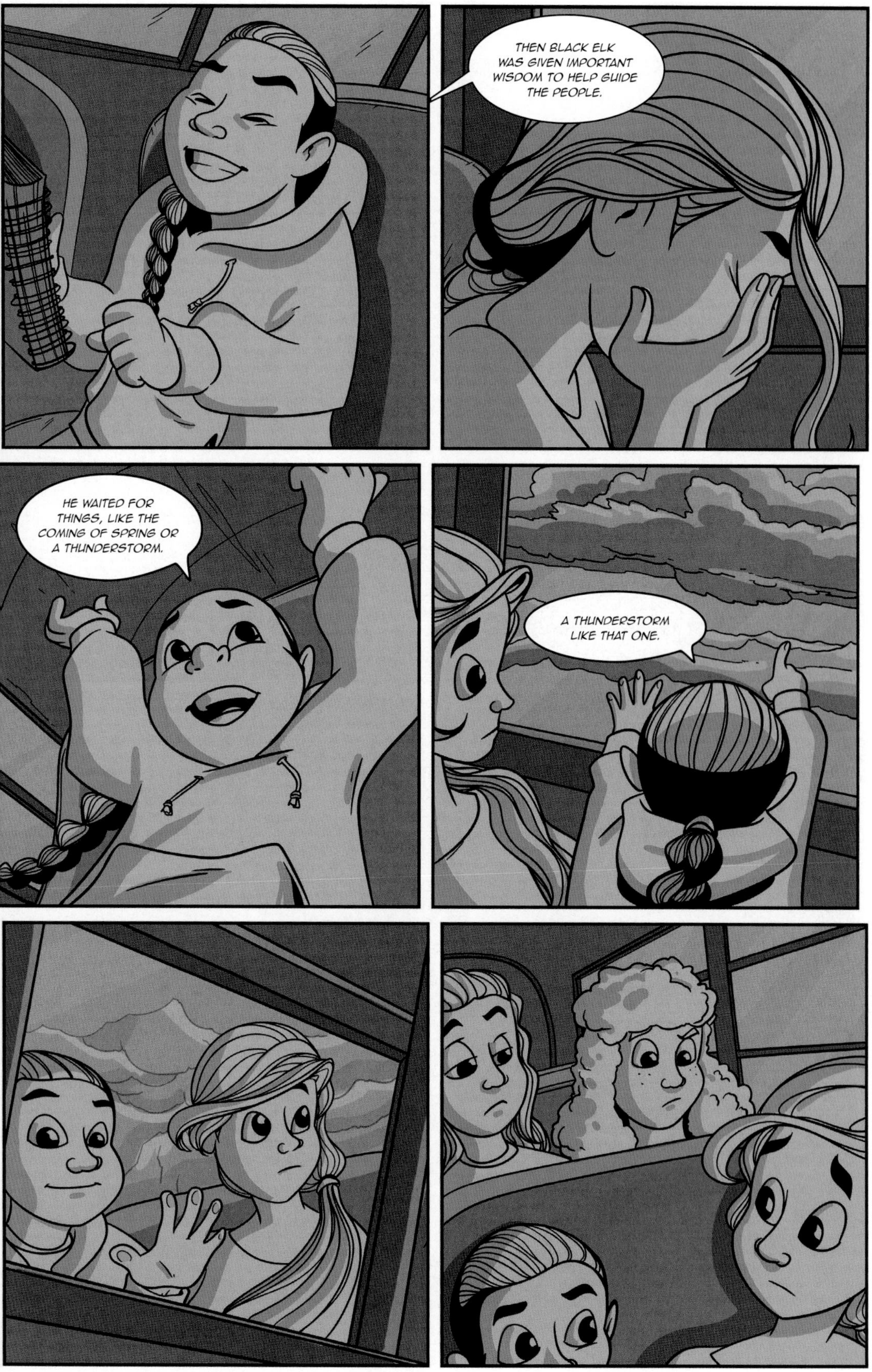
THEN BLACK ELK WAS GIVEN IMPORTANT WISDOM TO HELP GUIDE THE PEOPLE.
HE WAITED FOR THINGS, LIKE THE COMING OF SPRING OR A THUNDERSTORM.
A THUNDERSTORM LIKE THAT ONE.

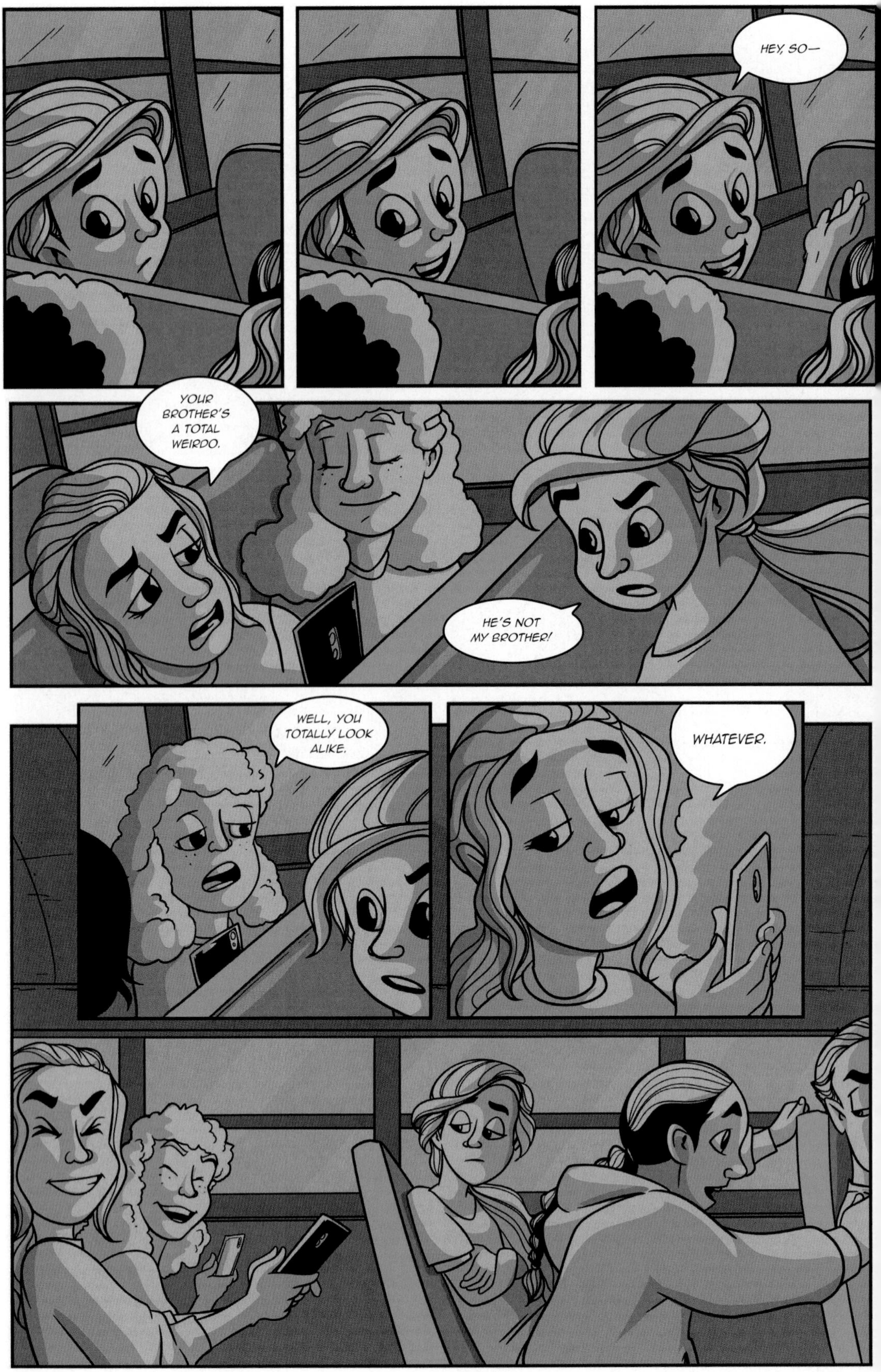
HEY, SO—
YOUR BROTHER'S A TOTAL WEIRDO.
HE'S NOT MY BROTHER!
WELL, YOU TOTALLY LOOK ALIKE.
WHATEVER.

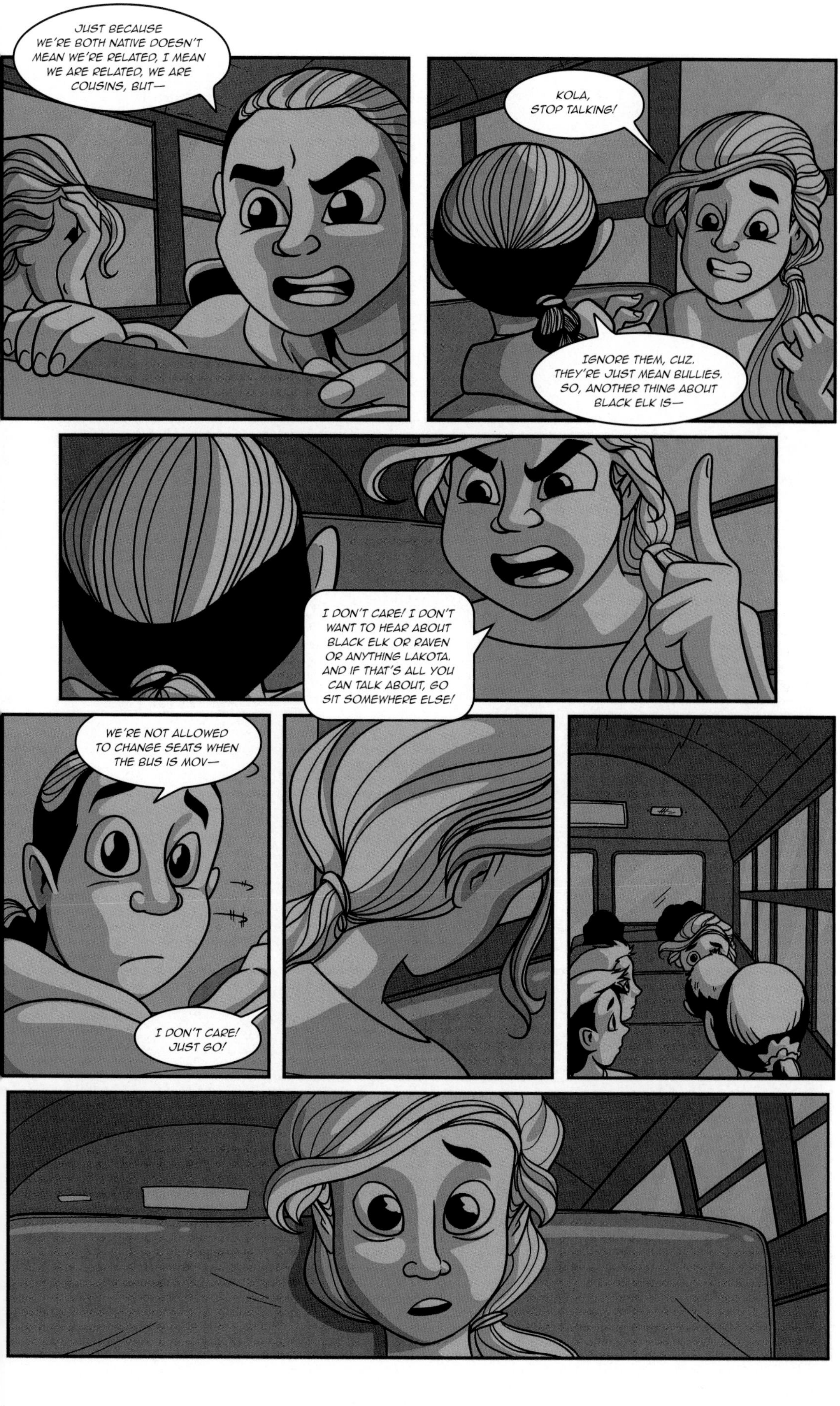
JUST BECAUSE WE'RE BOTH NATIVE DOESN'T MEAN WE'RE RELATED, I MEAN WE ARE RELATED, WE ARE COUSINS, BUT—
KOLA, STOP TALKING!
IGNORE THEM, CUZ. THEY'RE JUST MEAN BULLIES. SO, ANOTHER THING ABOUT BLACK ELK IS—
I DON'T CARE! I DON'T WANT TO HEAR ABOUT BLACK ELK OR RAVEN OR ANYTHING LAKOTA. AND IF THAT'S ALL YOU CAN TALK ABOUT, GO SIT SOMEWHERE ELSE!
WE'RE NOT ALLOWED TO CHANGE SEATS WHEN THE BUS IS MOV—
I DON'T CARE! JUST GO!

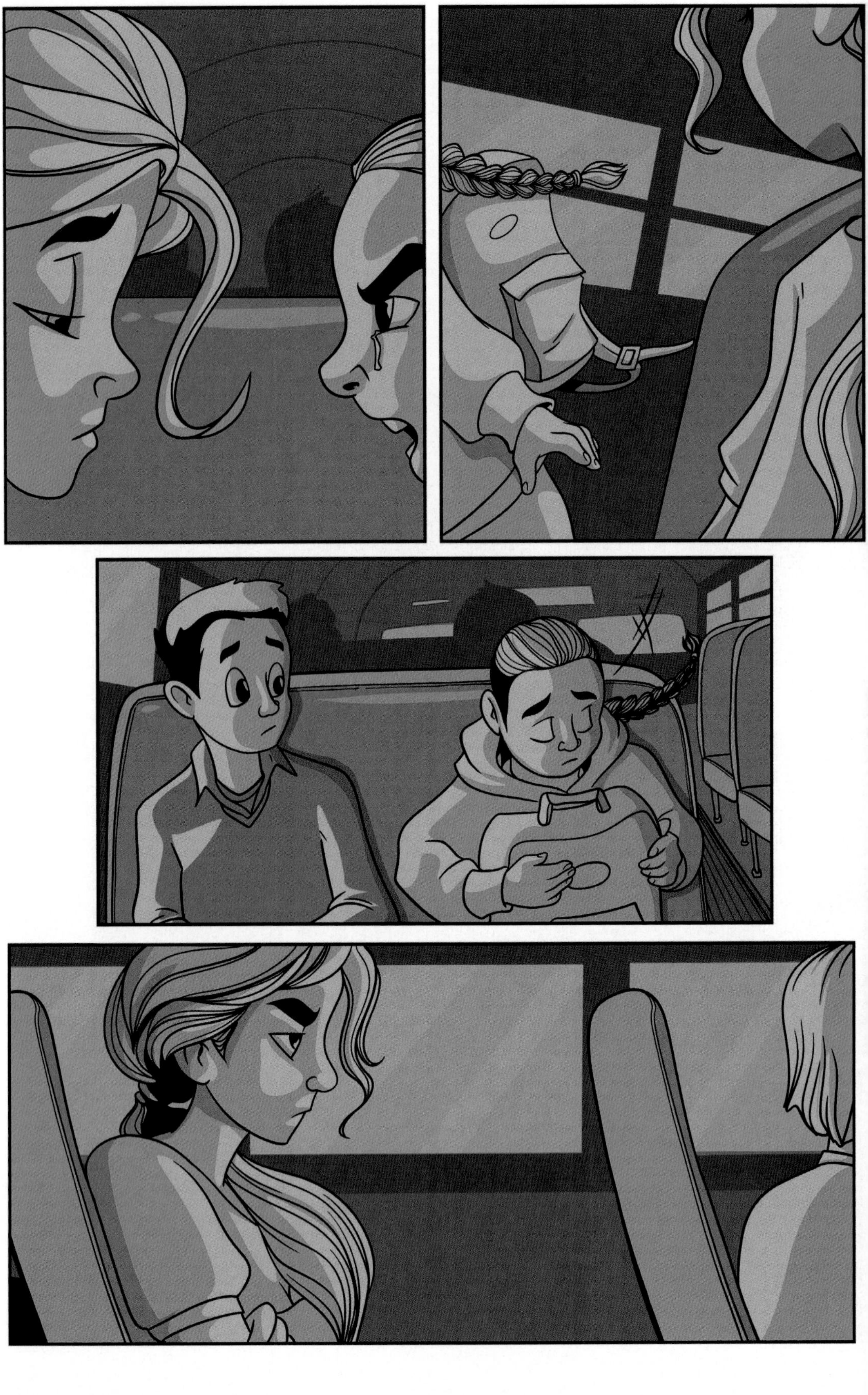

AT THE BLACK ELK PEAK TRAILHEAD.
BLACK ELK MTN TRAIL HEAD
OPEN
LISTEN UP! THIS IS RANGER RED CROW.
MORNING, KIDS. IT'S ABOUT A THREE-MILE HIKE FROM HERE TO THE PEAK ITSELF.
WE HAVE TO HIKE?
IS THERE, LIKE, AN ELEVATOR?
GROAN

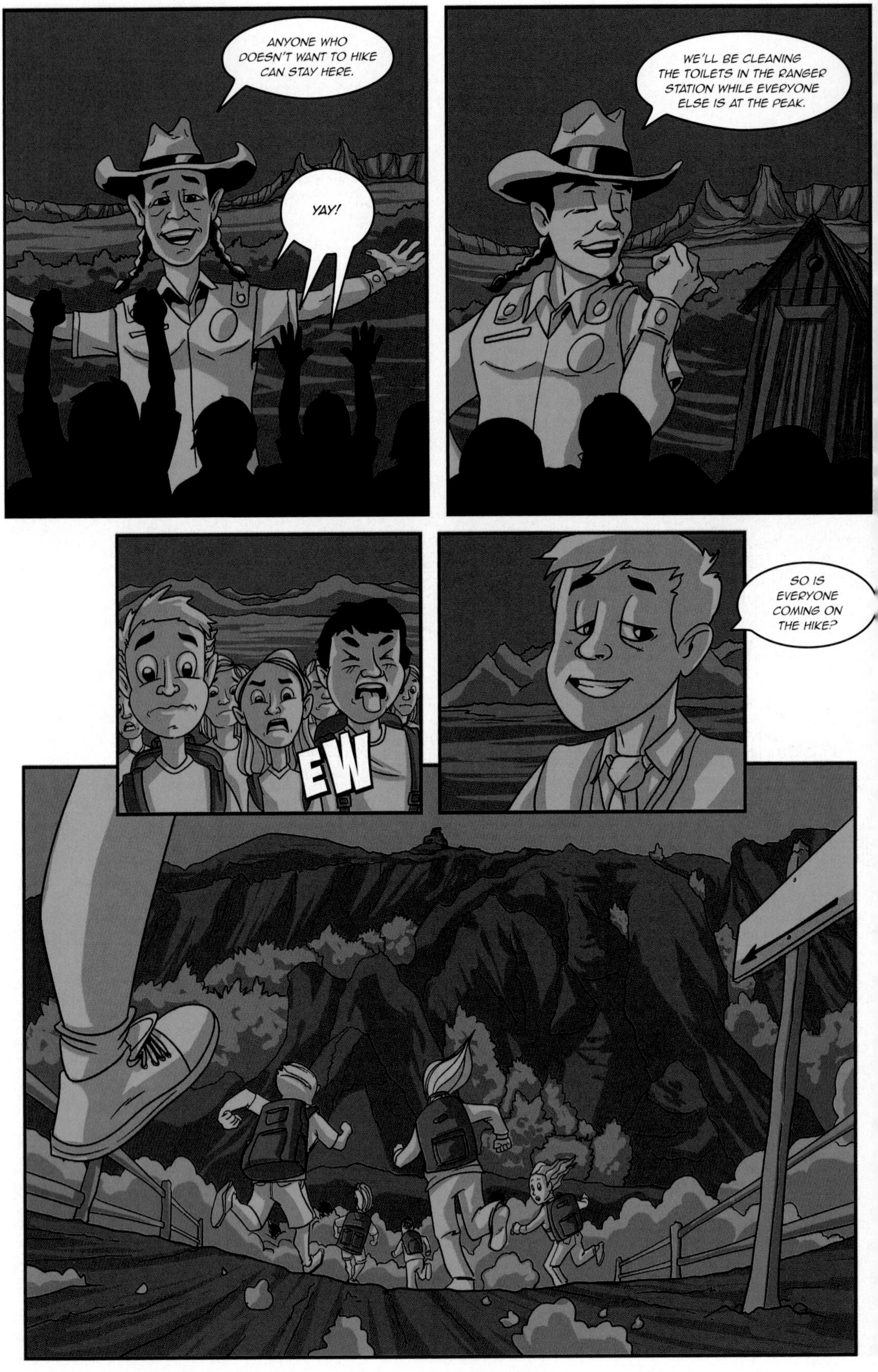
ANYONE WHO DOESN'T WANT TO HIKE CAN STAY HERE.
YAY!
WE'LL BE CLEANING THE TOILETS IN THE RANGER STATION WHILE EVERYONE ELSE IS AT THE PEAK.
EW
SO IS EVERYONE COMING ON THE HIKE?

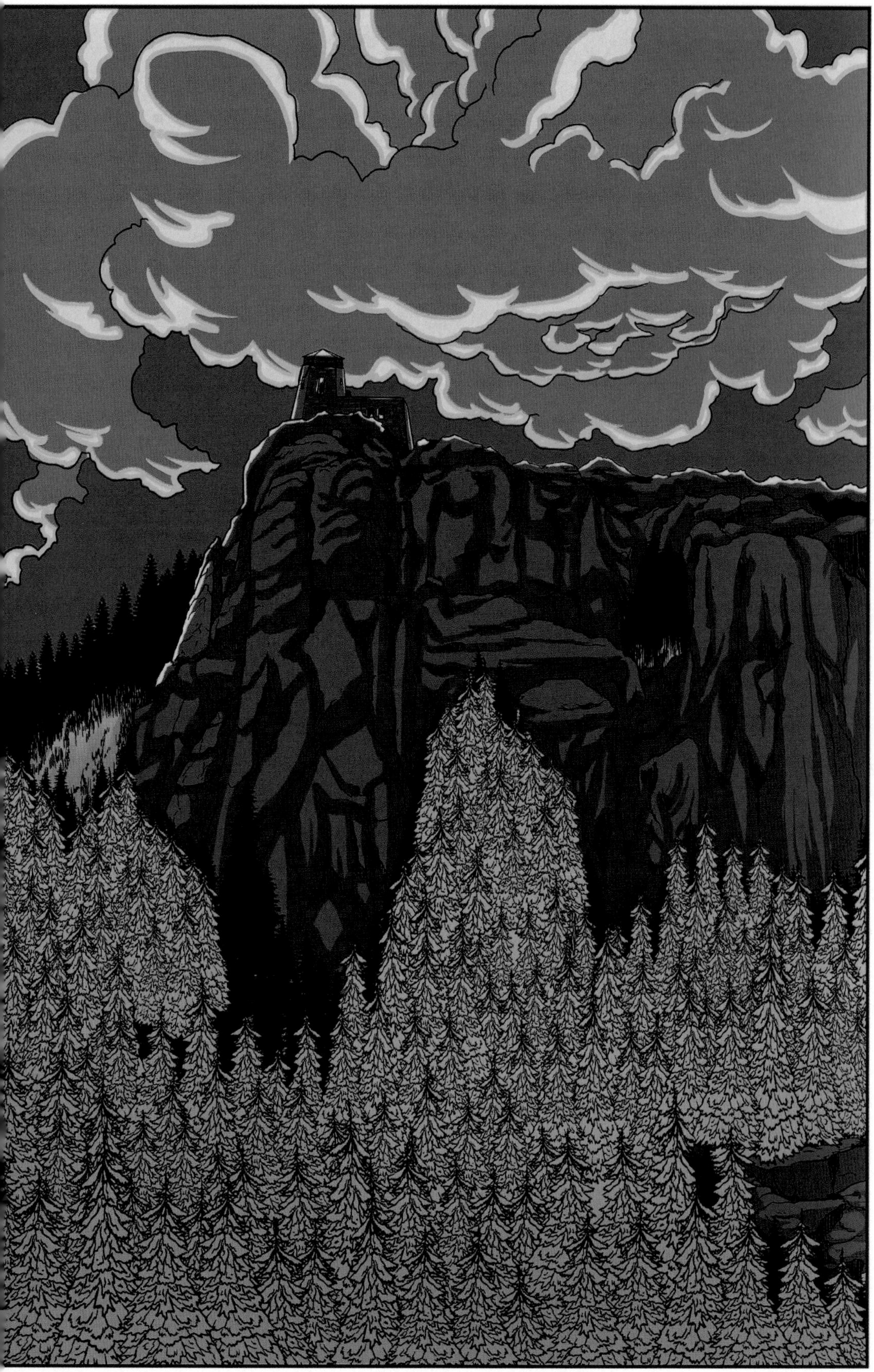

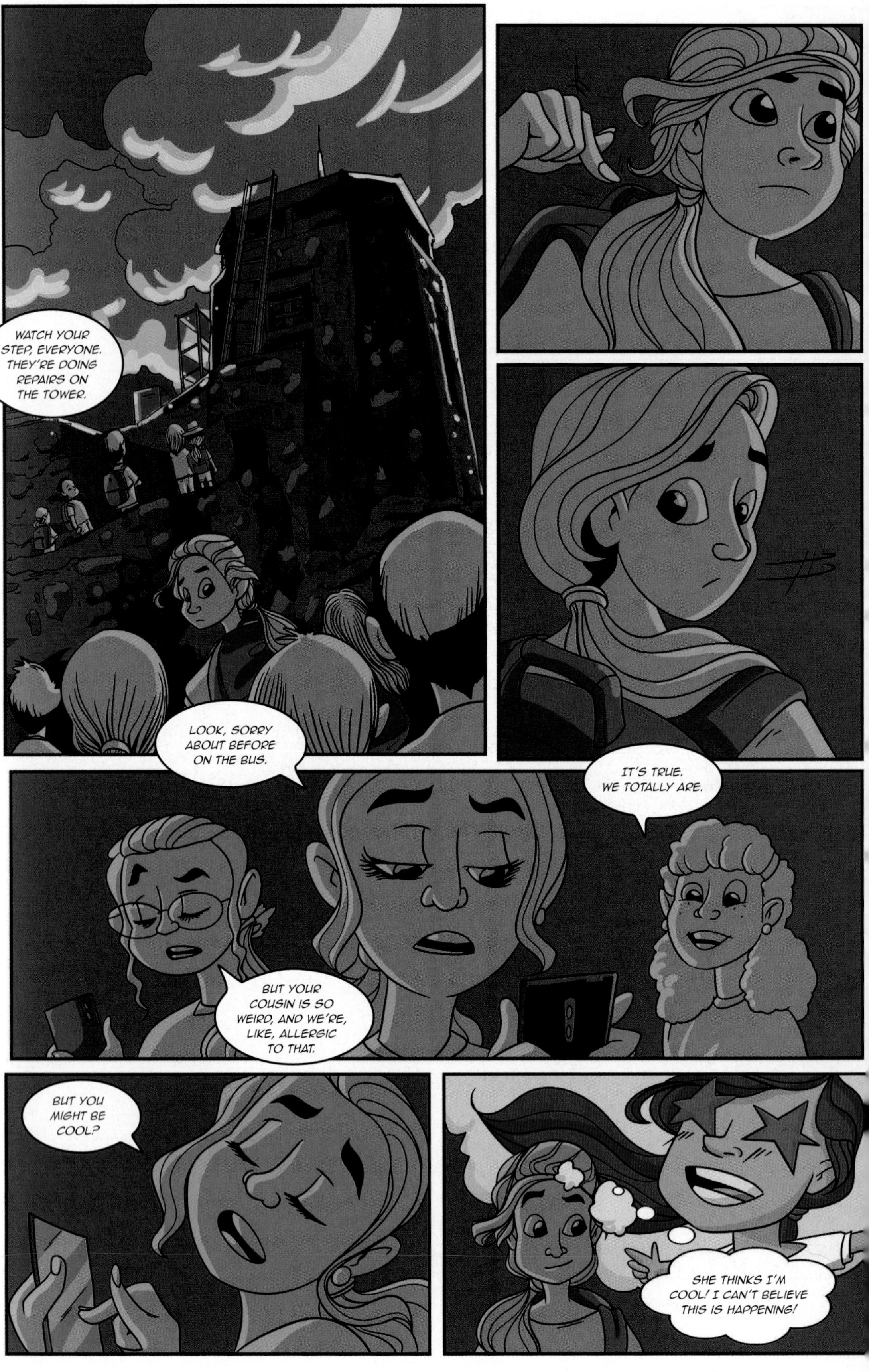
WATCH YOUR STEP, EVERYONE. THEY'RE DOING REPAIRS ON THE TOWER.
LOOK, SORRY ABOUT BEFORE ON THE BUS.
IT'S TRUE. WE TOTALLY ARE.
BUT YOUR COUSIN IS SO WEIRD, AND WE'RE, LIKE, ALLERGIC TO THAT.
BUT YOU MIGHT BE COOL?
SHE THINKS I'M COOL! I CAN'T BELIEVE THIS IS HAPPENING!

WHY DON'T YOU PROVE IT? TAKE A SELFIE FROM THE ROOF OF THAT TOWER.
BOOM
IT'LL MAKE A GREAT POST. BUT BETTER DO IT FAST.

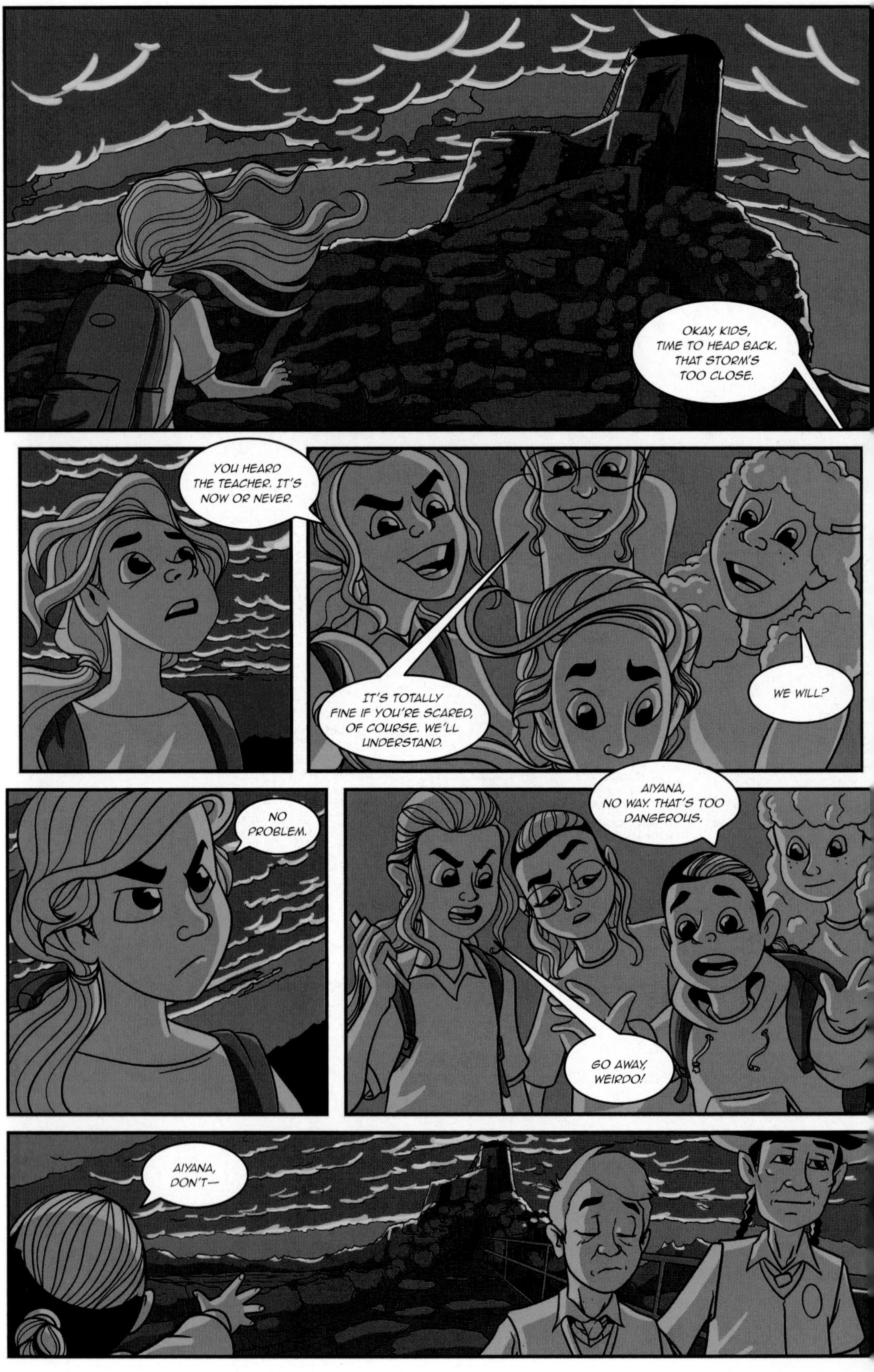
OKAY, KIDS, TIME TO HEAD BACK. THAT STORM'S TOO CLOSE.
YOU HEARD THE TEACHER. IT'S NOW OR NEVER.
IT'S TOTALLY FINE IF YOU'RE SCARED, OF COURSE. WE'LL UNDERSTAND.
WE WILL?
NO PROBLEM.
AIYANA, NO WAY. THAT'S TOO DANGEROUS.
GO AWAY, WEIRDO!
AIYANA, DON'T—

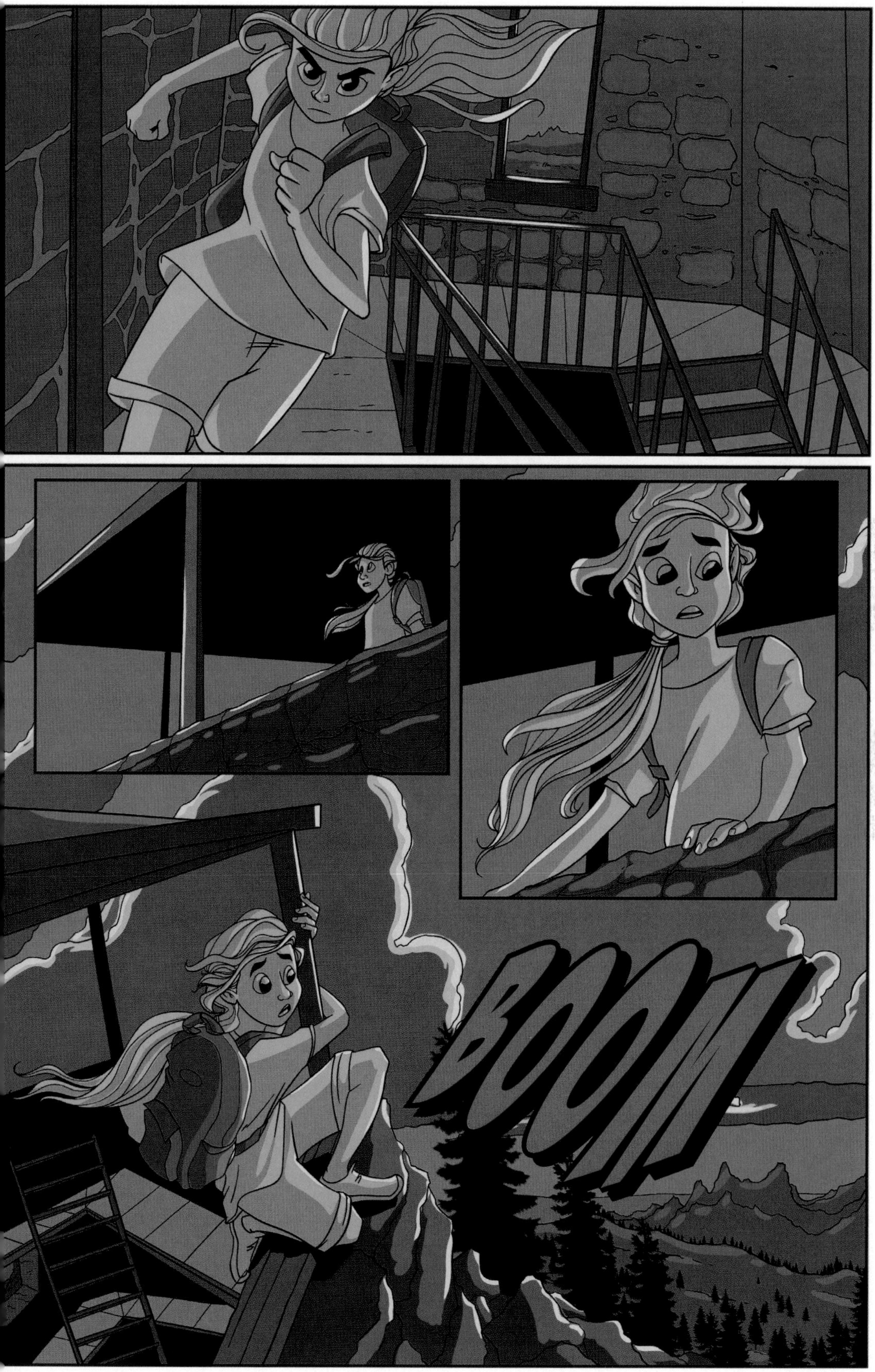
BOOM

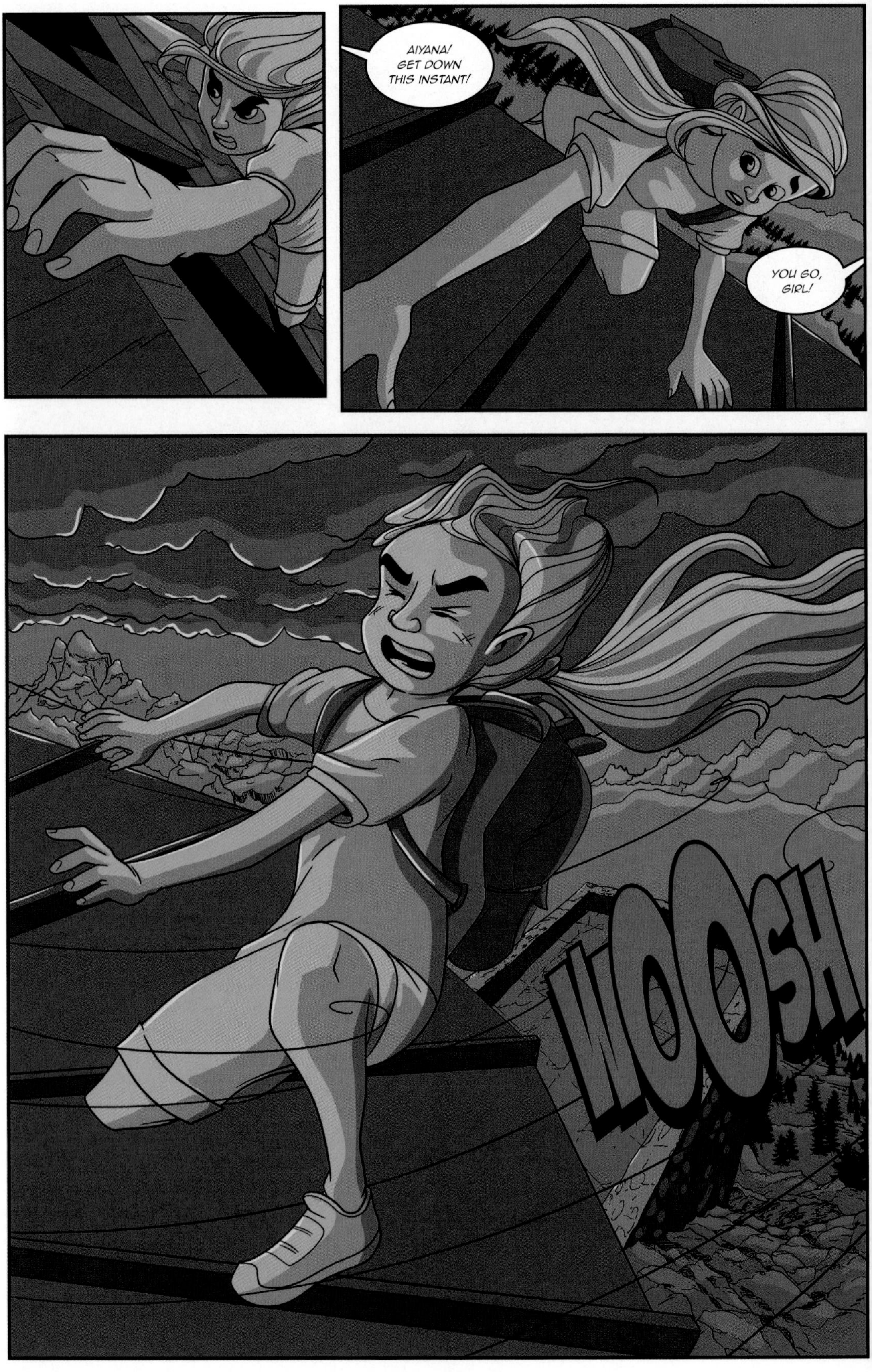
AIYANA! GET DOWN THIS INSTANT!
YOU GO, GIRL!
WOOSH

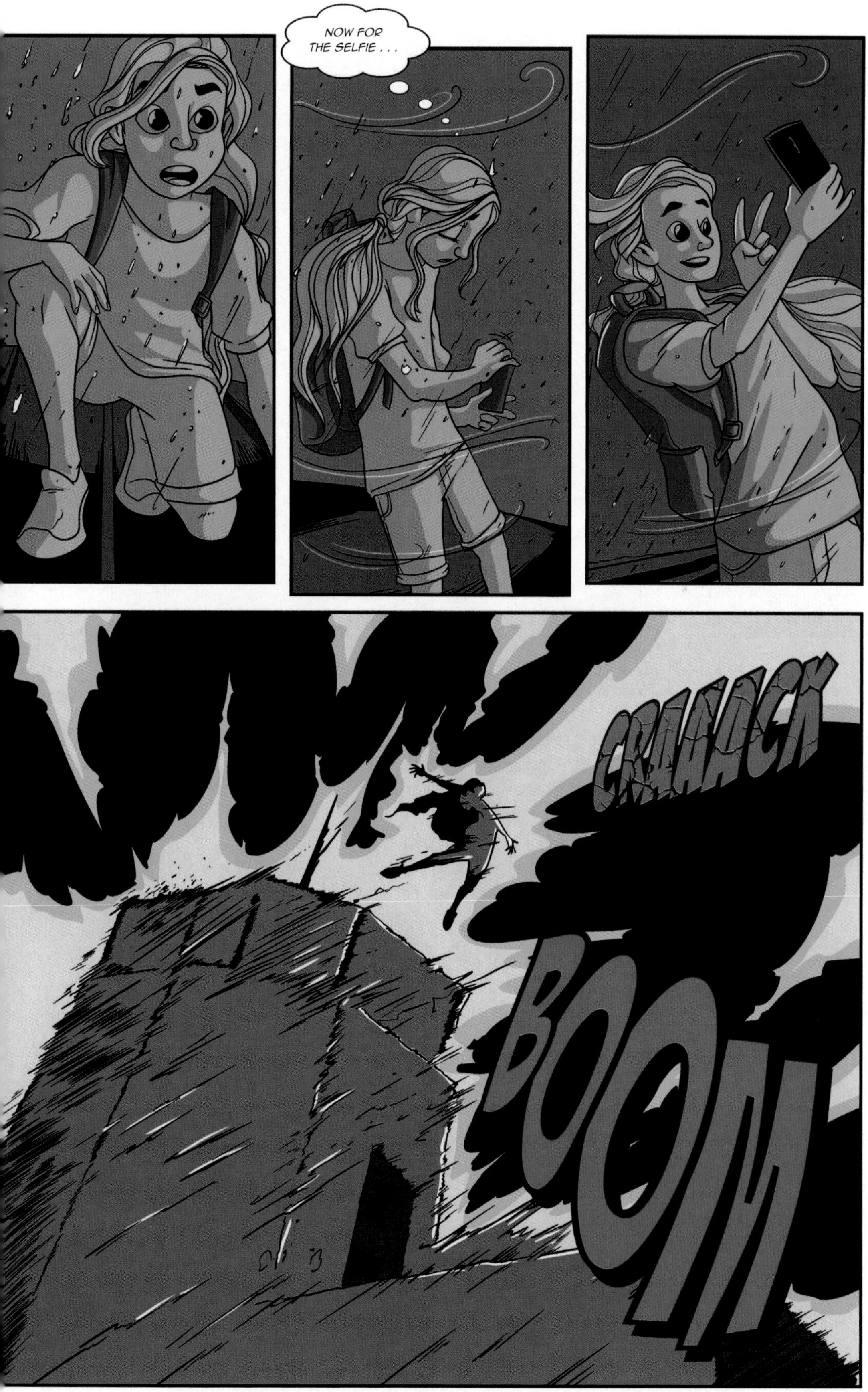
NOW FOR THE SELFIE . . .
CRAAACK
BOOOM

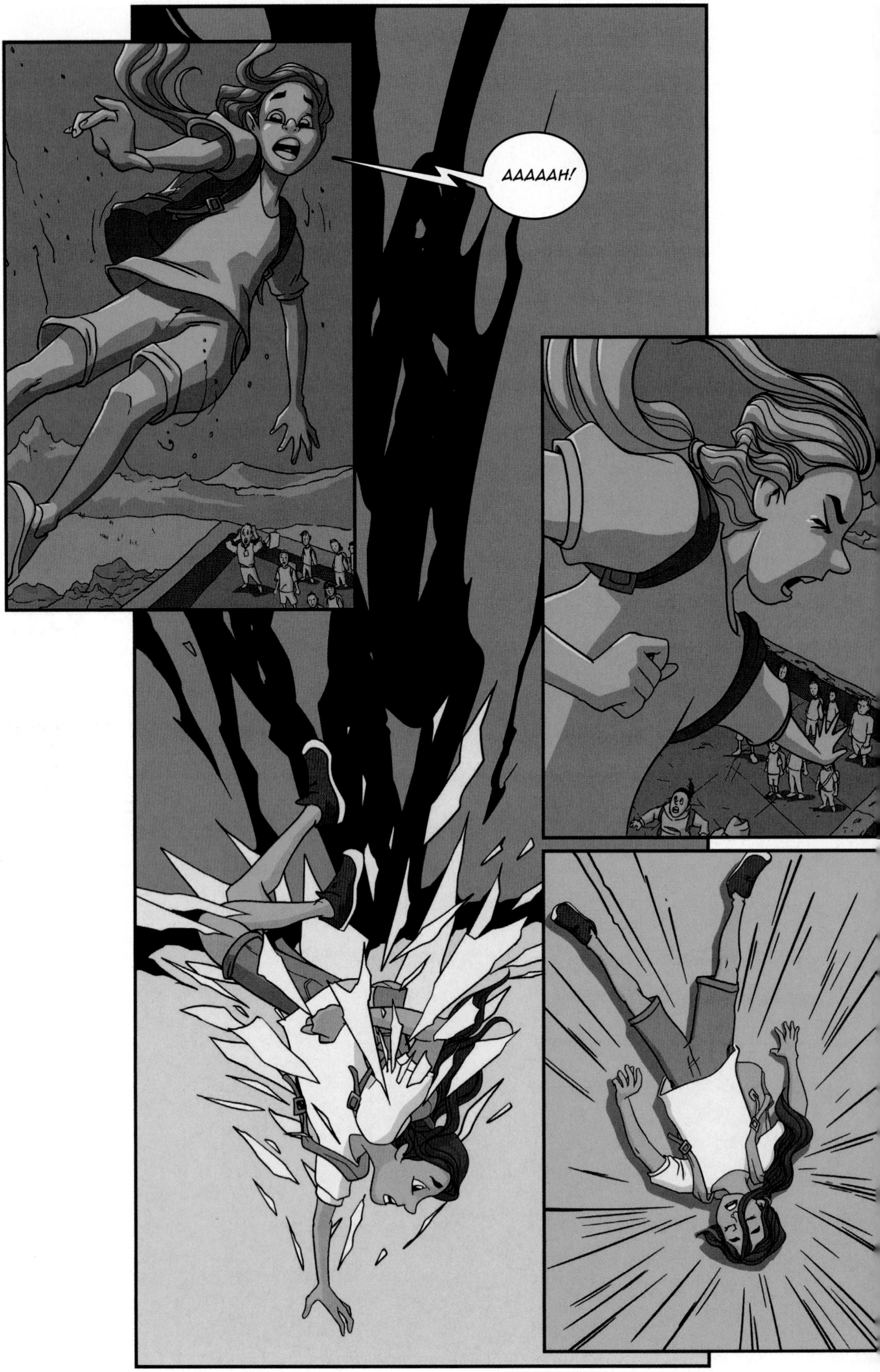
AAAAAH!

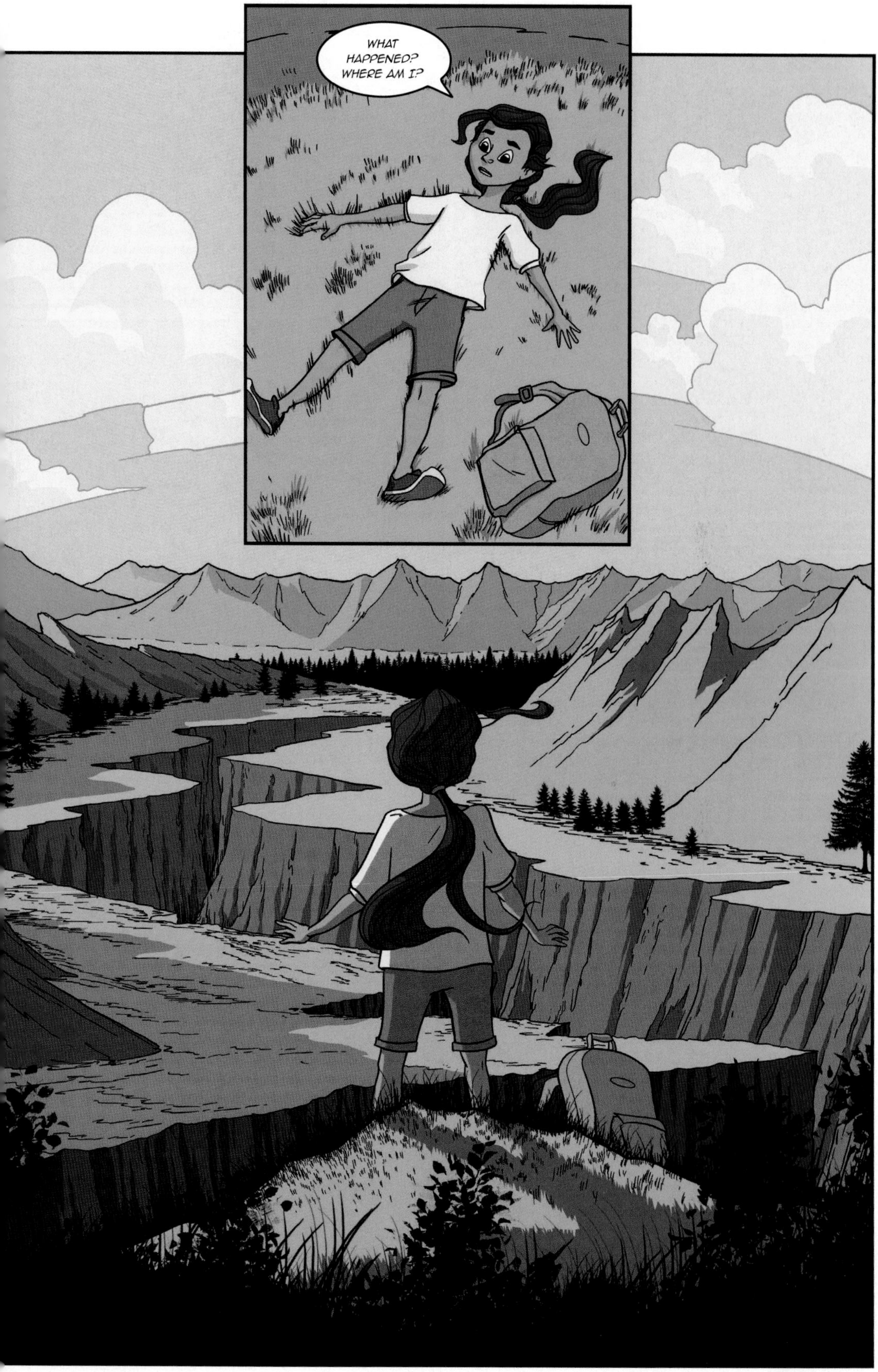
WHAT HAPPENED? WHERE AM I?

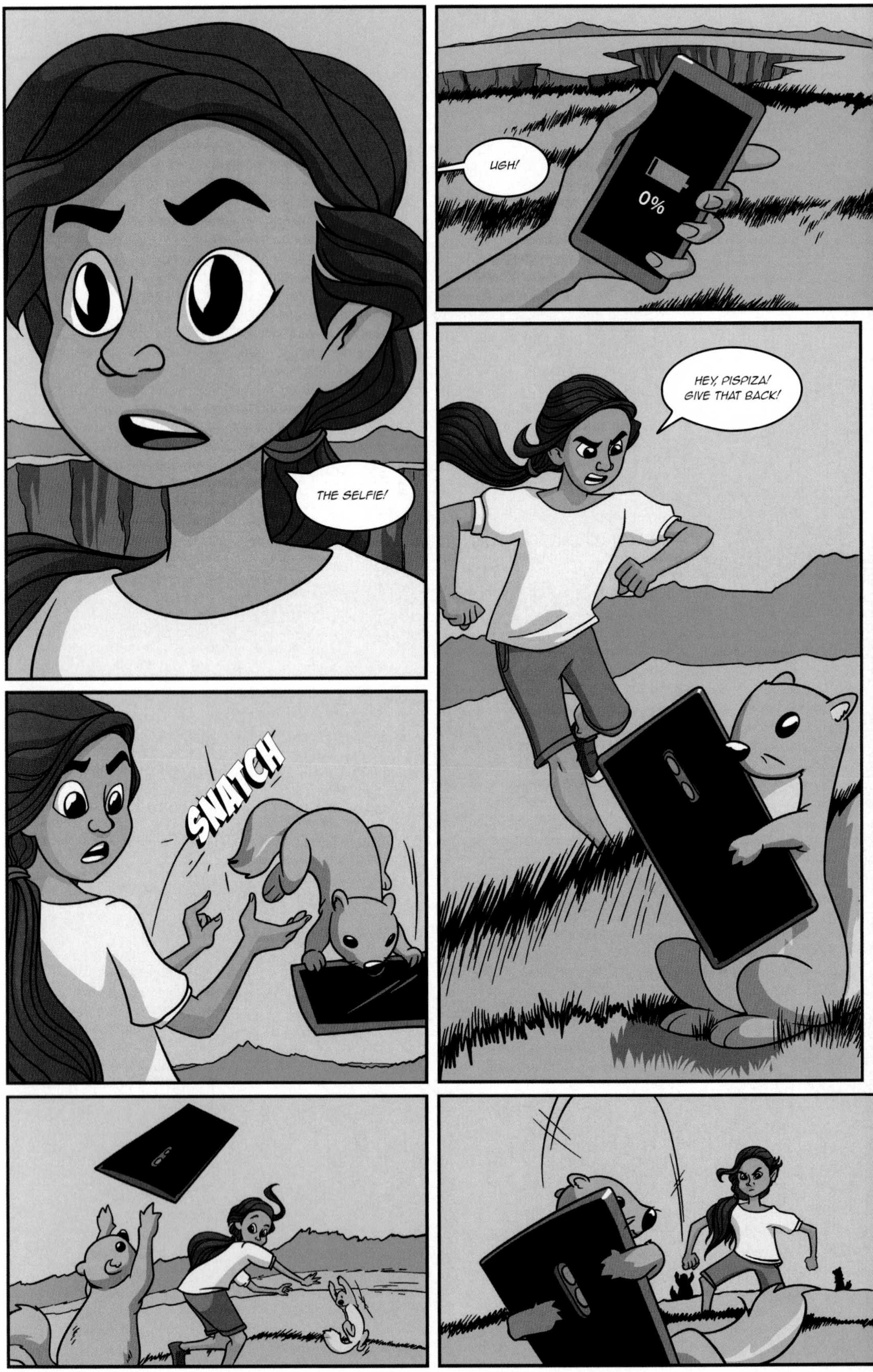
THE SELFIE!
UGH!
0%
SNATCH
HEY, PISPIZA!
GIVE THAT BACK!

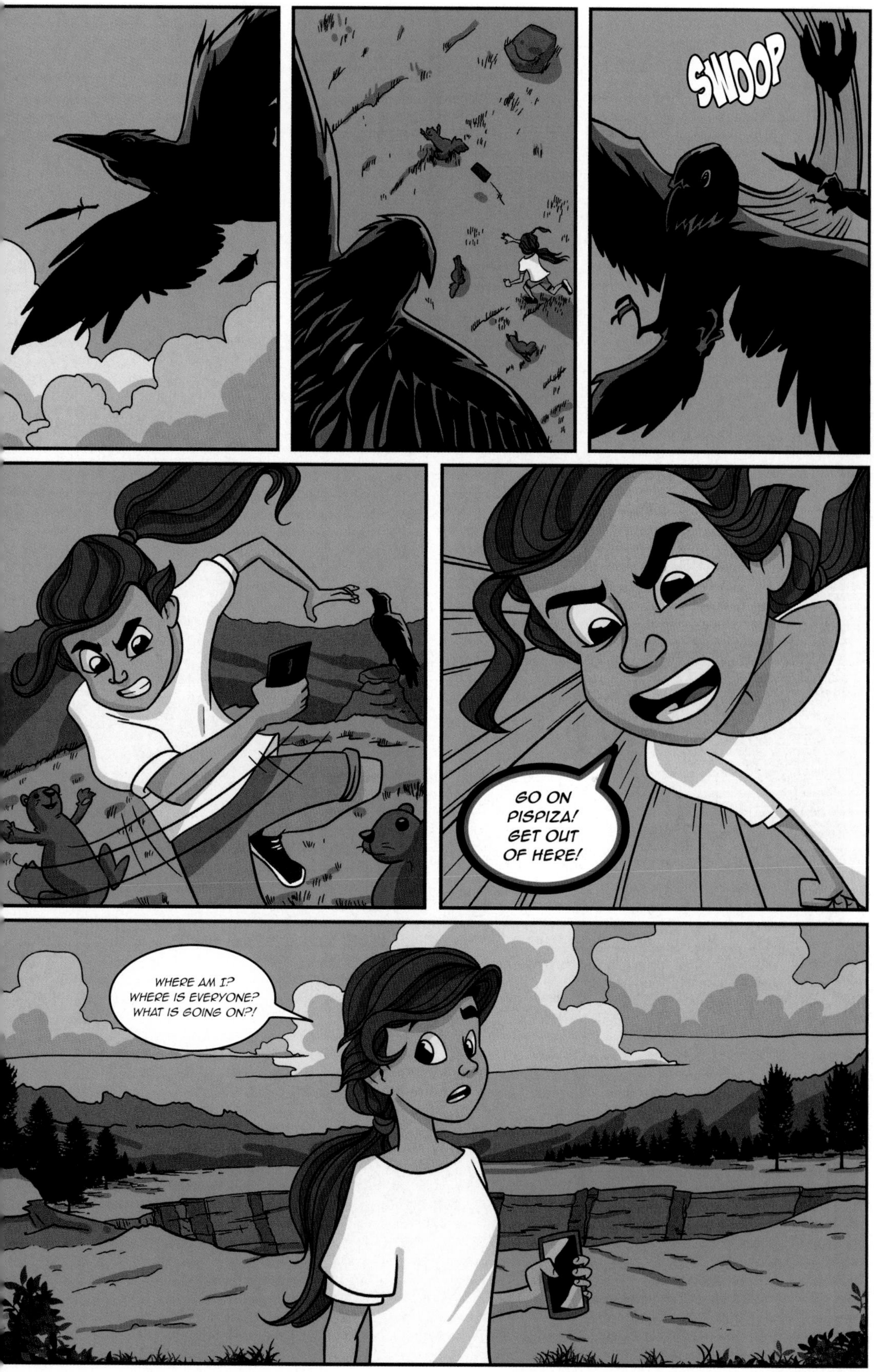
SWOOP
GO ON PISPIZA! GET OUT OF HERE!
WHERE AM I? WHERE IS EVERYONE? WHAT IS GOING ON?!

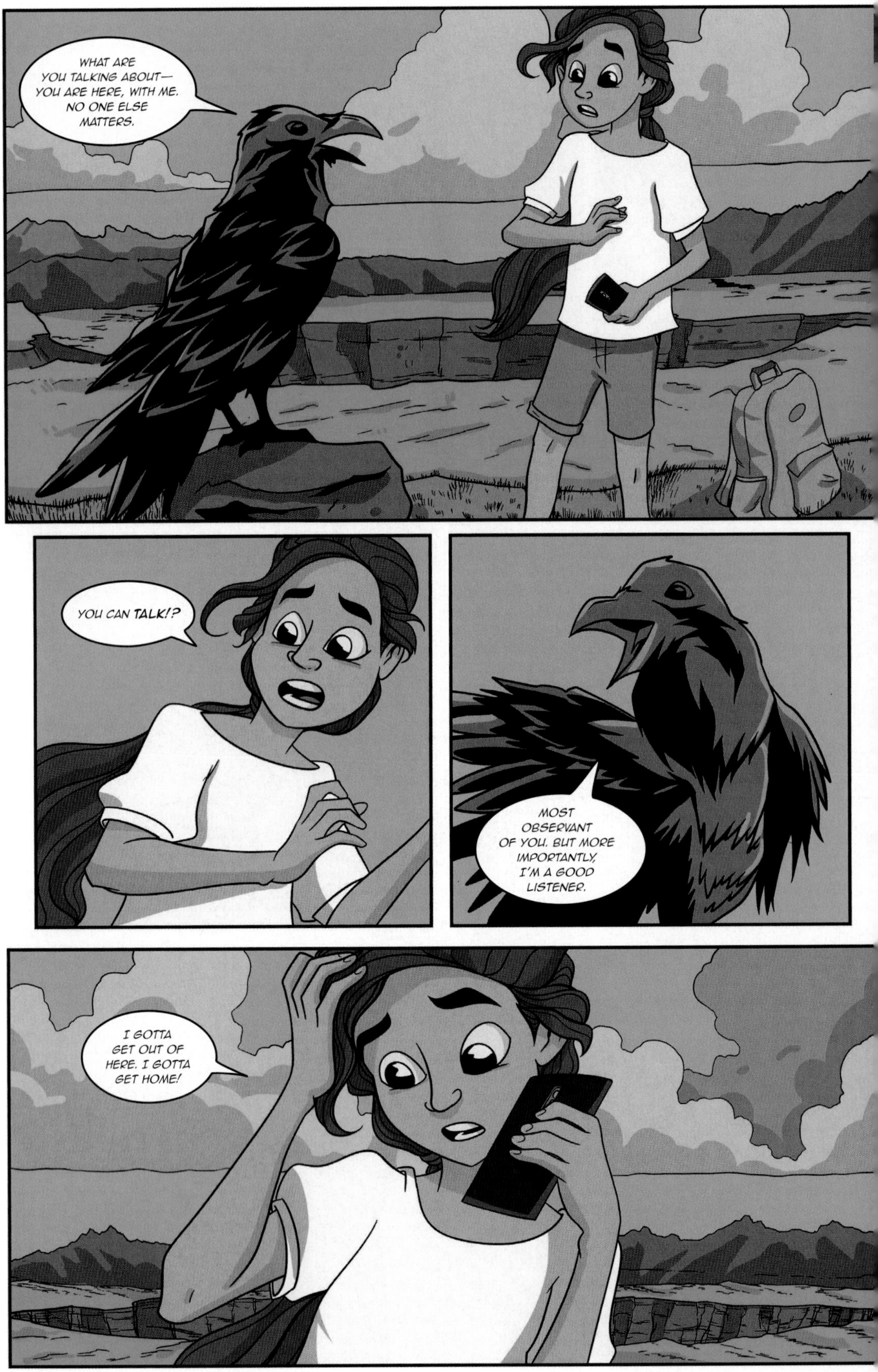
WHAT ARE YOU TALKING ABOUT— YOU ARE HERE, WITH ME. NO ONE ELSE MATTERS.
YOU CAN TALK!?
MOST OBSERVANT OF YOU. BUT MORE IMPORTANTLY, I'M A GOOD LISTENER.
I GOTTA GET OUT OF HERE. I GOTTA GET HOME!

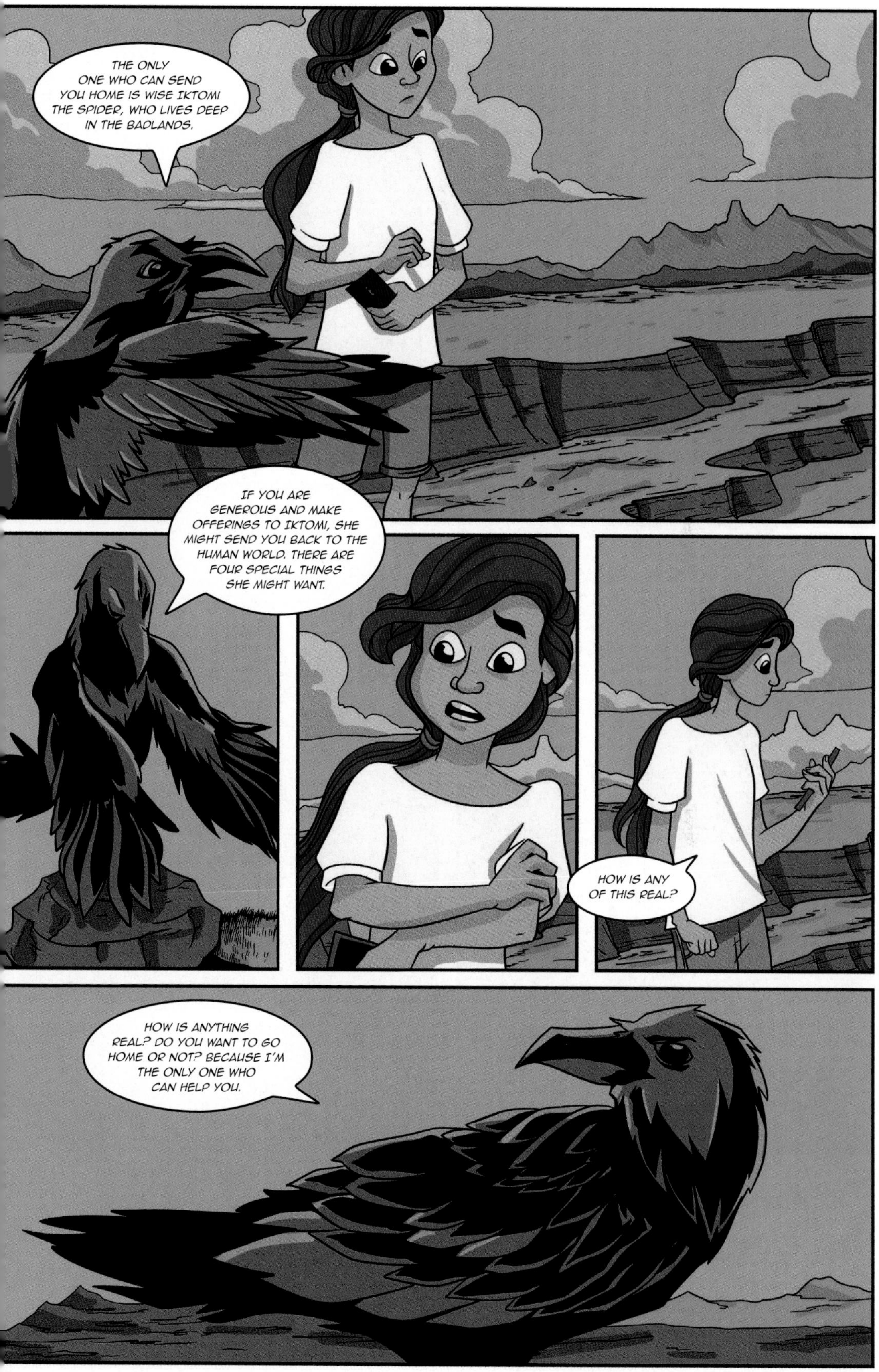
THE ONLY ONE WHO CAN SEND YOU HOME IS WISE IKTOMI THE SPIDER, WHO LIVES DEEP IN THE BADLANDS.
IF YOU ARE GENEROUS AND MAKE OFFERINGS TO IKTOMI, SHE MIGHT SEND YOU BACK TO THE HUMAN WORLD. THERE ARE FOUR SPECIAL THINGS SHE MIGHT WANT.
HOW IS ANY OF THIS REAL?
HOW IS ANYTHING REAL? DO YOU WANT TO GO HOME OR NOT? BECAUSE I'M THE ONLY ONE WHO CAN HELP YOU.

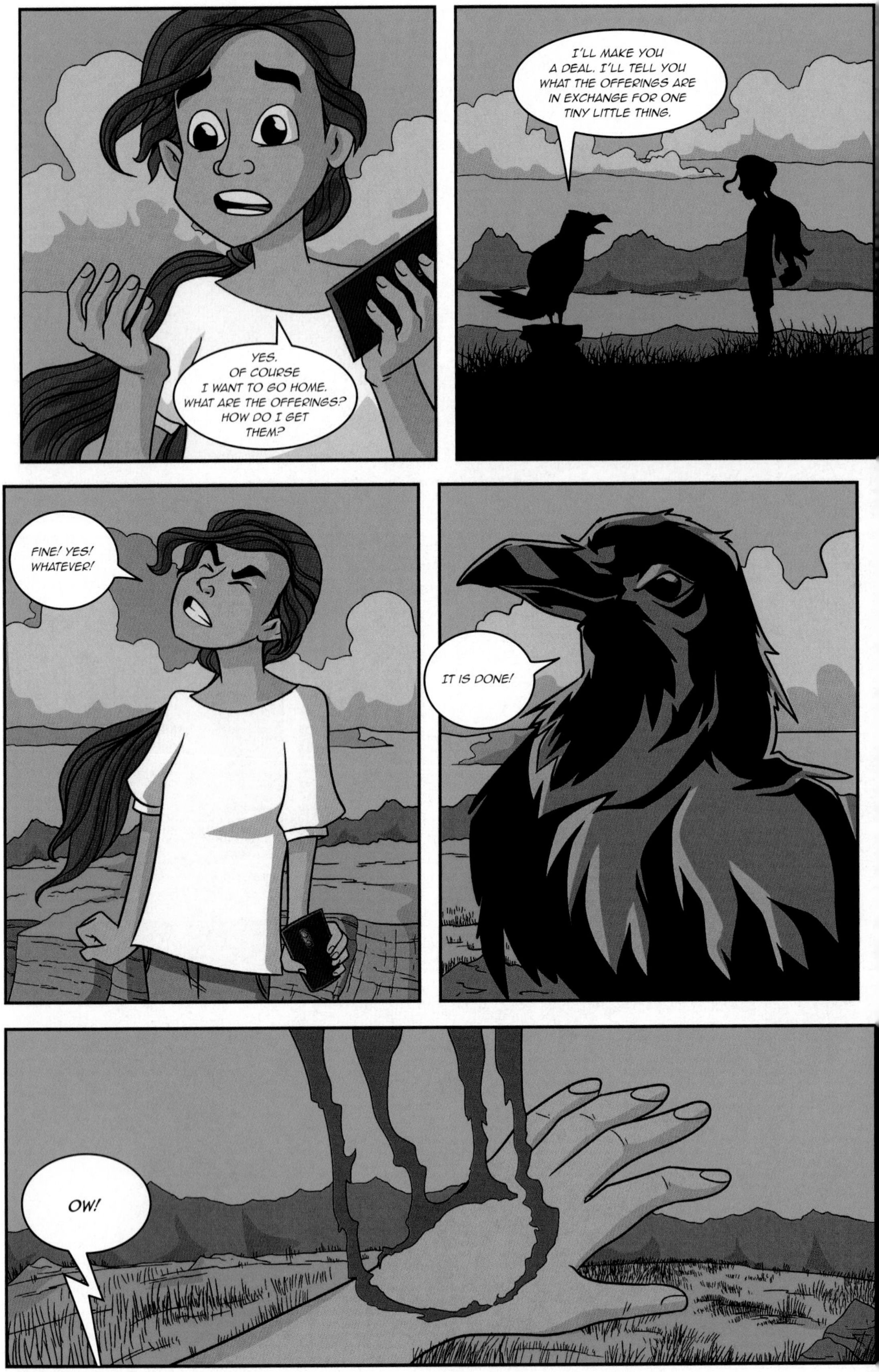
YES. OF COURSE I WANT TO GO HOME. WHAT ARE THE OFFERINGS? HOW DO I GET THEM?
I'LL MAKE YOU A DEAL. I'LL TELL YOU WHAT THE OFFERINGS ARE IN EXCHANGE FOR ONE TINY LITTLE THING.
FINE! YES! WHATEVER!
IT IS DONE!
OW!

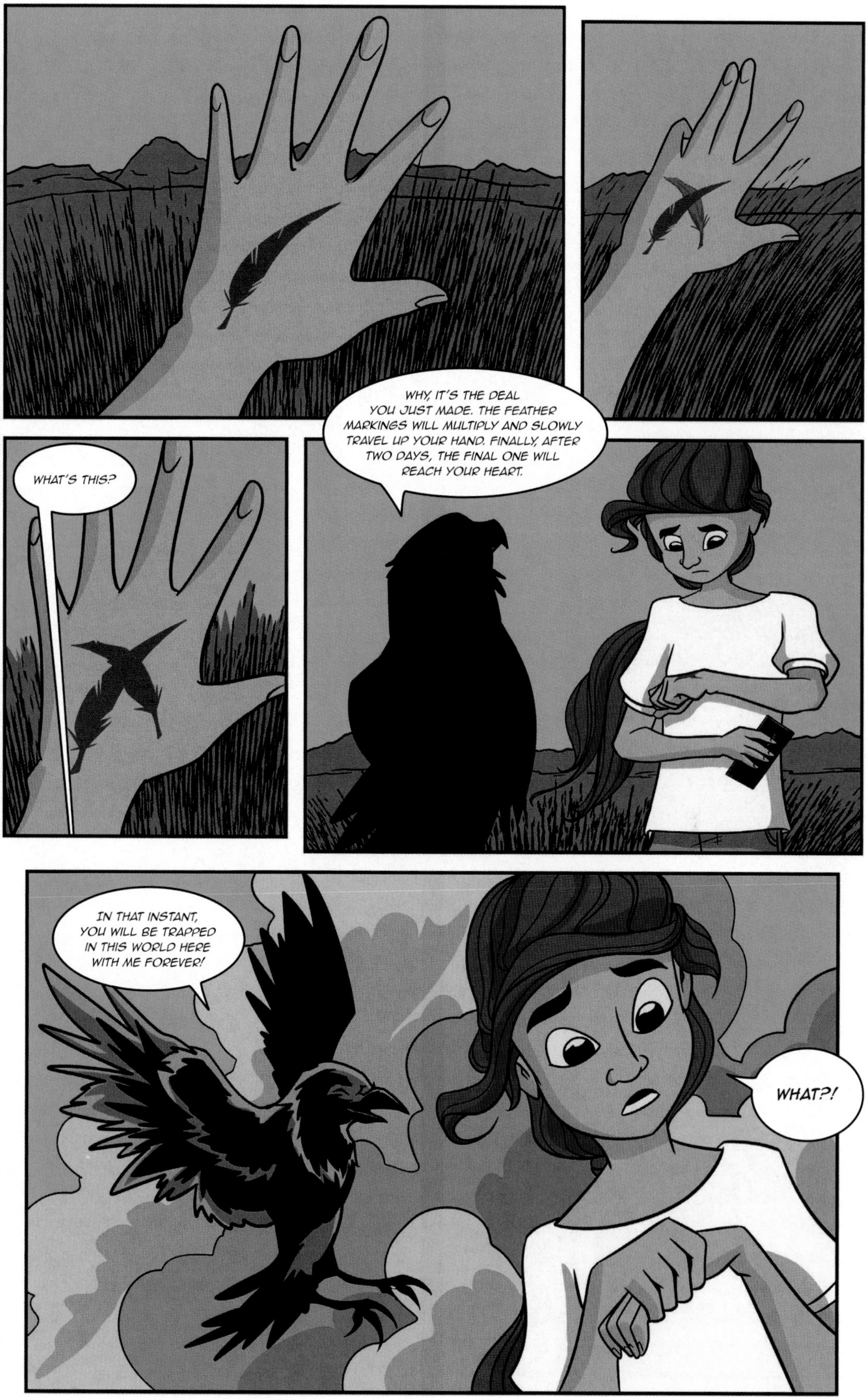
WHAT'S THIS?
WHY, IT'S THE DEAL YOU JUST MADE. THE FEATHER MARKINGS WILL MULTIPLY AND SLOWLY TRAVEL UP YOUR HAND. FINALLY, AFTER TWO DAYS, THE FINAL ONE WILL REACH YOUR HEART.
IN THAT INSTANT, YOU WILL BE TRAPPED IN THIS WORLD HERE WITH ME FOREVER!
WHAT?!

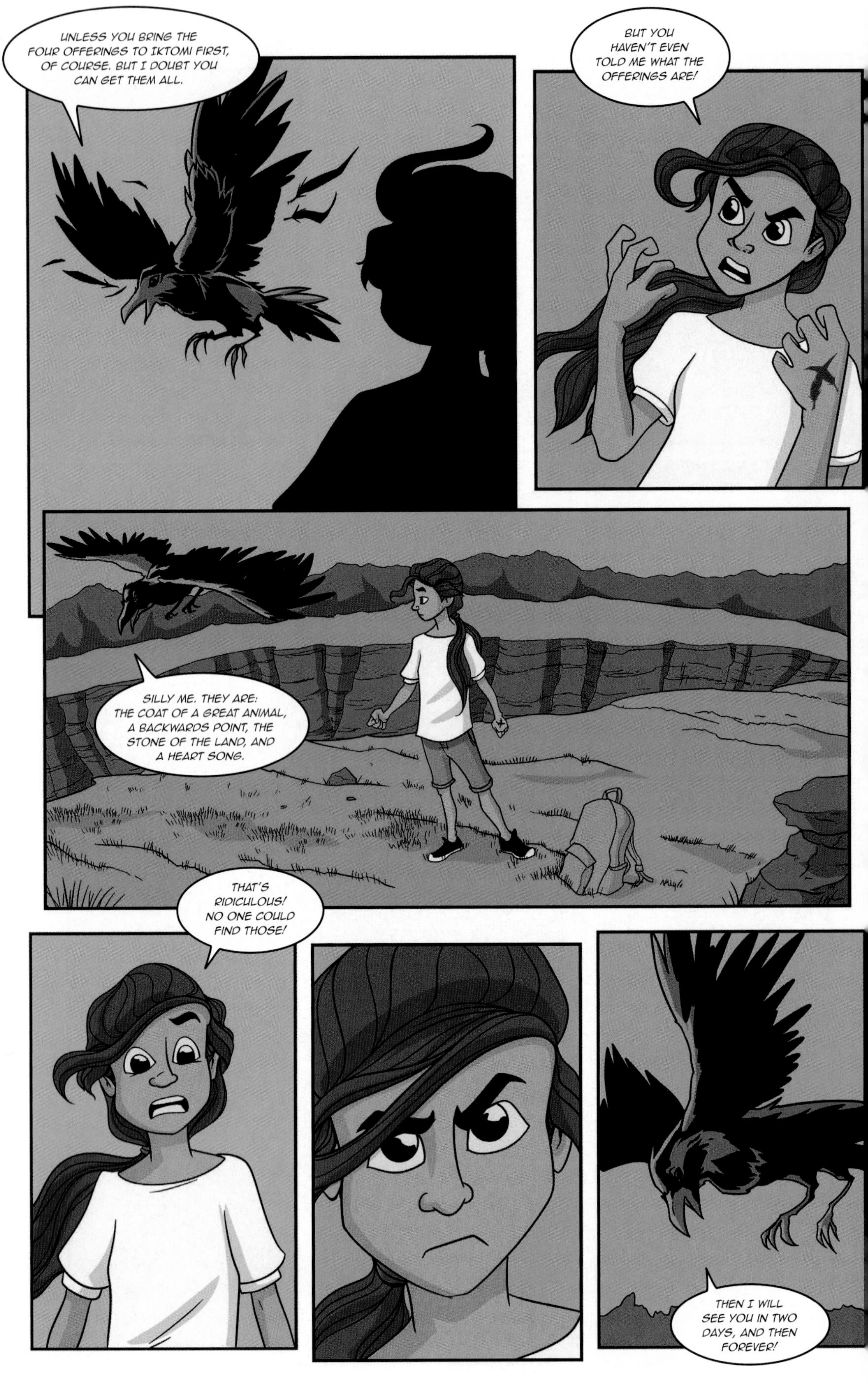
UNLESS YOU BRING THE FOUR OFFERINGS TO IKTOMI FIRST, OF COURSE. BUT I DOUBT YOU CAN GET THEM ALL.
BUT YOU HAVEN'T EVEN TOLD ME WHAT THE OFFERINGS ARE!
SILLY ME. THEY ARE: THE COAT OF A GREAT ANIMAL, A BACKWARDS POINT, THE STONE OF THE LAND, AND A HEART SONG.
THAT'S RIDICULOUS! NO ONE COULD FIND THOSE!
THEN I WILL SEE YOU IN TWO DAYS, AND THEN FOREVER!

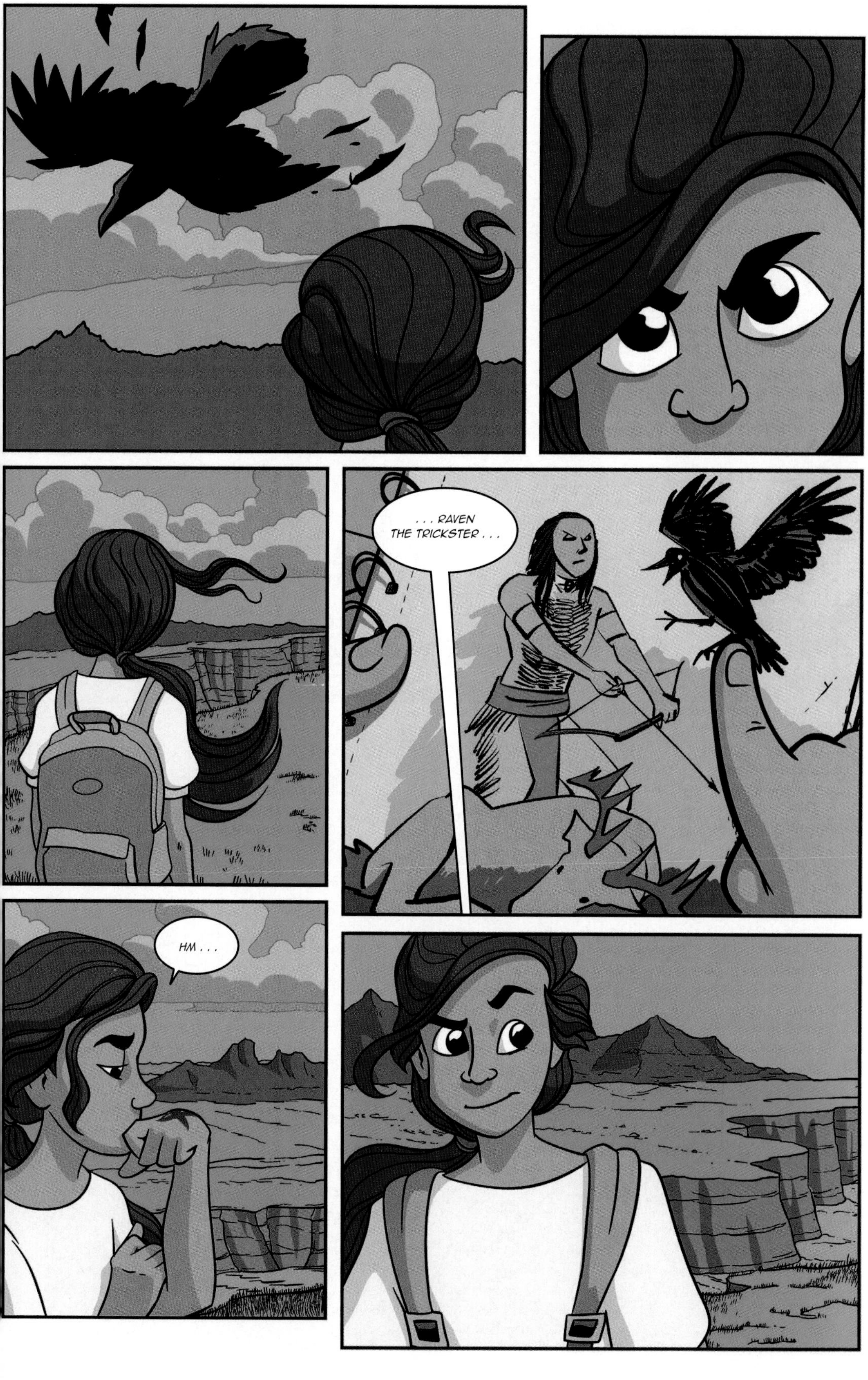
. . . RAVEN THE TRICKSTER . . .
HM . . .

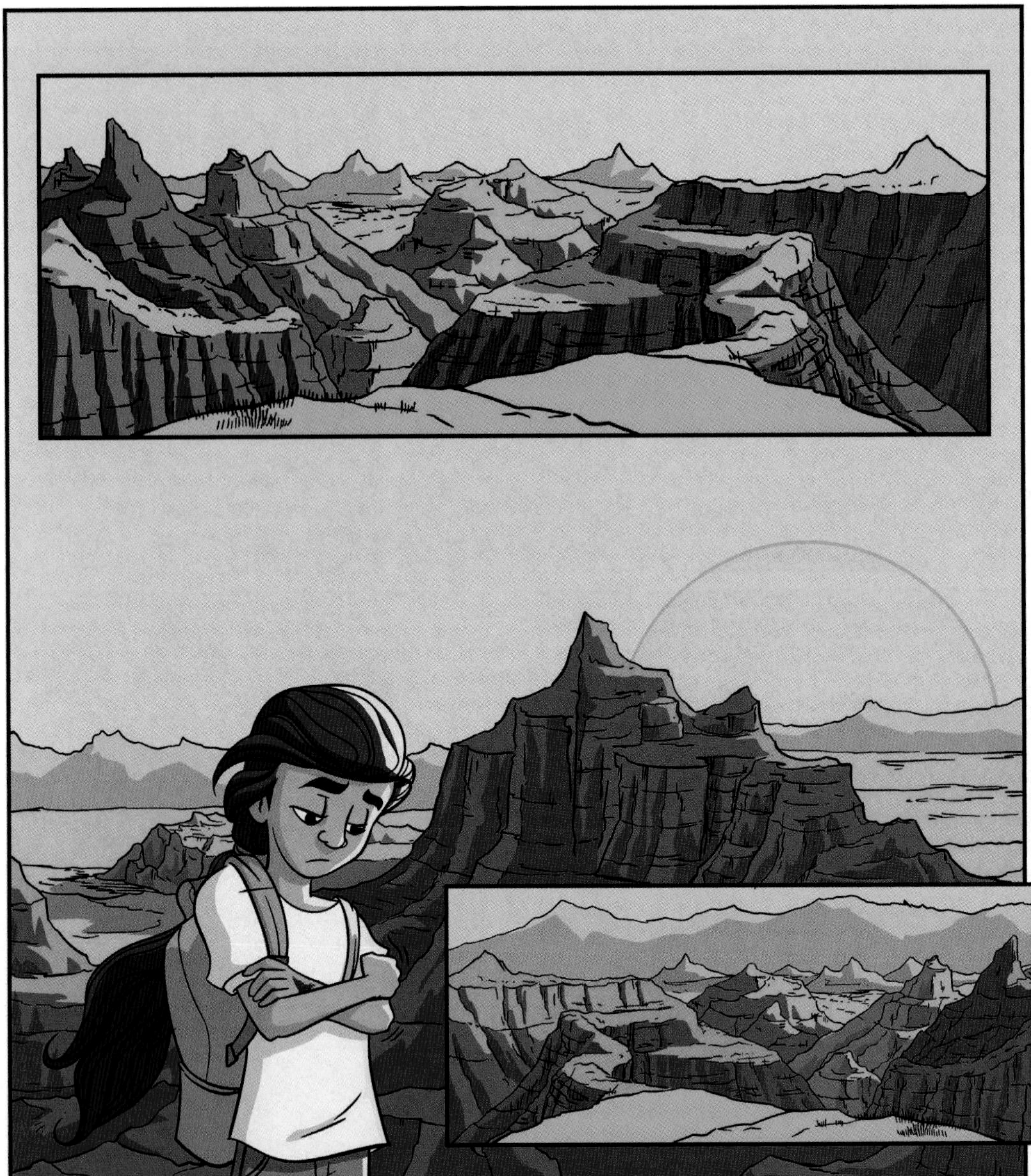
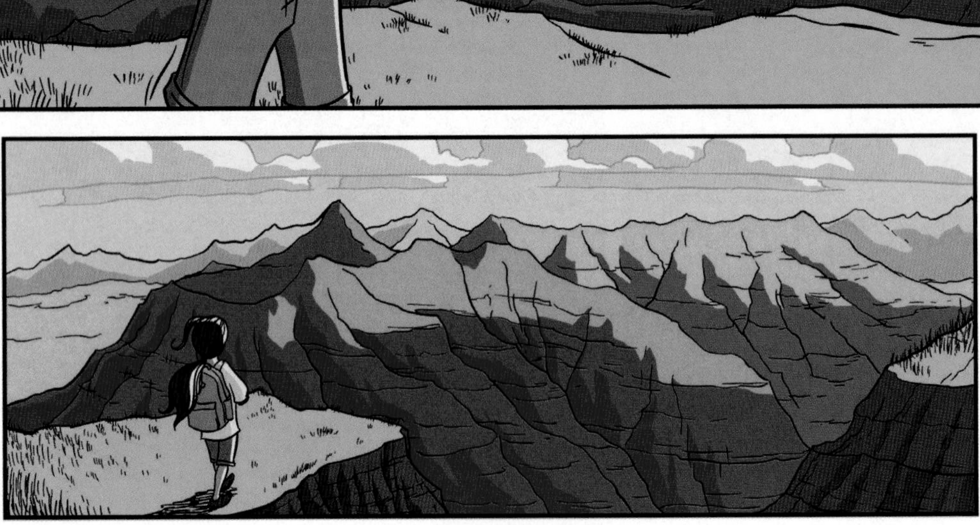

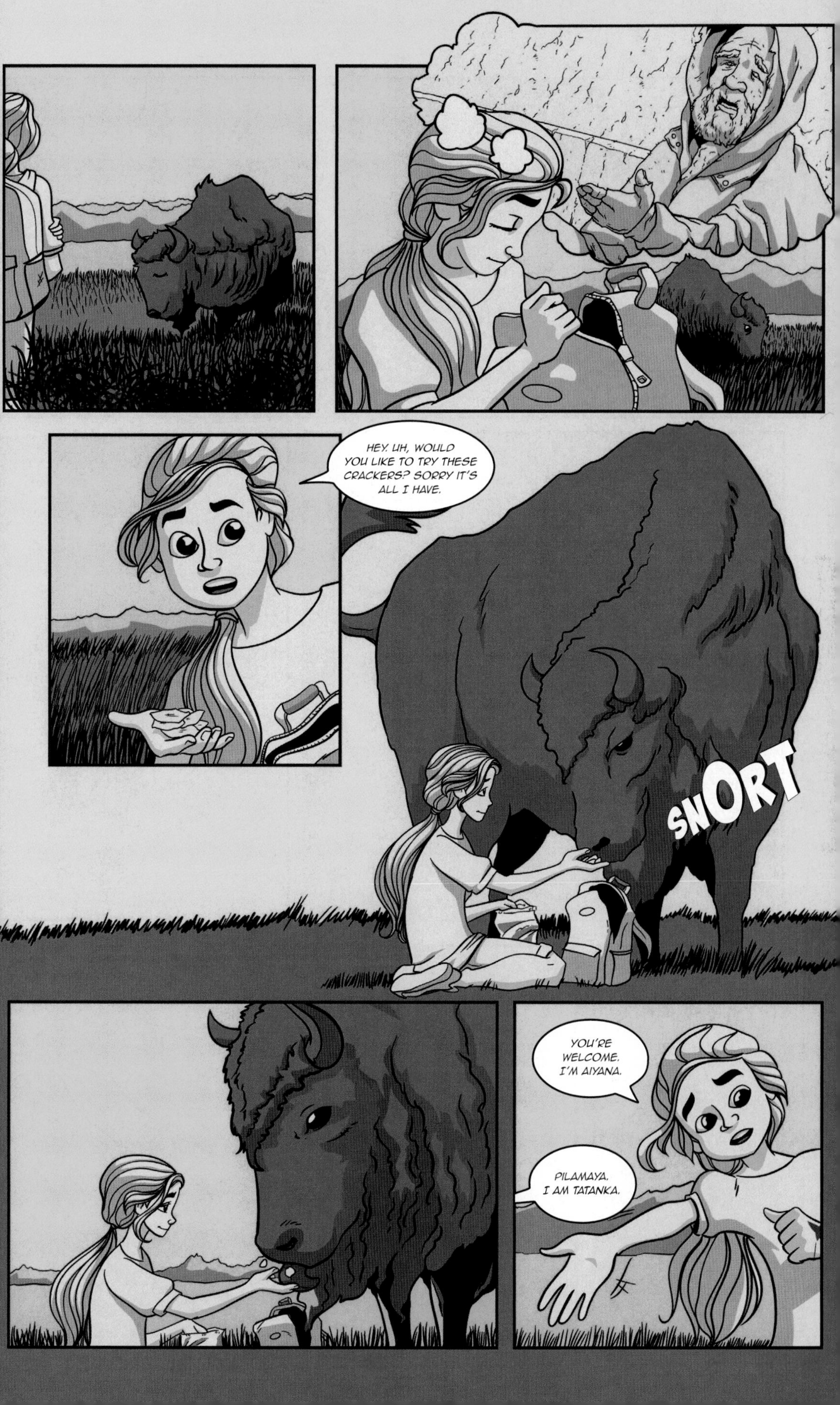
HEY. UH, WOULD YOU LIKE TO TRY THESE CRACKERS? SORRY IT'S ALL I HAVE.
SNORT
YOU'RE WELCOME. I'M AIYANA.
PILAMAYA. I AM TATANKA.

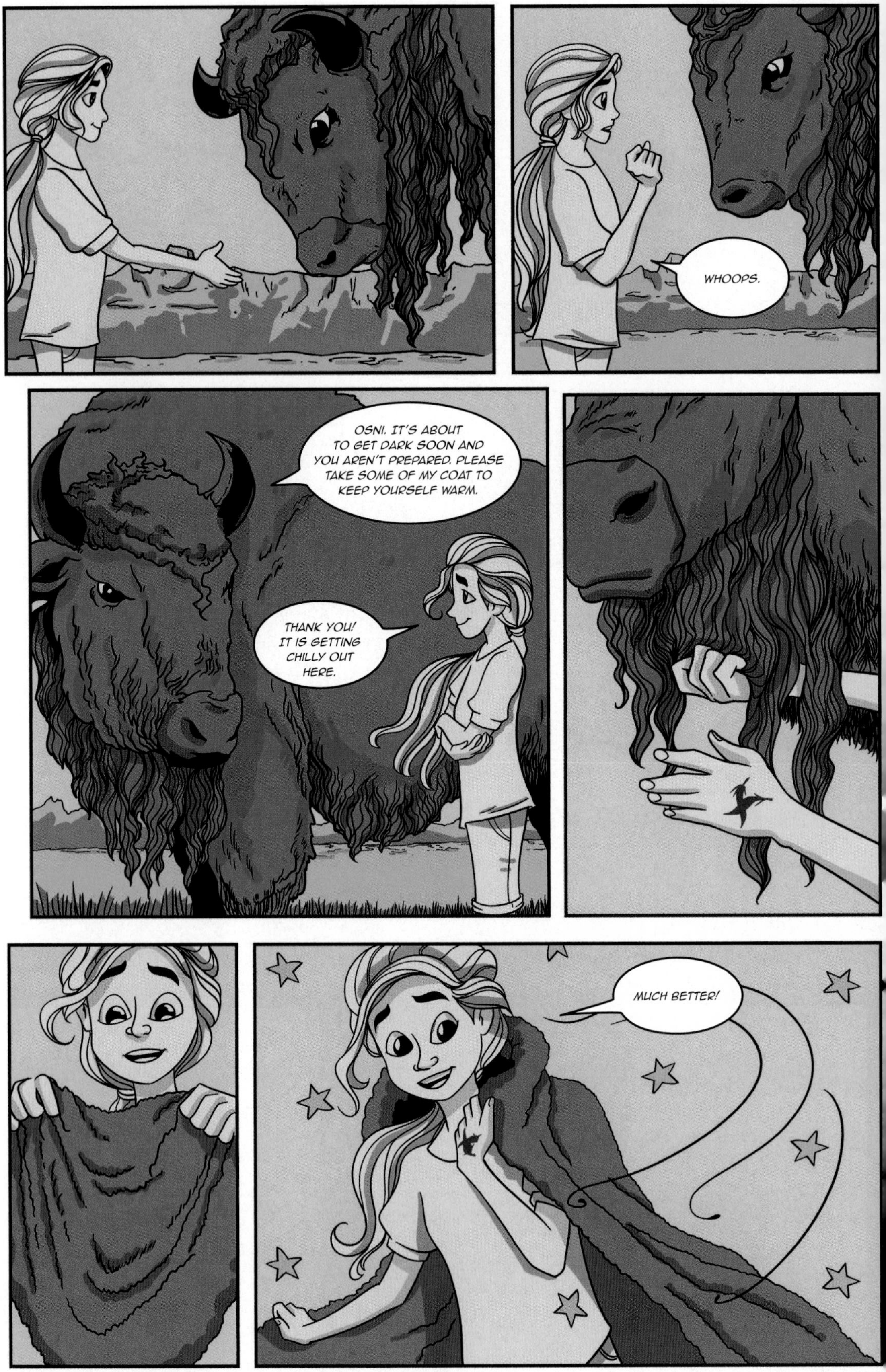
WHOOPS.
OSNI. IT'S ABOUT TO GET DARK SOON AND YOU AREN'T PREPARED. PLEASE TAKE SOME OF MY COAT TO KEEP YOURSELF WARM.
THANK YOU! IT IS GETTING CHILLY OUT HERE.
MUCH BETTER!

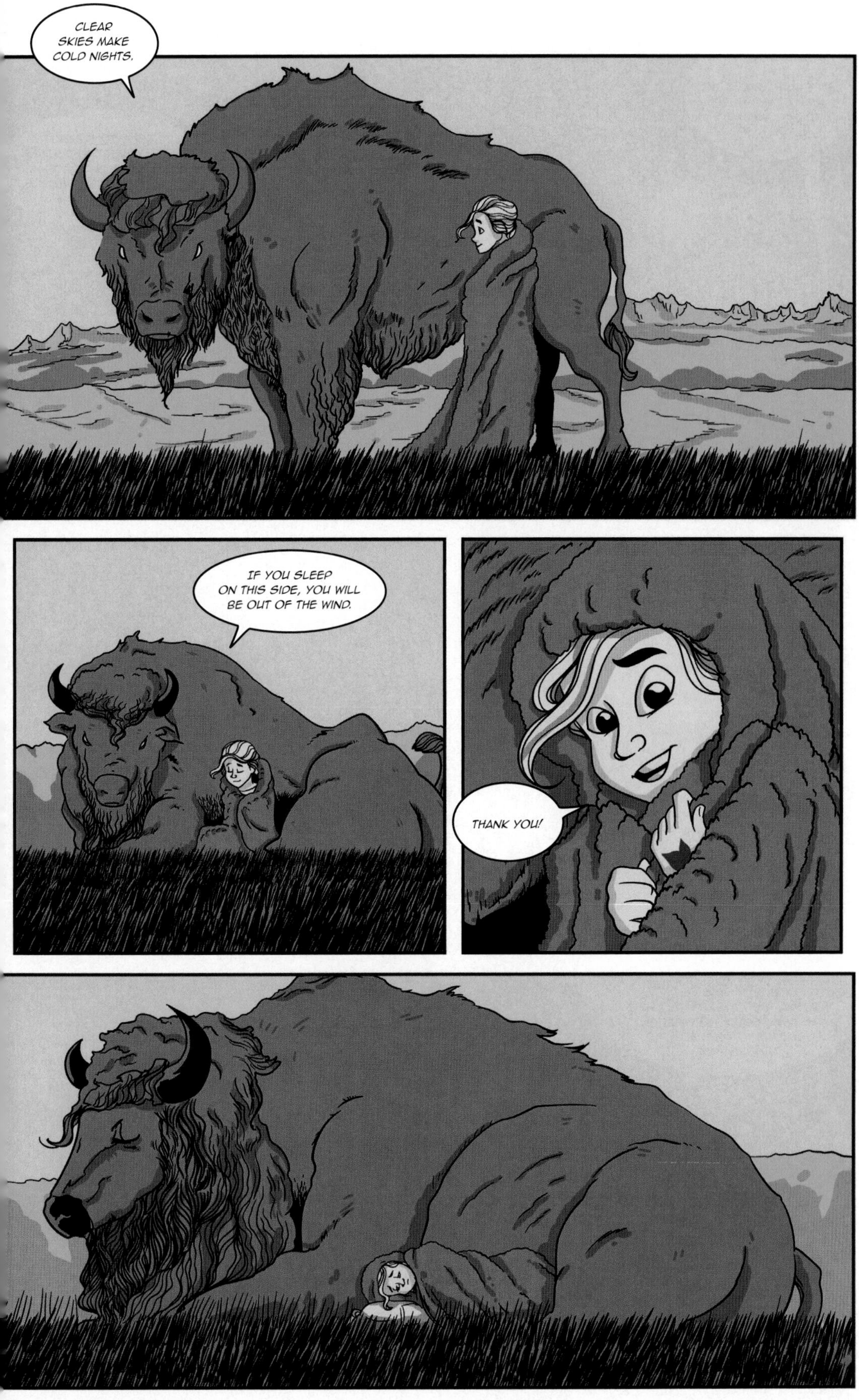
CLEAR SKIES MAKE COLD NIGHTS.
IF YOU SLEEP ON THIS SIDE, YOU WILL BE OUT OF THE WIND.
THANK YOU!

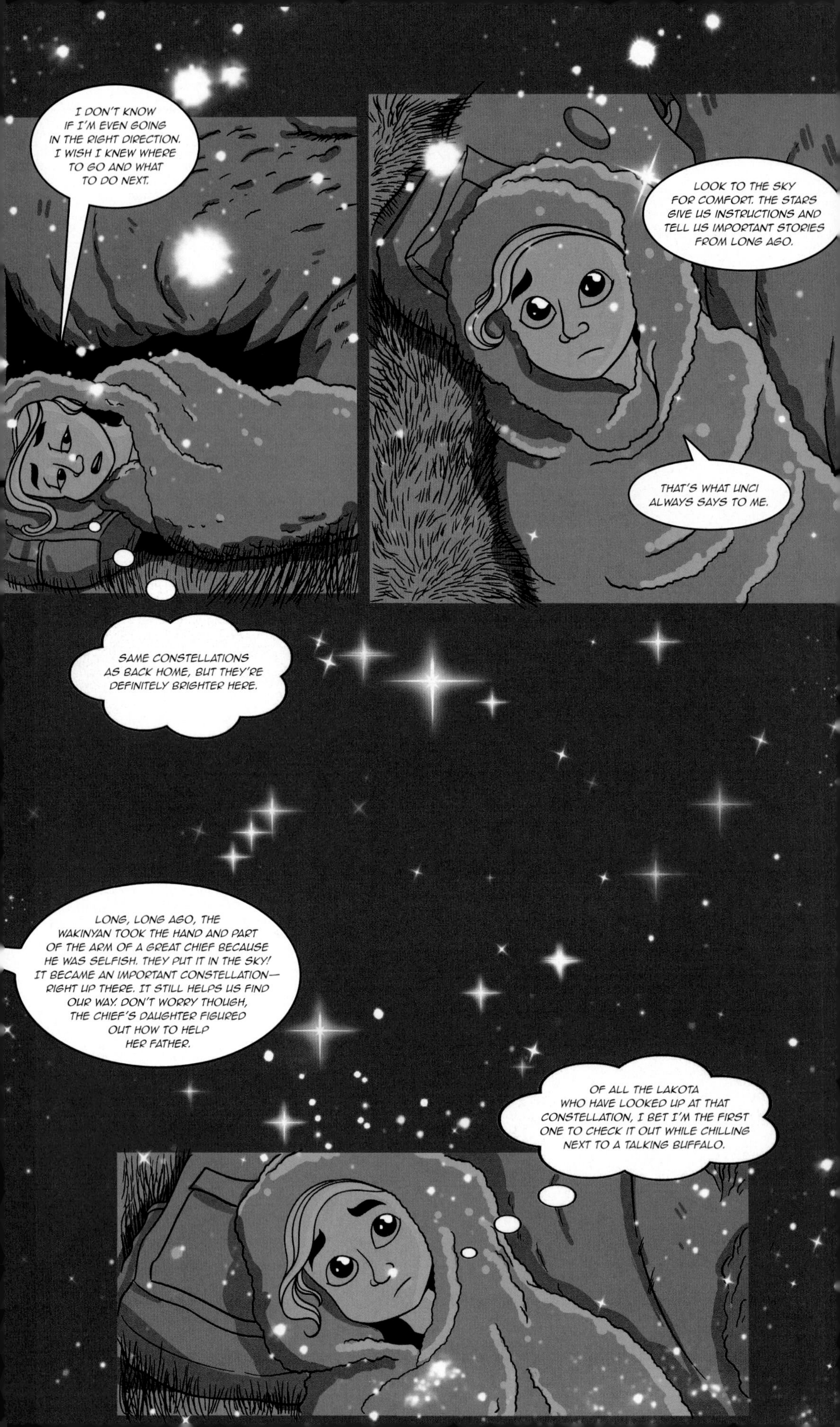
I DON'T KNOW IF I'M EVEN GOING IN THE RIGHT DIRECTION. I WISH I KNEW WHERE TO GO AND WHAT TO DO NEXT.
LOOK TO THE SKY FOR COMFORT. THE STARS GIVE US INSTRUCTIONS AND TELL US IMPORTANT STORIES FROM LONG AGO.
THAT'S WHAT UNCI ALWAYS SAYS TO ME.
SAME CONSTELLATIONS AS BACK HOME, BUT THEY'RE DEFINITELY BRIGHTER HERE.
LONG, LONG AGO, THE WAKINYAN TOOK THE HAND AND PART OF THE ARM OF A GREAT CHIEF BECAUSE HE WAS SELFISH. THEY PUT IT IN THE SKY! IT BECAME AN IMPORTANT CONSTELLATION—RIGHT UP THERE. IT STILL HELPS US FIND OUR WAY. DON'T WORRY THOUGH, THE CHIEF'S DAUGHTER FIGURED OUT HOW TO HELP HER FATHER.
OF ALL THE LAKOTA WHO HAVE LOOKED UP AT THAT CONSTELLATION, I BET I'M THE FIRST ONE TO CHECK IT OUT WHILE CHILLING NEXT TO A TALKING BUFFALO.

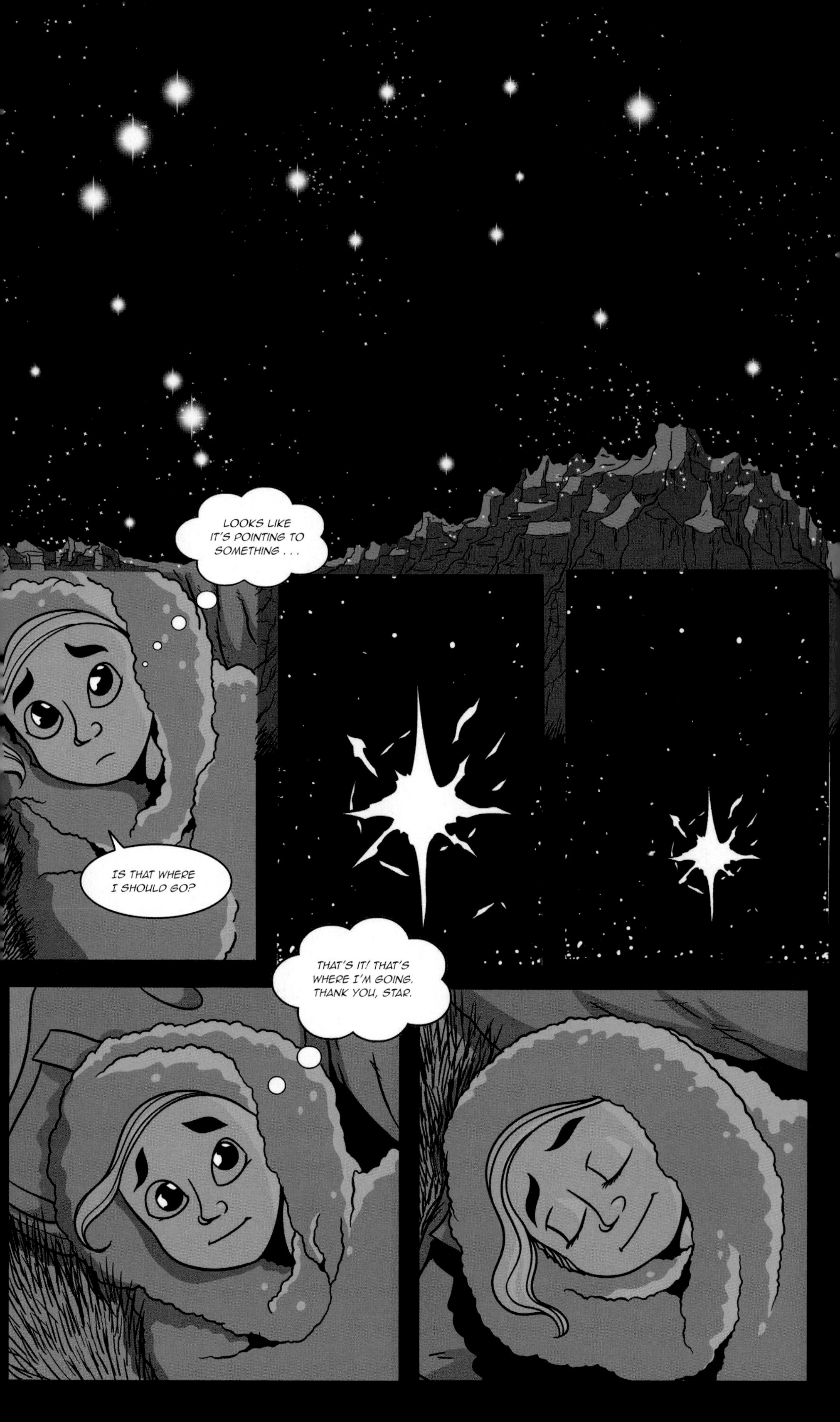

LOOKS LIKE IT'S POINTING TO SOMETHING . . .
IS THAT WHERE I SHOULD GO?
THAT'S IT! THAT'S WHERE I'M GOING. THANK YOU, STAR.

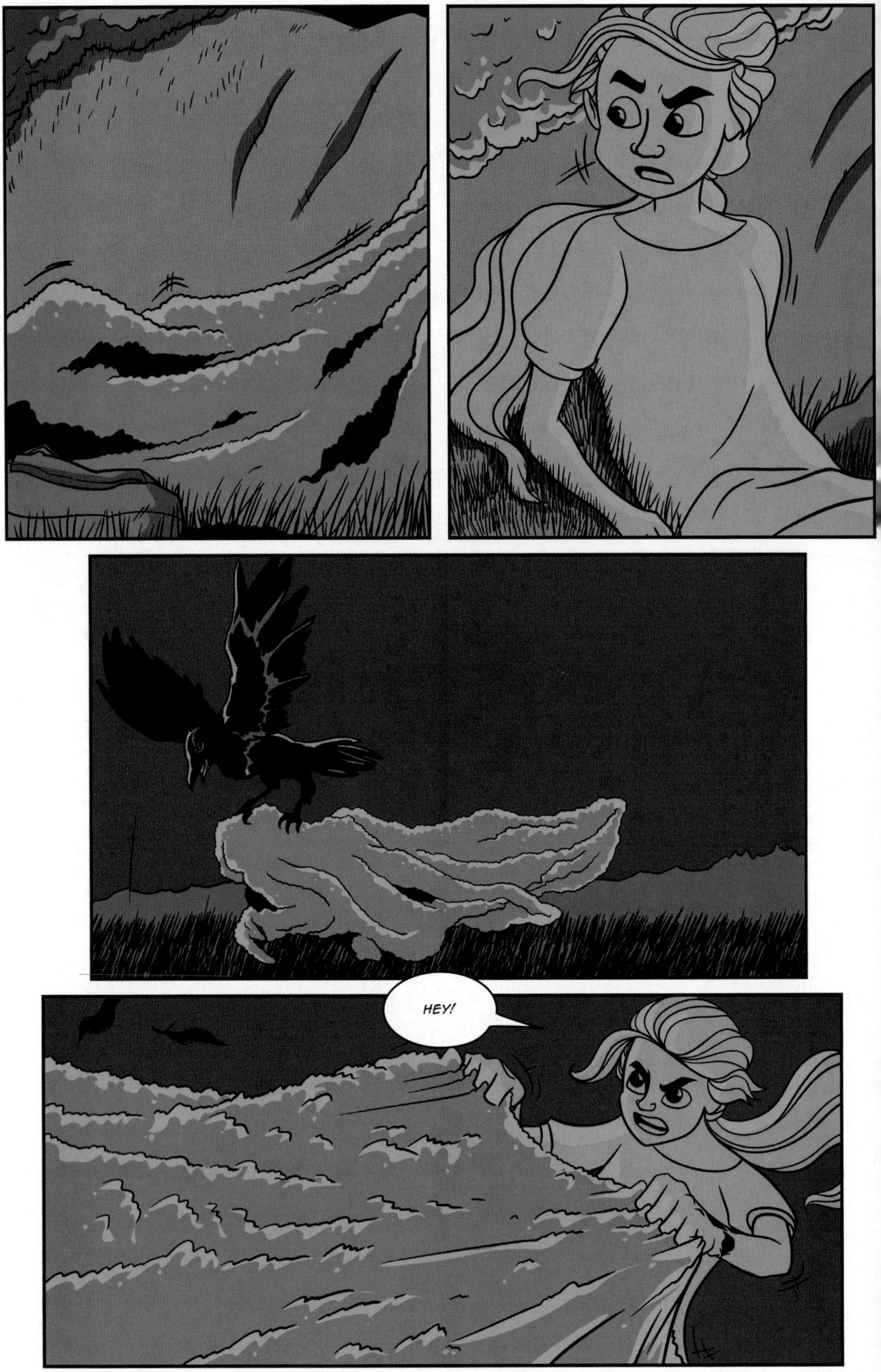
HEY!

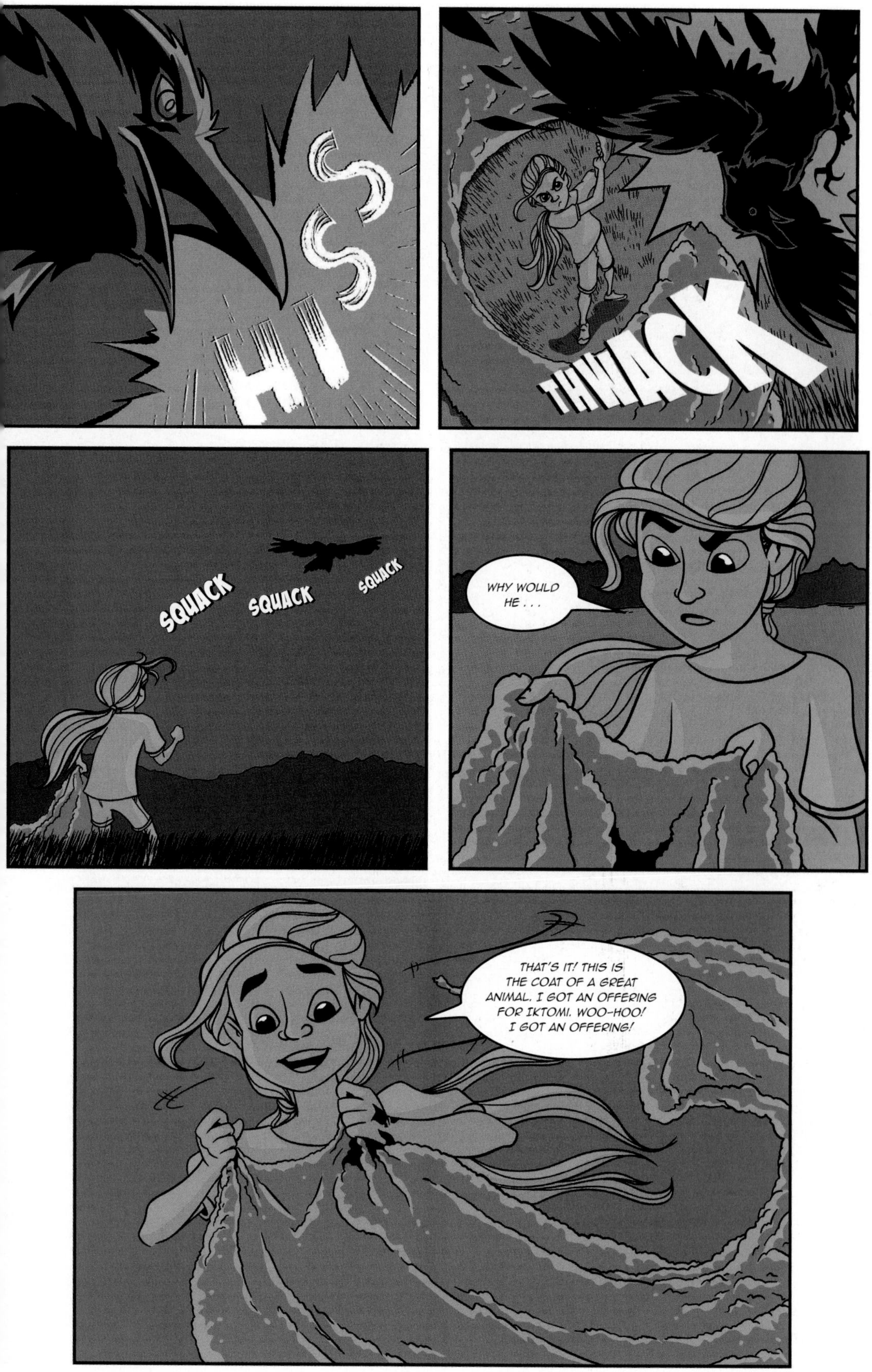
HISS
THWACK
SQUACK
SQUACK
SQUACK
WHY WOULD HE . . .
THAT'S IT! THIS IS THE COAT OF A GREAT ANIMAL. I GOT AN OFFERING FOR IKTOMI. WOO-HOO! I GOT AN OFFERING!

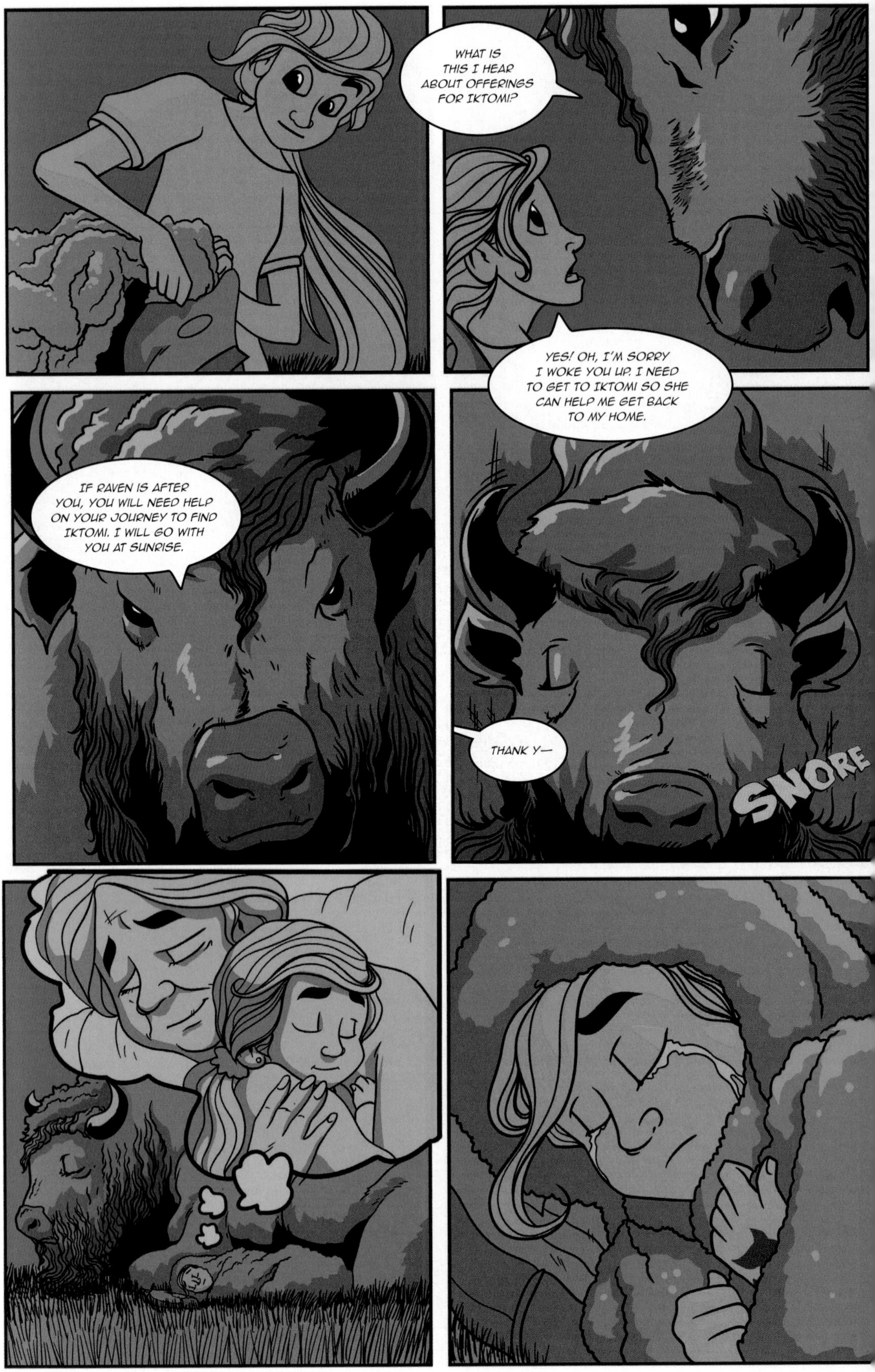
WHAT IS THIS I HEAR ABOUT OFFERINGS FOR IKTOMI?
YES! OH, I'M SORRY I WOKE YOU UP. I NEED TO GET TO IKTOMI SO SHE CAN HELP ME GET BACK TO MY HOME.
IF RAVEN IS AFTER YOU, YOU WILL NEED HELP ON YOUR JOURNEY TO FIND IKTOMI. I WILL GO WITH YOU AT SUNRISE.
THANK Y—
SNORE

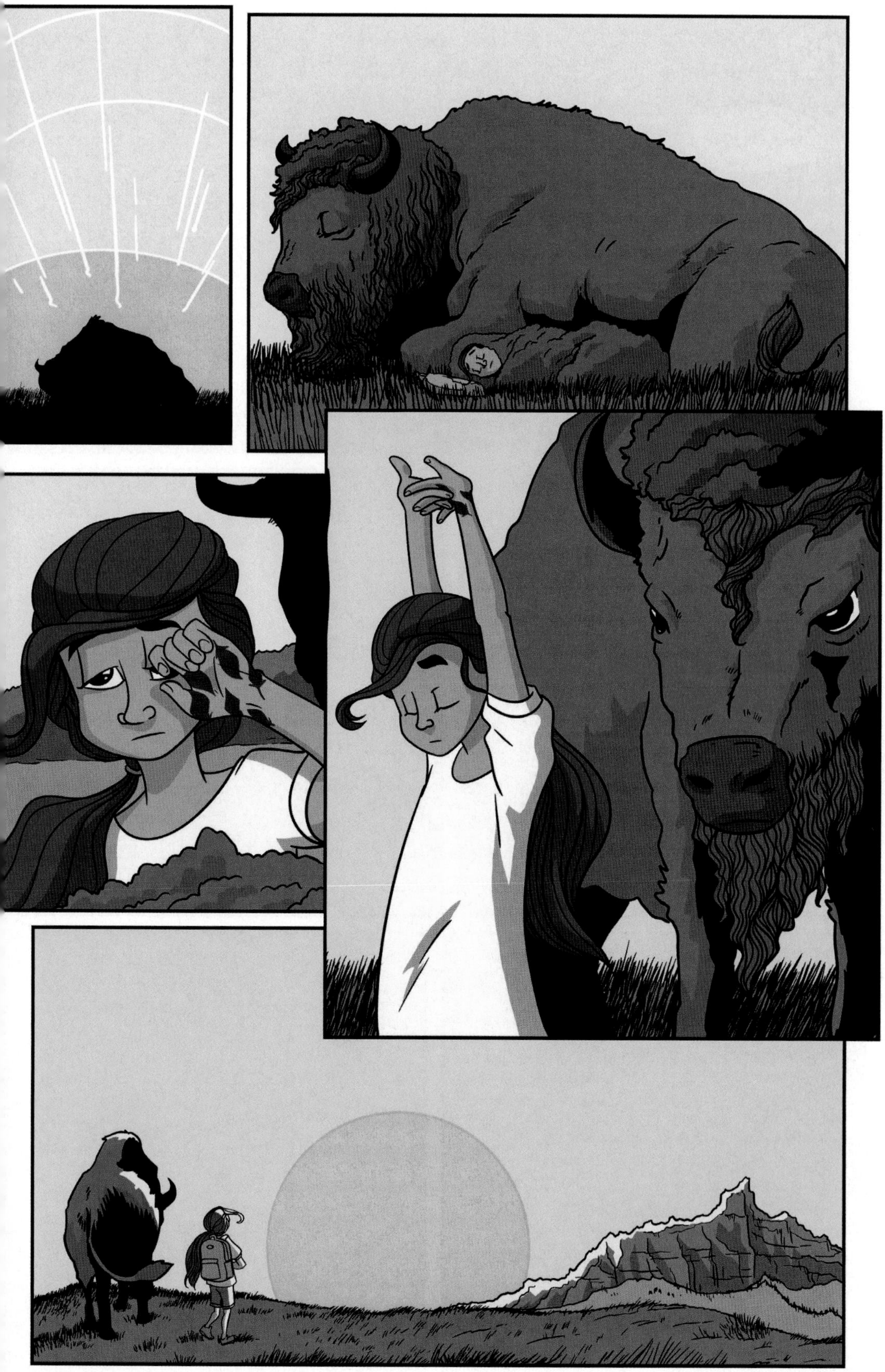

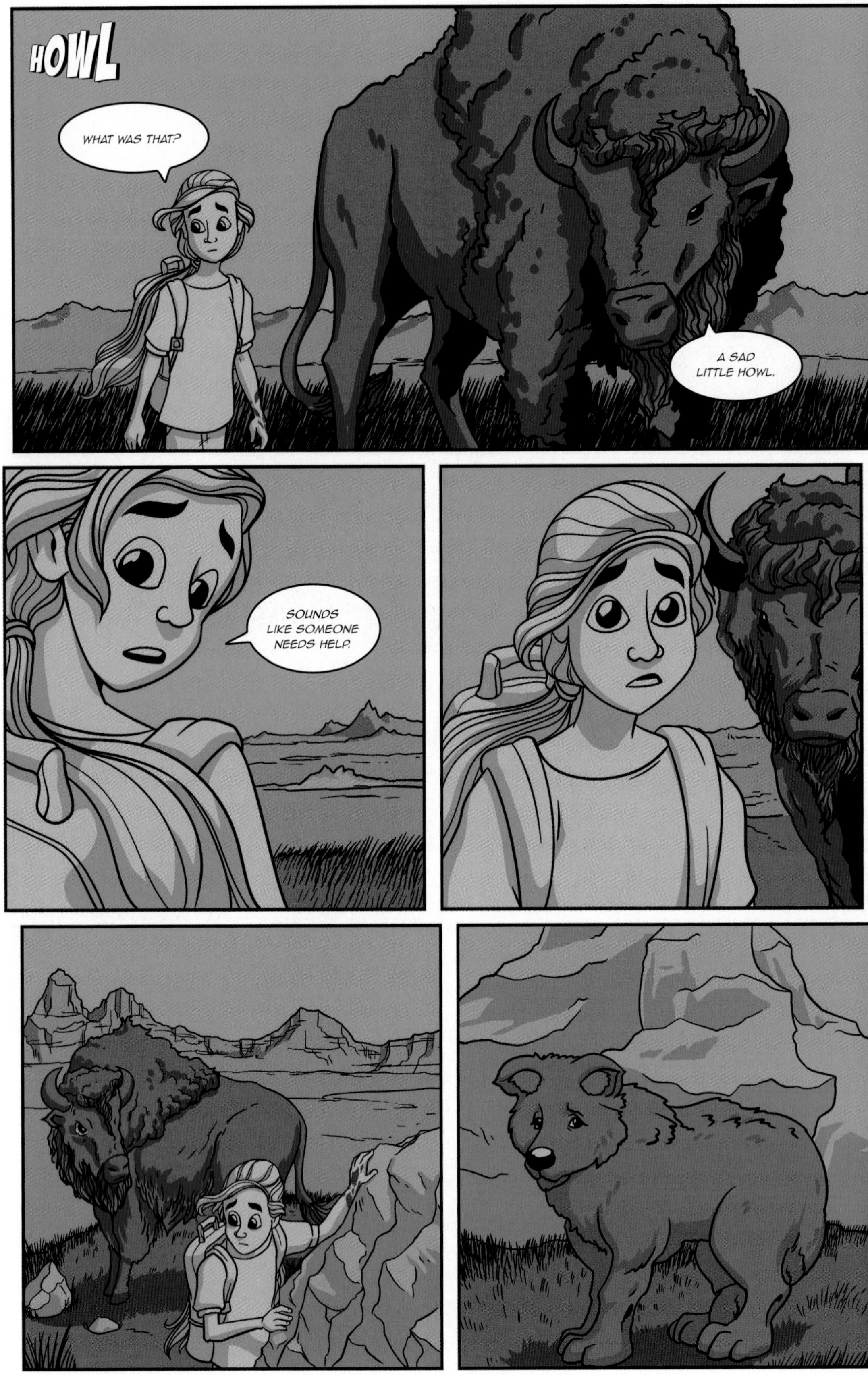
HOWL
WHAT WAS THAT?
A SAD LITTLE HOWL.
SOUNDS LIKE SOMEONE NEEDS HELP.

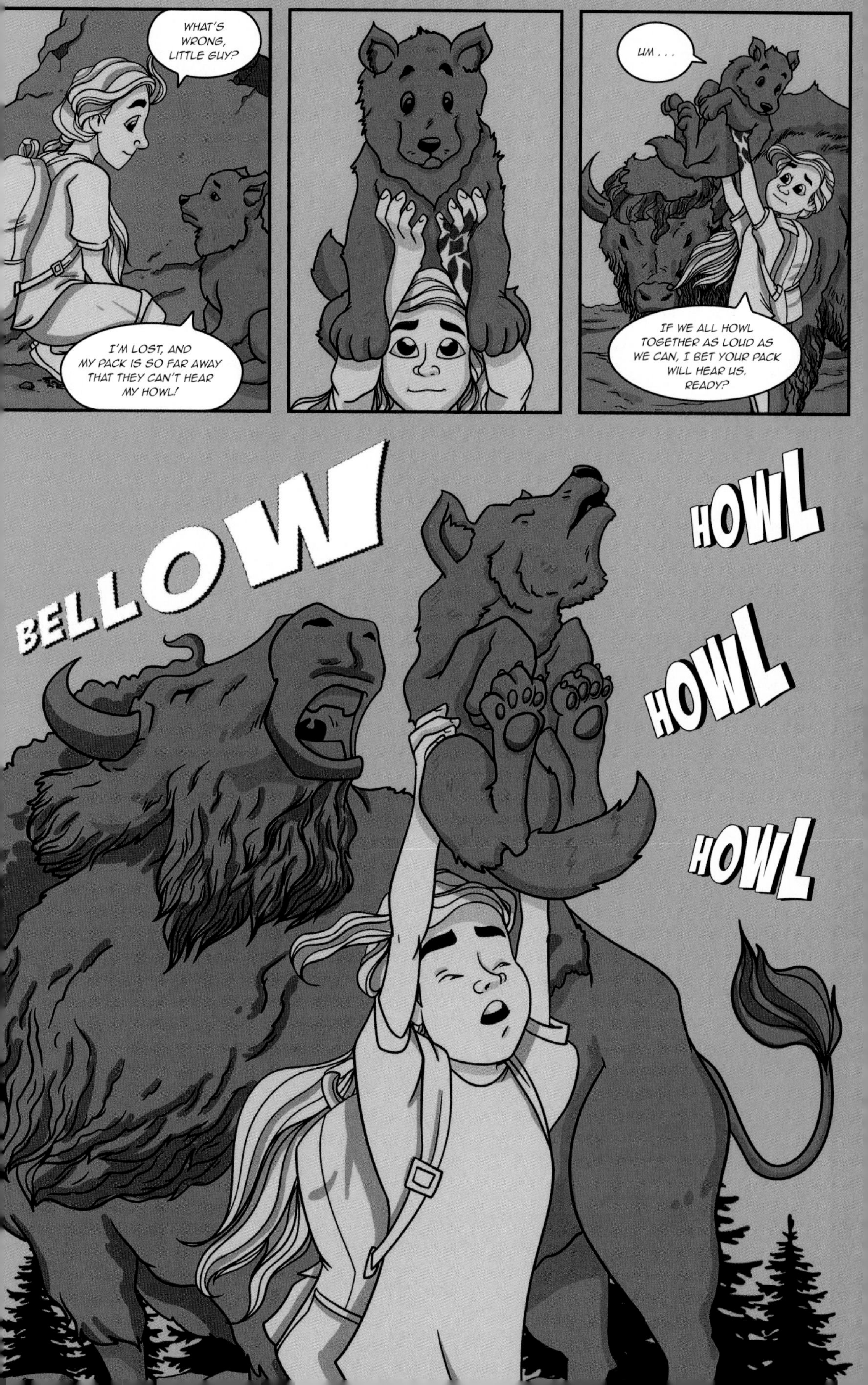
WHAT'S WRONG, LITTLE GUY?
I'M LOST, AND MY PACK IS SO FAR AWAY THAT THEY CAN'T HEAR MY HOWL!
UM . . .
IF WE ALL HOWL TOGETHER AS LOUD AS WE CAN, I BET YOUR PACK WILL HEAR US. READY?
BELLOW
HOWL
HOWL
HOWL

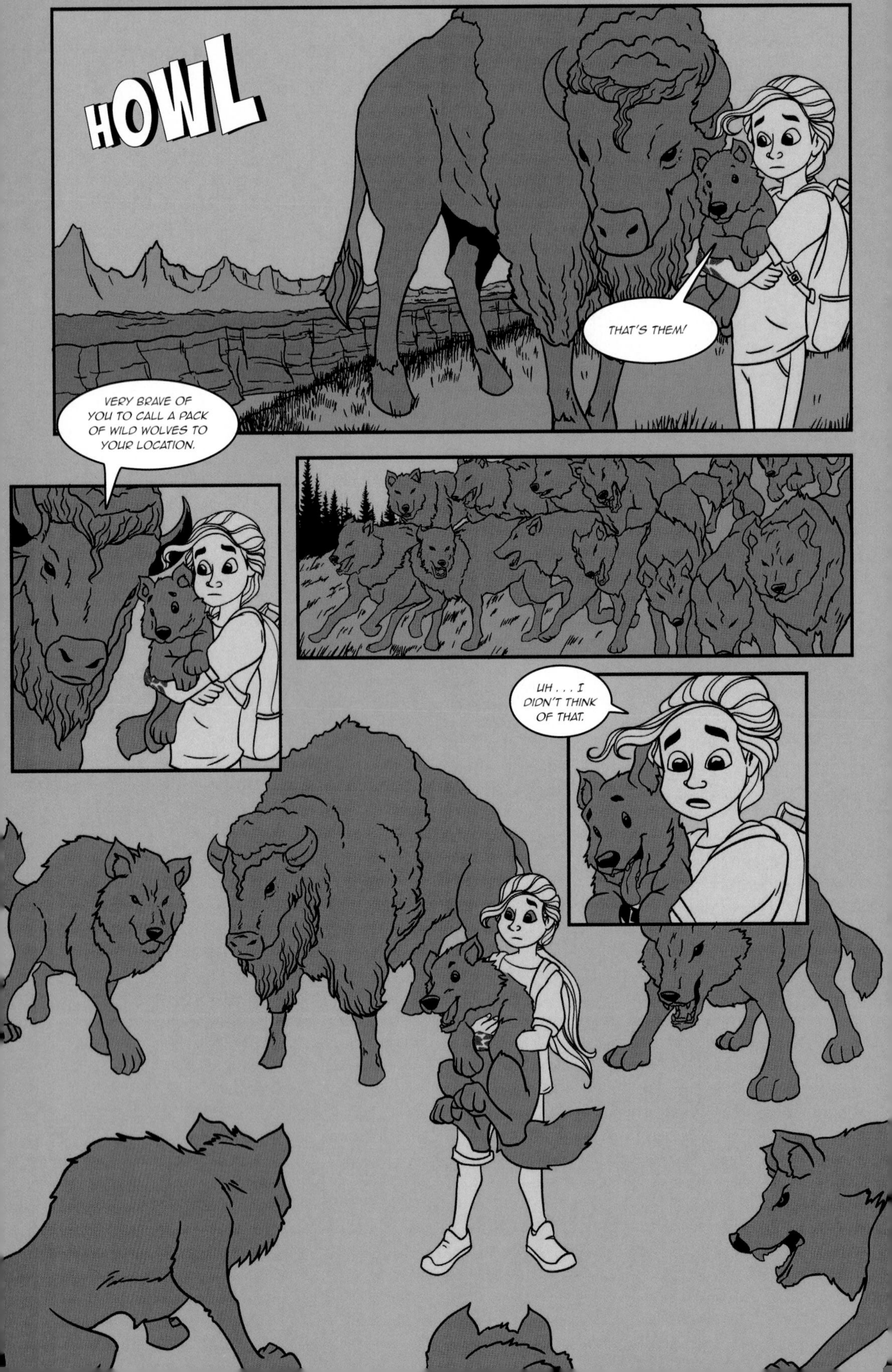
HOWL
THAT'S THEM!
VERY BRAVE OF YOU TO CALL A PACK OF WILD WOLVES TO YOUR LOCATION.
UH . . . I DIDN'T THINK OF THAT.

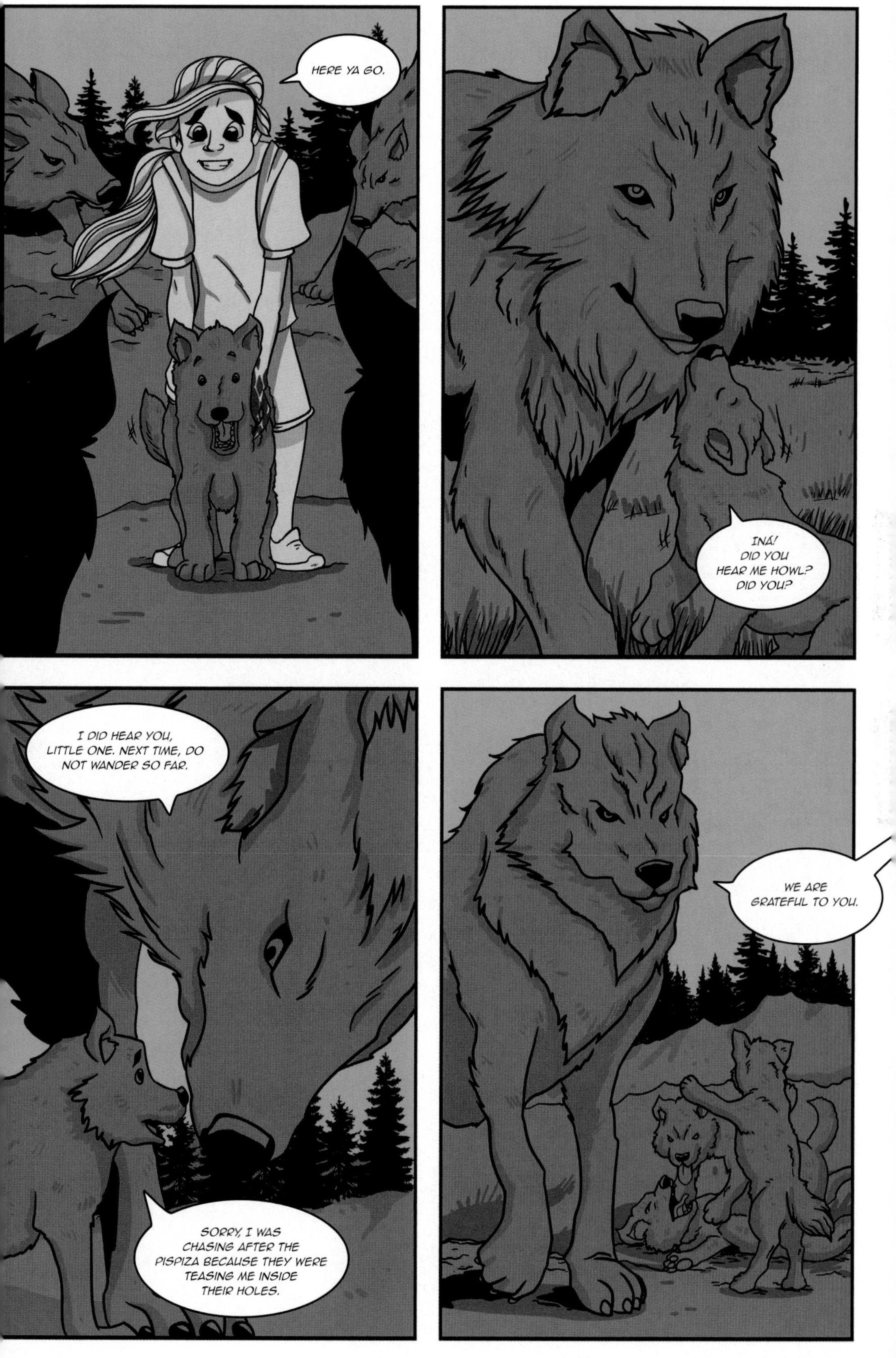
HERE YA GO.
INÁ! DID YOU HEAR ME HOWL? DID YOU?
I DID HEAR YOU, LITTLE ONE. NEXT TIME, DO NOT WANDER SO FAR.
SORRY, I WAS CHASING AFTER THE PISPIZA BECAUSE THEY WERE TEASING ME INSIDE THEIR HOLES.
WE ARE GRATEFUL TO YOU.

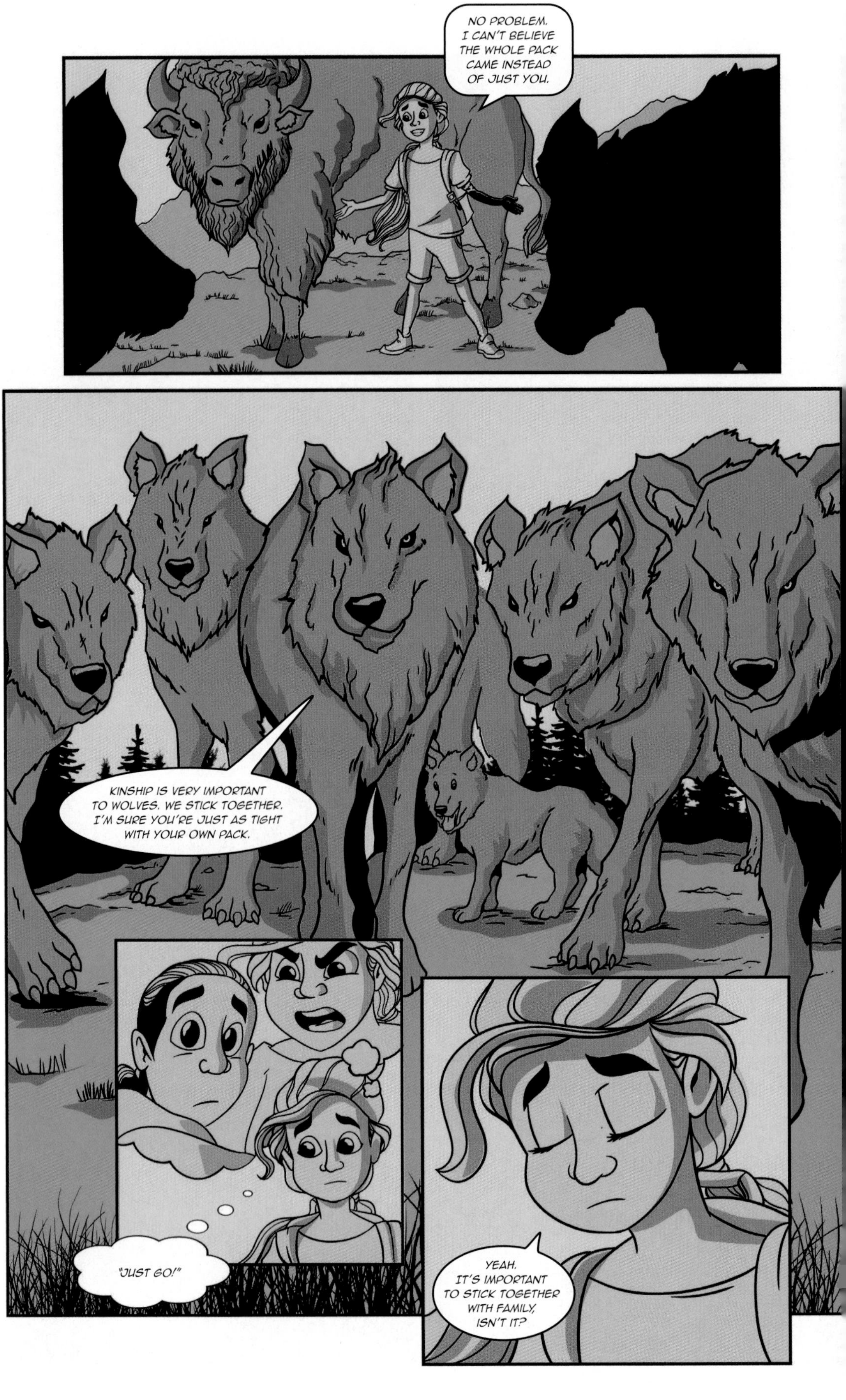
NO PROBLEM. I CAN'T BELIEVE THE WHOLE PACK CAME INSTEAD OF JUST YOU.
KINSHIP IS VERY IMPORTANT TO WOLVES. WE STICK TOGETHER. I'M SURE YOU'RE JUST AS TIGHT WITH YOUR OWN PACK.
"JUST GO!"
YEAH. IT'S IMPORTANT TO STICK TOGETHER WITH FAMILY, ISN'T IT?

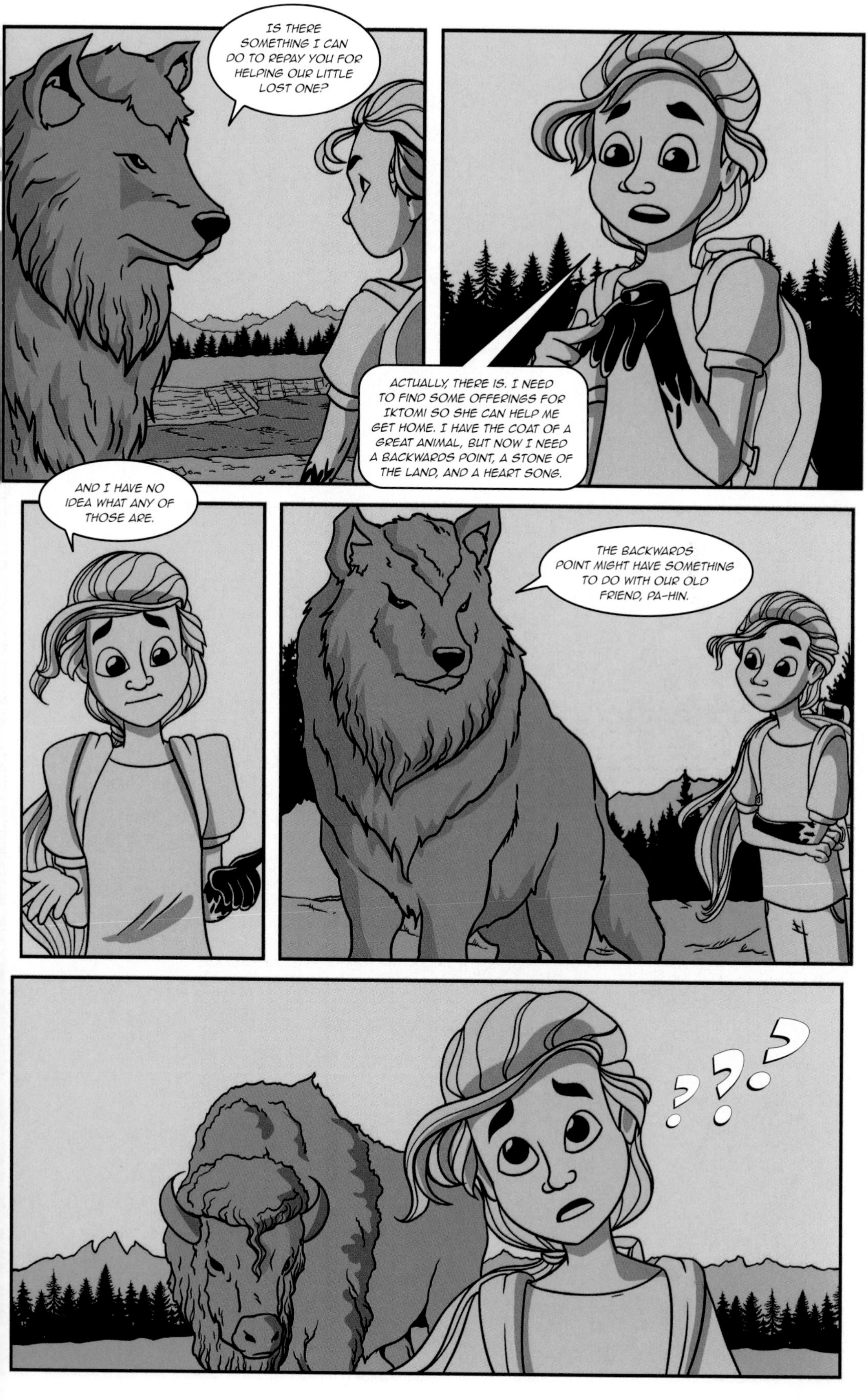
IS THERE SOMETHING I CAN DO TO REPAY YOU FOR HELPING OUR LITTLE LOST ONE?
ACTUALLY, THERE IS. I NEED TO FIND SOME OFFERINGS FOR IKTOMI SO SHE CAN HELP ME GET HOME. I HAVE THE COAT OF A GREAT ANIMAL, BUT NOW I NEED A BACKWARDS POINT, A STONE OF THE LAND, AND A HEART SONG.
AND I HAVE NO IDEA WHAT ANY OF THOSE ARE.
THE BACKWARDS POINT MIGHT HAVE SOMETHING TO DO WITH OUR OLD FRIEND, PA-HIN.
???

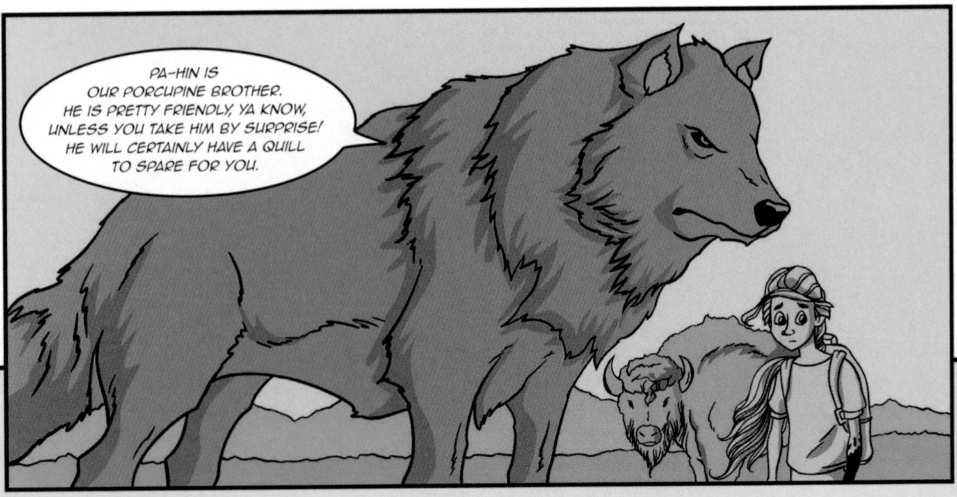
PA-HIN IS
OUR PORCUPINE BROTHER.
HE IS PRETTY FRIENDLY, YA KNOW,
UNLESS YOU TAKE HIM BY SURPRISE!
HE WILL CERTAINLY HAVE A QUILL
TO SPARE FOR YOU.

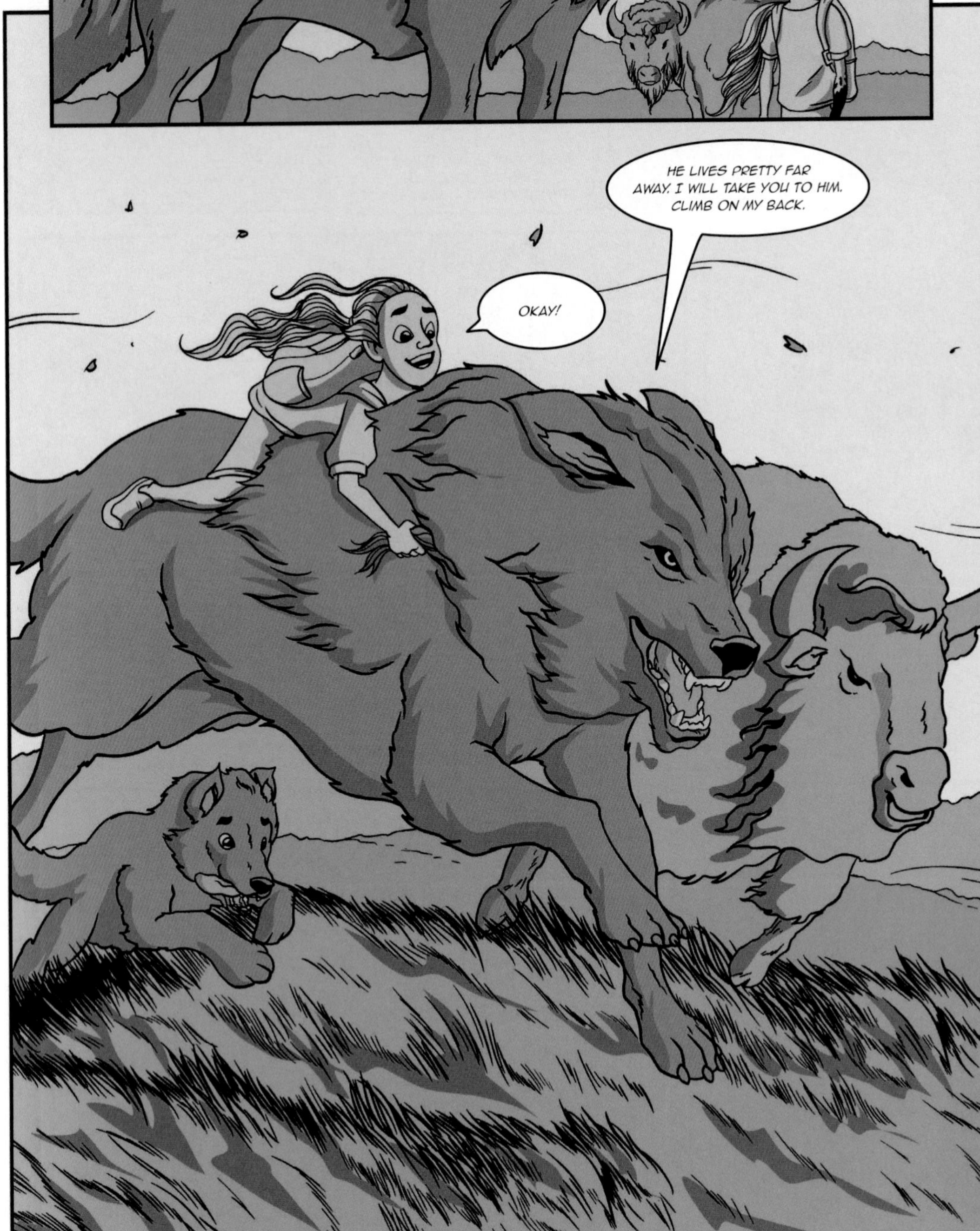
HE LIVES PRETTY FAR
AWAY. I WILL TAKE YOU TO HIM.
CLIMB ON MY BACK.
OKAY!

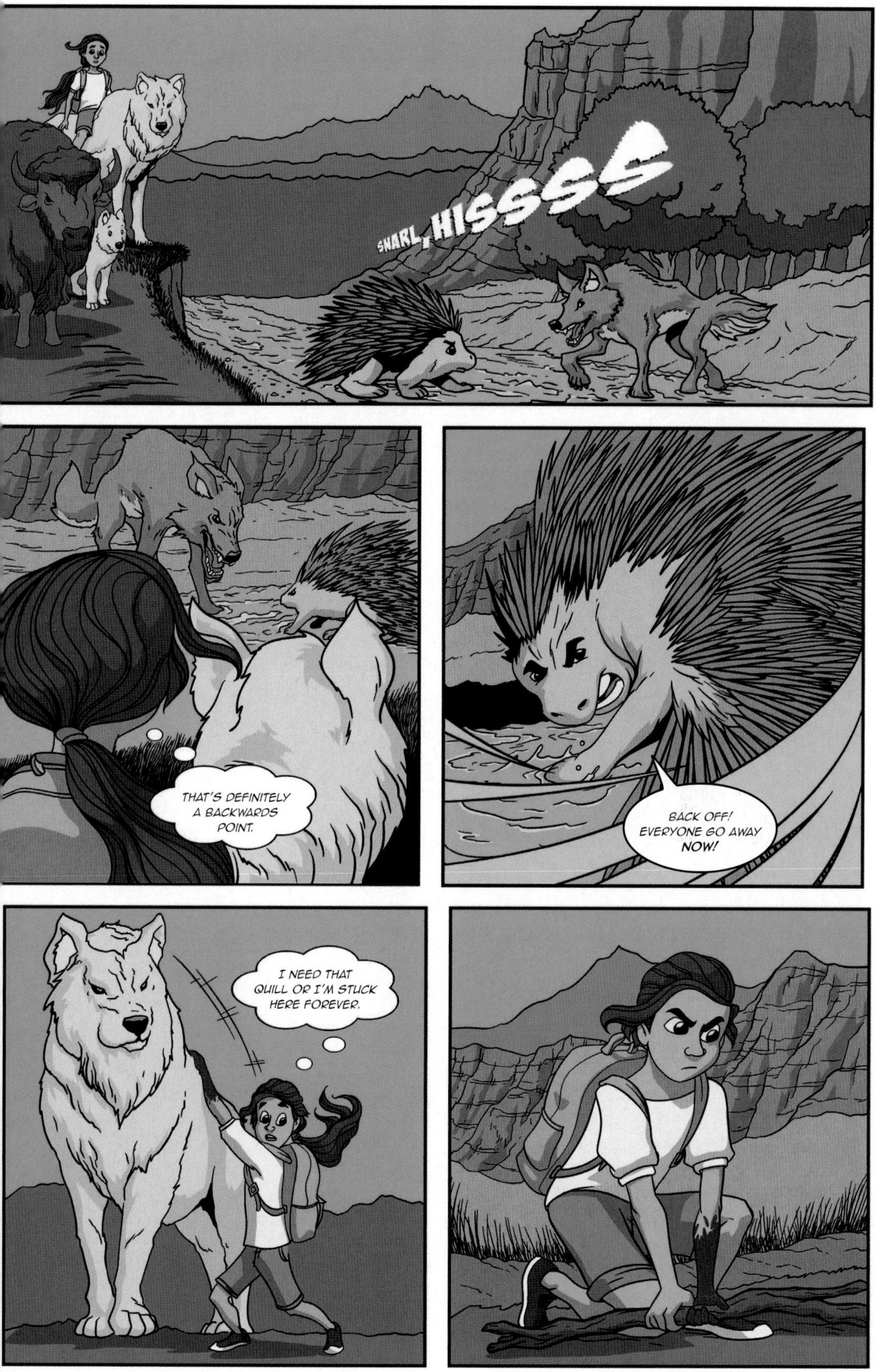
SNARL, HISSSSS
THAT'S DEFINITELY A BACKWARDS POINT.
BACK OFF! EVERYONE GO AWAY NOW!
I NEED THAT QUILL OR I'M STUCK HERE FOREVER.

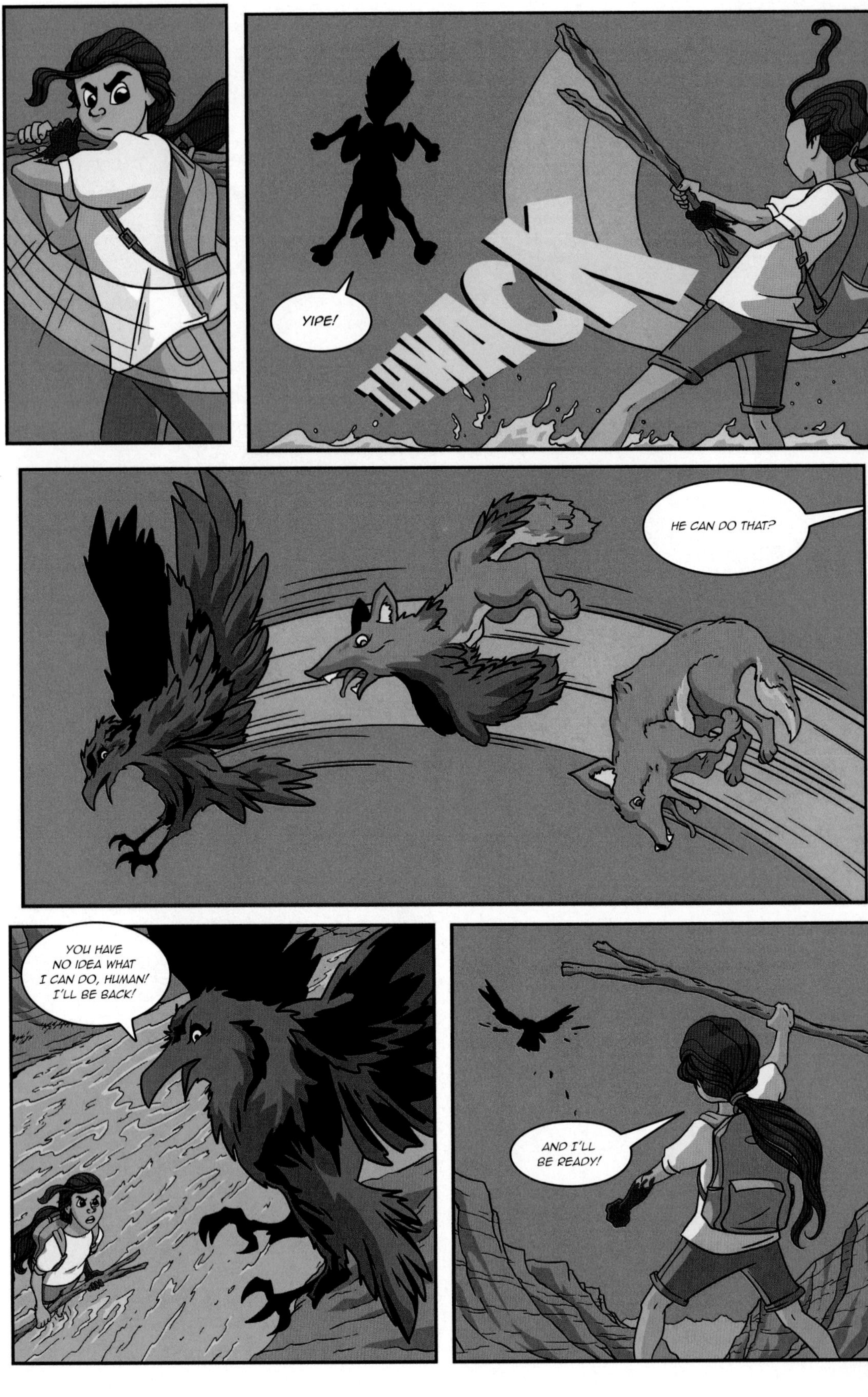
YIPE!
THWACK
HE CAN DO THAT?
YOU HAVE NO IDEA WHAT I CAN DO, HUMAN! I'LL BE BACK!
AND I'LL BE READY!

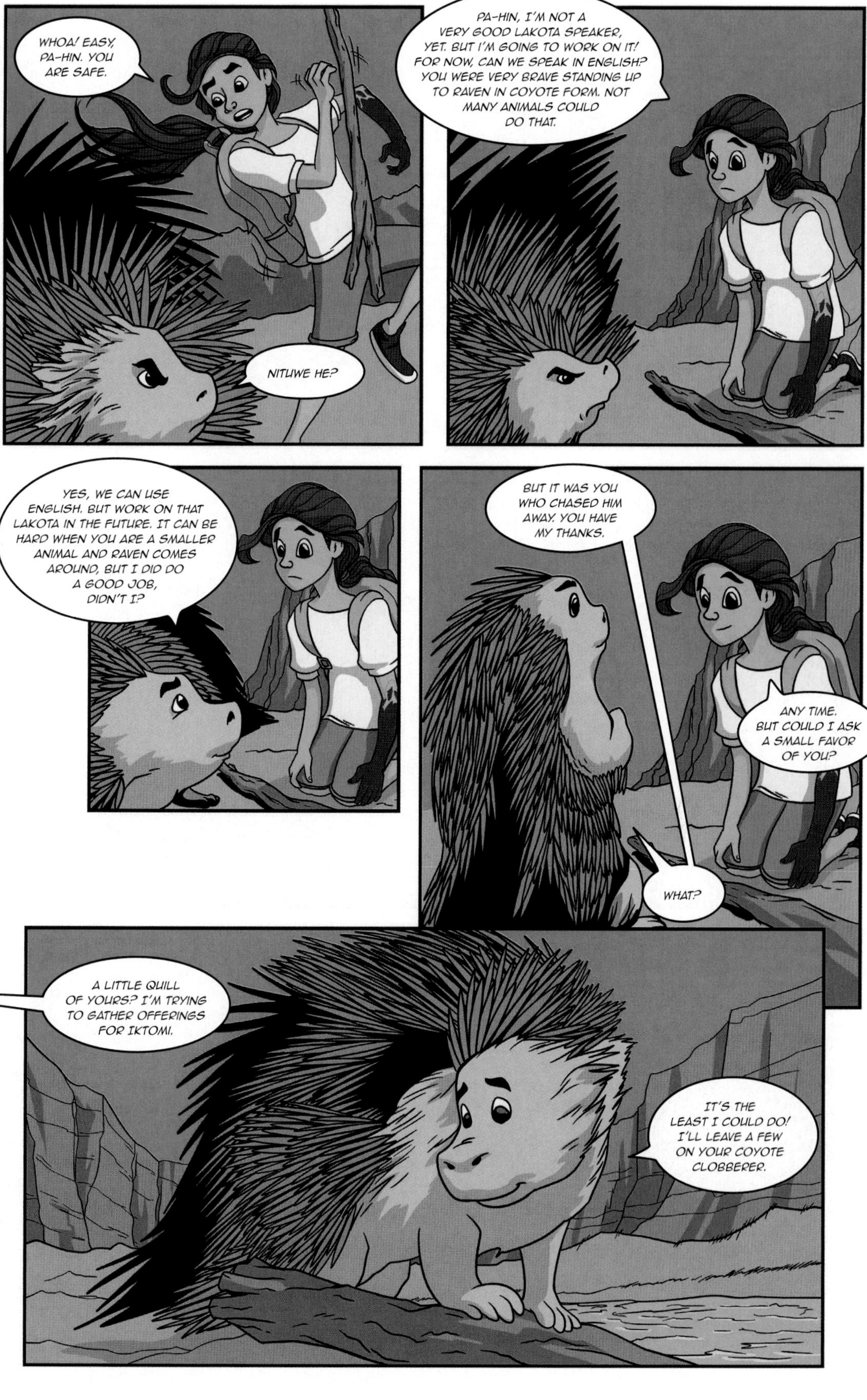
WHOA! EASY, PA-HIN. YOU ARE SAFE.
NITUWE HE?
PA-HIN, I'M NOT A VERY GOOD LAKOTA SPEAKER, YET. BUT I'M GOING TO WORK ON IT! FOR NOW, CAN WE SPEAK IN ENGLISH? YOU WERE VERY BRAVE STANDING UP TO RAVEN IN COYOTE FORM. NOT MANY ANIMALS COULD DO THAT.
YES, WE CAN USE ENGLISH. BUT WORK ON THAT LAKOTA IN THE FUTURE. IT CAN BE HARD WHEN YOU ARE A SMALLER ANIMAL AND RAVEN COMES AROUND, BUT I DID DO A GOOD JOB, DIDN'T I?
BUT IT WAS YOU WHO CHASED HIM AWAY. YOU HAVE MY THANKS.
ANY TIME. BUT COULD I ASK A SMALL FAVOR OF YOU?
WHAT?
A LITTLE QUILL OF YOURS? I'M TRYING TO GATHER OFFERINGS FOR IKTOMI.
IT'S THE LEAST I COULD DO! I'LL LEAVE A FEW ON YOUR COYOTE CLOBBERER.

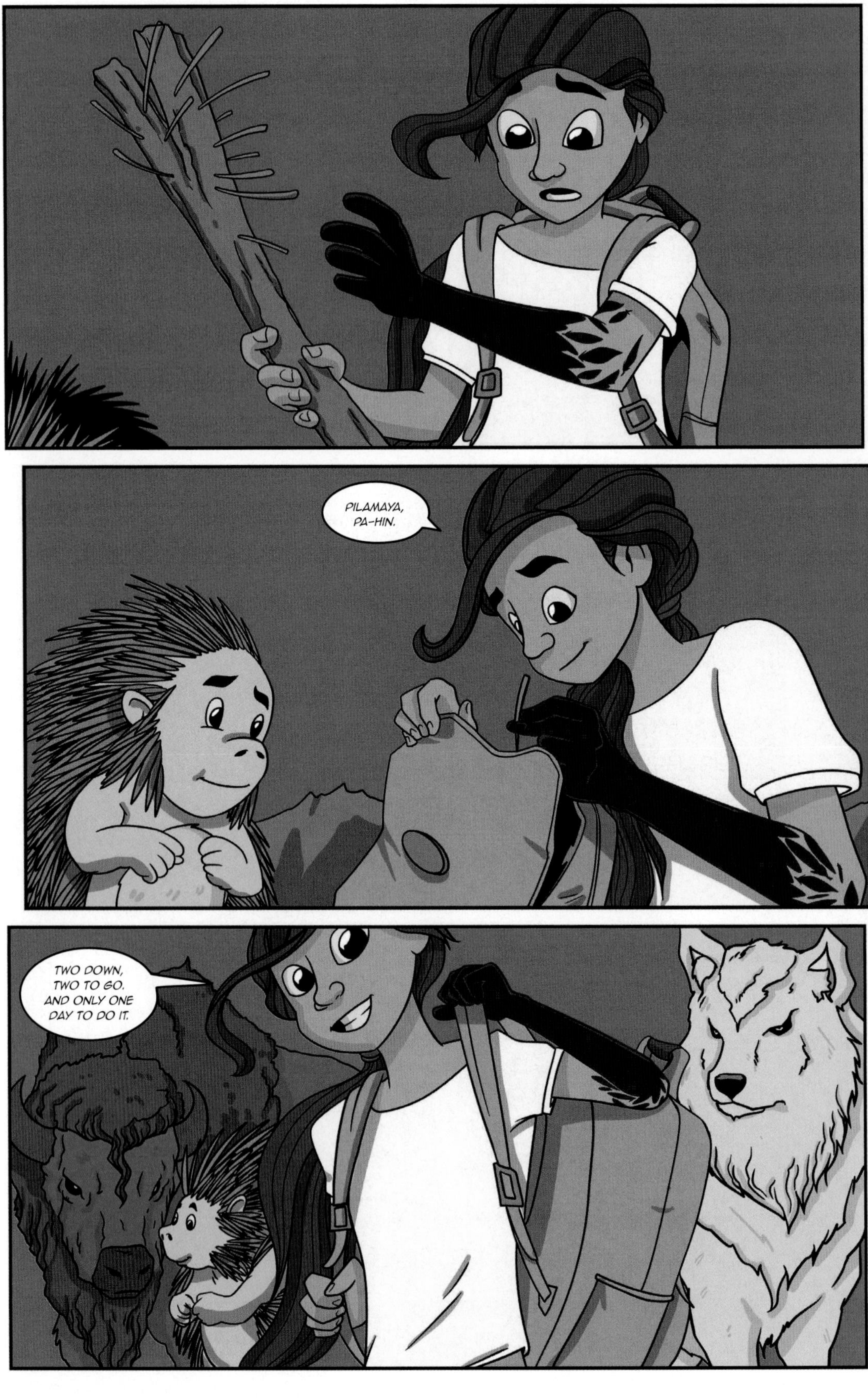
PILAMAYA, PA-HIN.
TWO DOWN, TWO TO GO. AND ONLY ONE DAY TO DO IT.

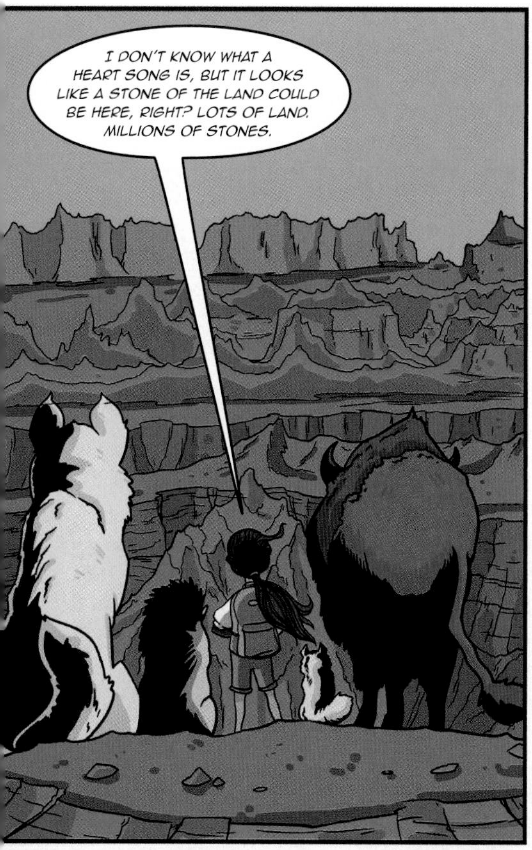
I DON'T KNOW WHAT A HEART SONG IS, BUT IT LOOKS LIKE A STONE OF THE LAND COULD BE HERE, RIGHT? LOTS OF LAND. MILLIONS OF STONES.

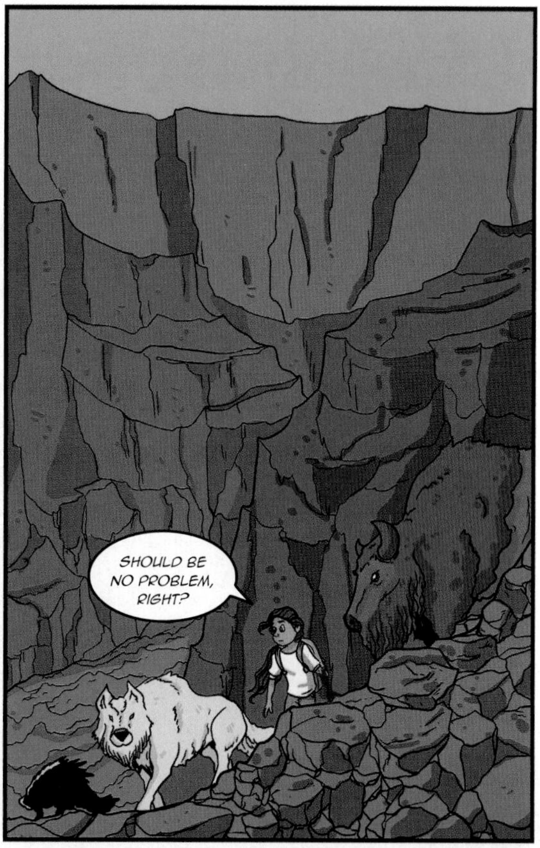
SHOULD BE NO PROBLEM, RIGHT?

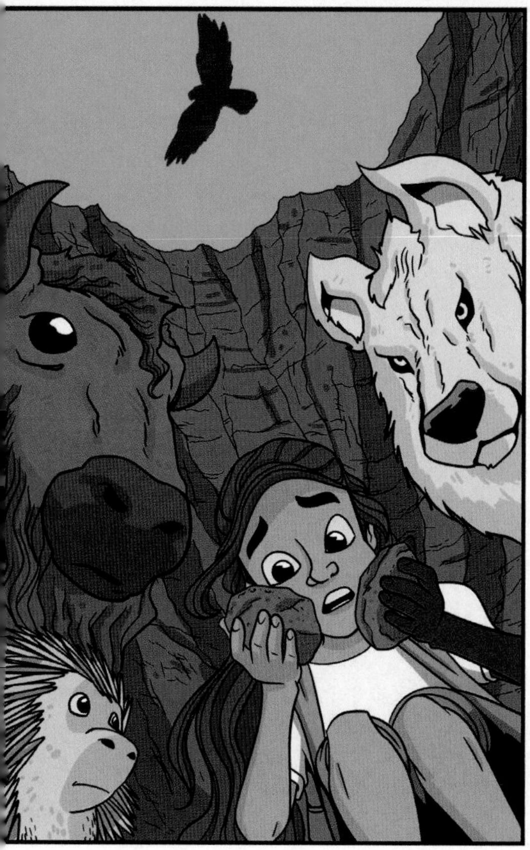

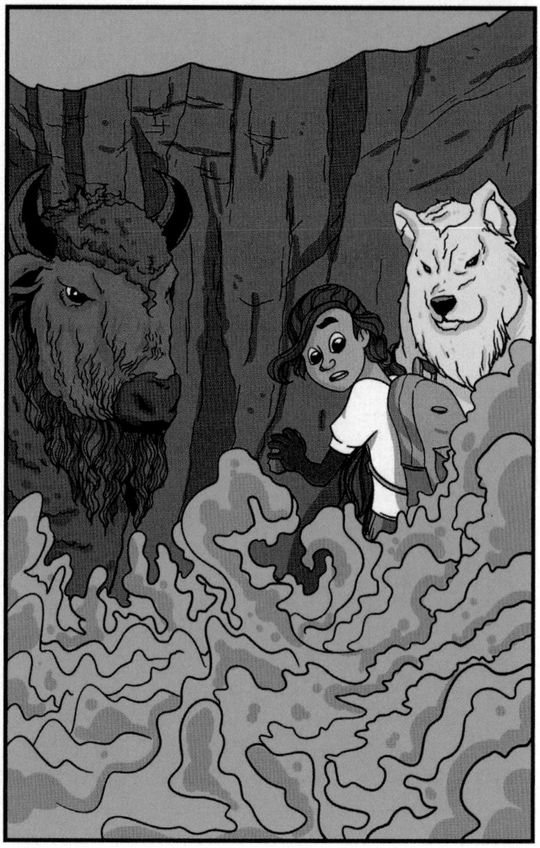

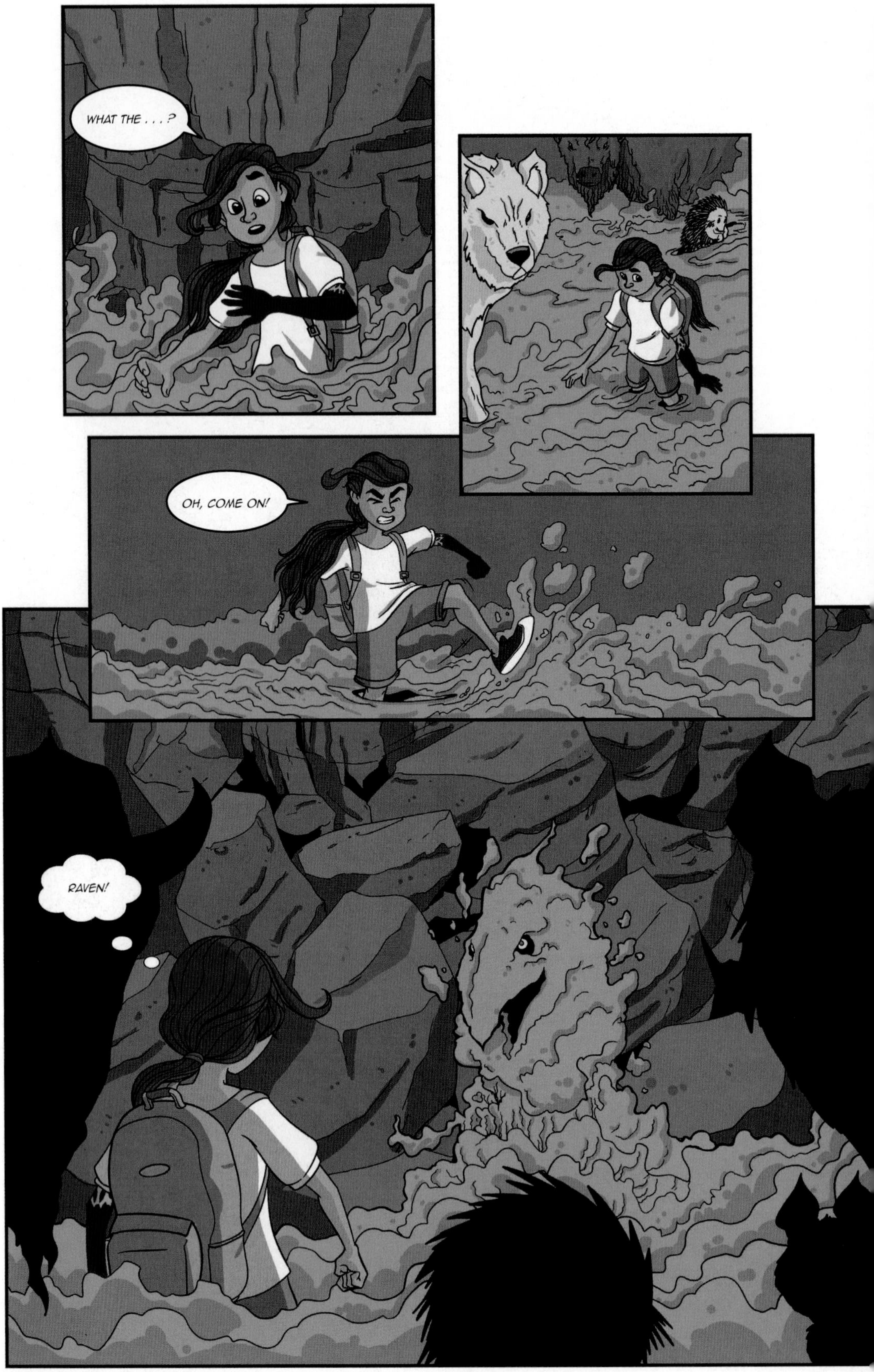
WHAT THE . . . ?
OH, COME ON!
RAVEN!

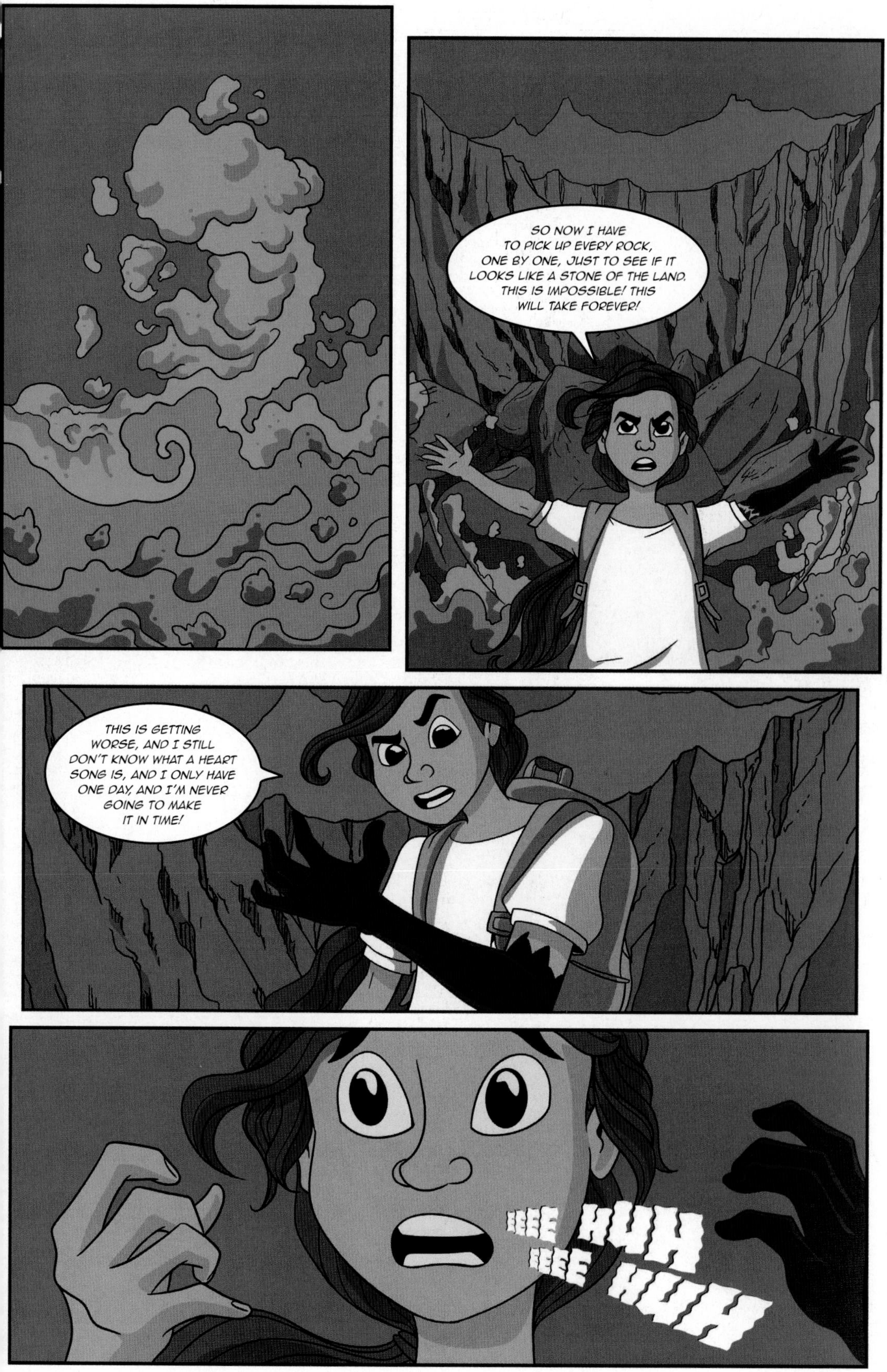
SO NOW I HAVE TO PICK UP EVERY ROCK, ONE BY ONE, JUST TO SEE IF IT LOOKS LIKE A STONE OF THE LAND. THIS IS IMPOSSIBLE! THIS WILL TAKE FOREVER!
THIS IS GETTING WORSE, AND I STILL DON'T KNOW WHAT A HEART SONG IS, AND I ONLY HAVE ONE DAY, AND I'M NEVER GOING TO MAKE IT IN TIME!
EEEE HUH
EEEE HUH

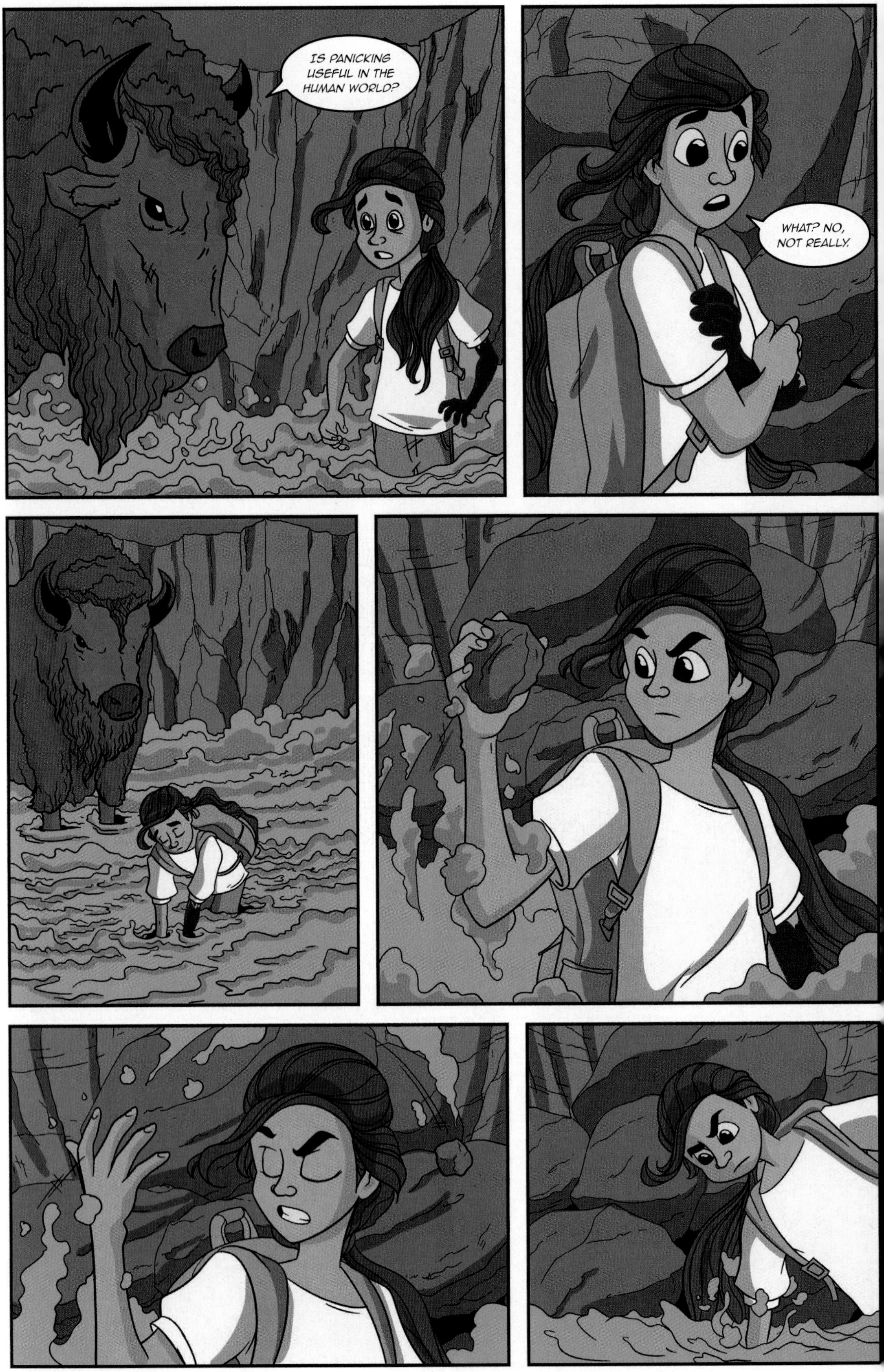
IS PANICKING USEFUL IN THE HUMAN WORLD?
WHAT? NO, NOT REALLY.

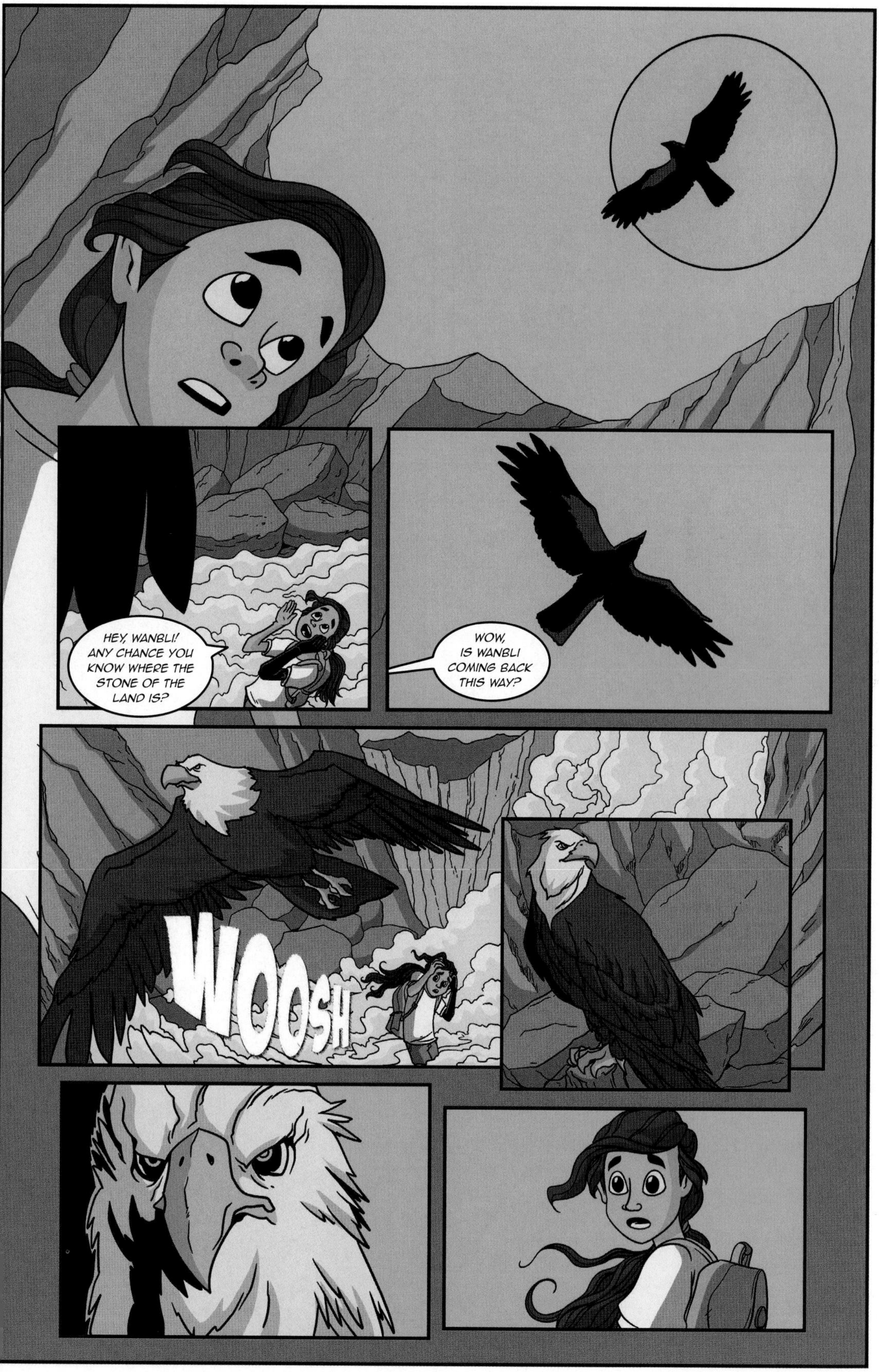
HEY, WANBLI! ANY CHANCE YOU KNOW WHERE THE STONE OF THE LAND IS?
WOW, IS WANBLI COMING BACK THIS WAY?
WOOSH

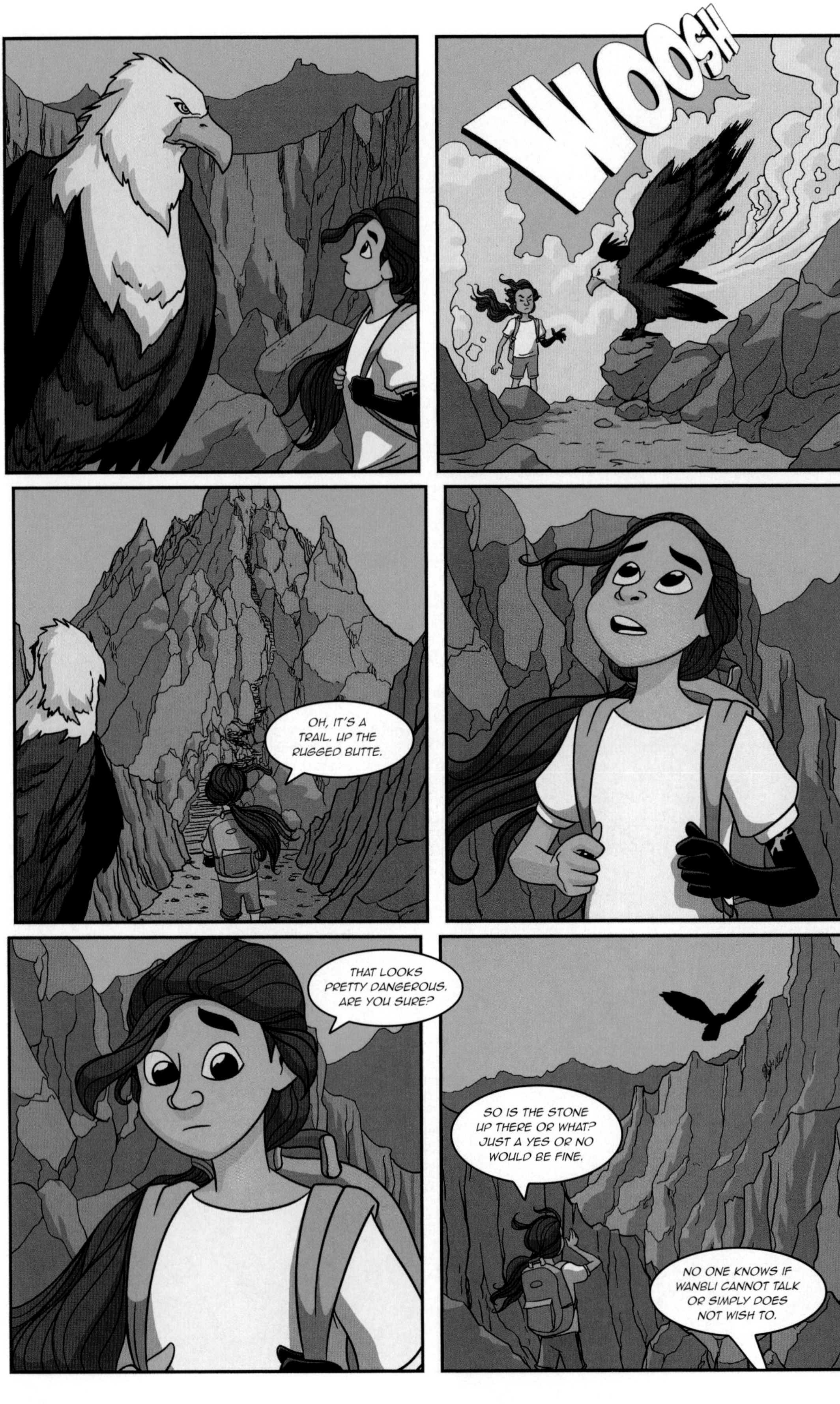
WOOSH
OH, IT'S A TRAIL. UP THE RUGGED BUTTE.
THAT LOOKS PRETTY DANGEROUS. ARE YOU SURE?
SO IS THE STONE UP THERE OR WHAT? JUST A YES OR NO WOULD BE FINE.
NO ONE KNOWS IF WANBLI CANNOT TALK OR SIMPLY DOES NOT WISH TO.

OKAY, THEN.

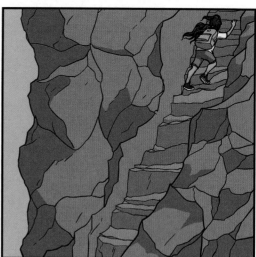

WOW . . .

KOLA WOULD LOVE ALL OF THIS.

CAN'T BELIEVE HOW MUCH I'M MISSING THEM RIGHT NOW.

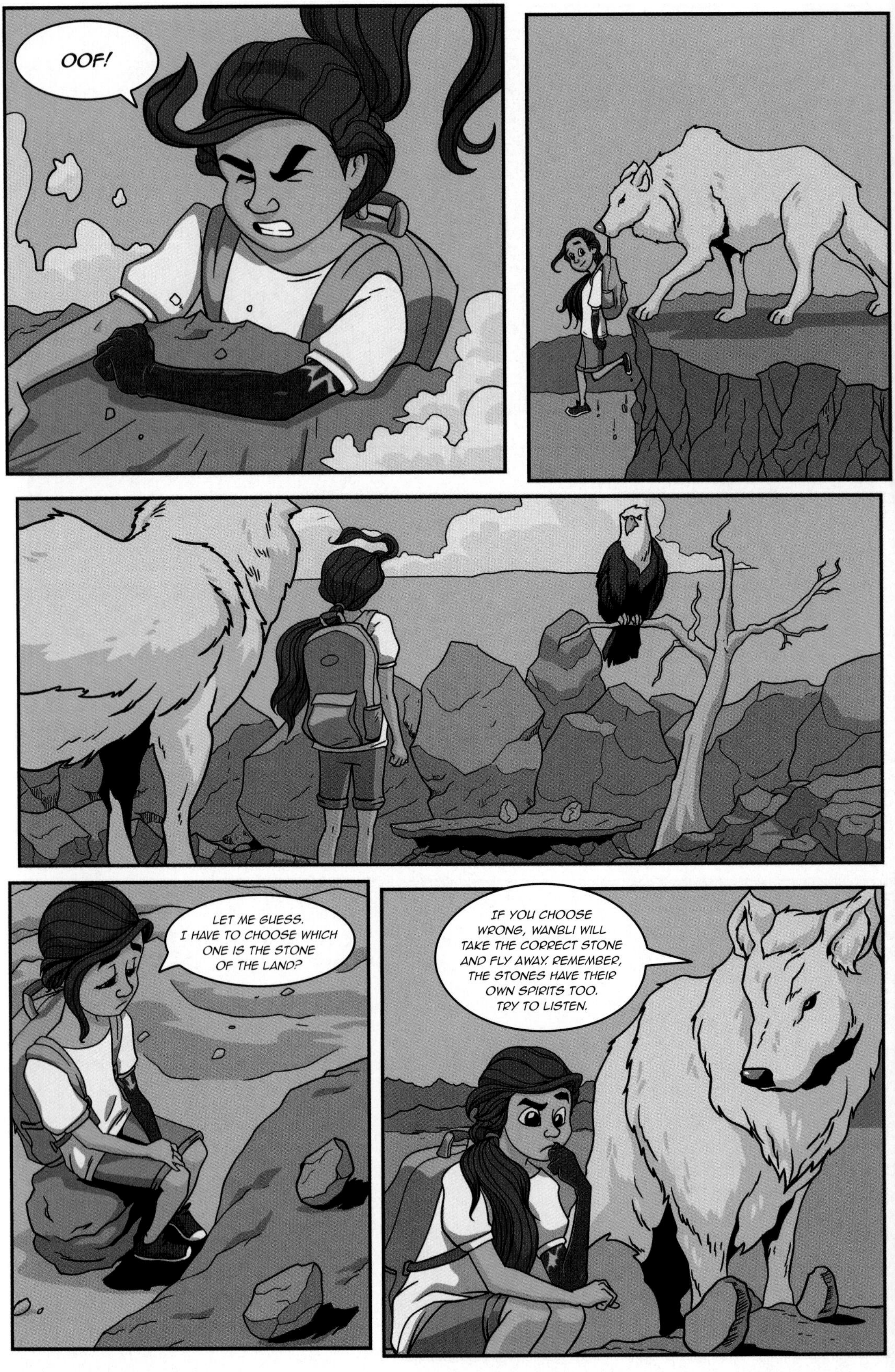
OOF!
LET ME GUESS. I HAVE TO CHOOSE WHICH ONE IS THE STONE OF THE LAND?
IF YOU CHOOSE WRONG, WANBLI WILL TAKE THE CORRECT STONE AND FLY AWAY. REMEMBER, THE STONES HAVE THEIR OWN SPIRITS TOO. TRY TO LISTEN.

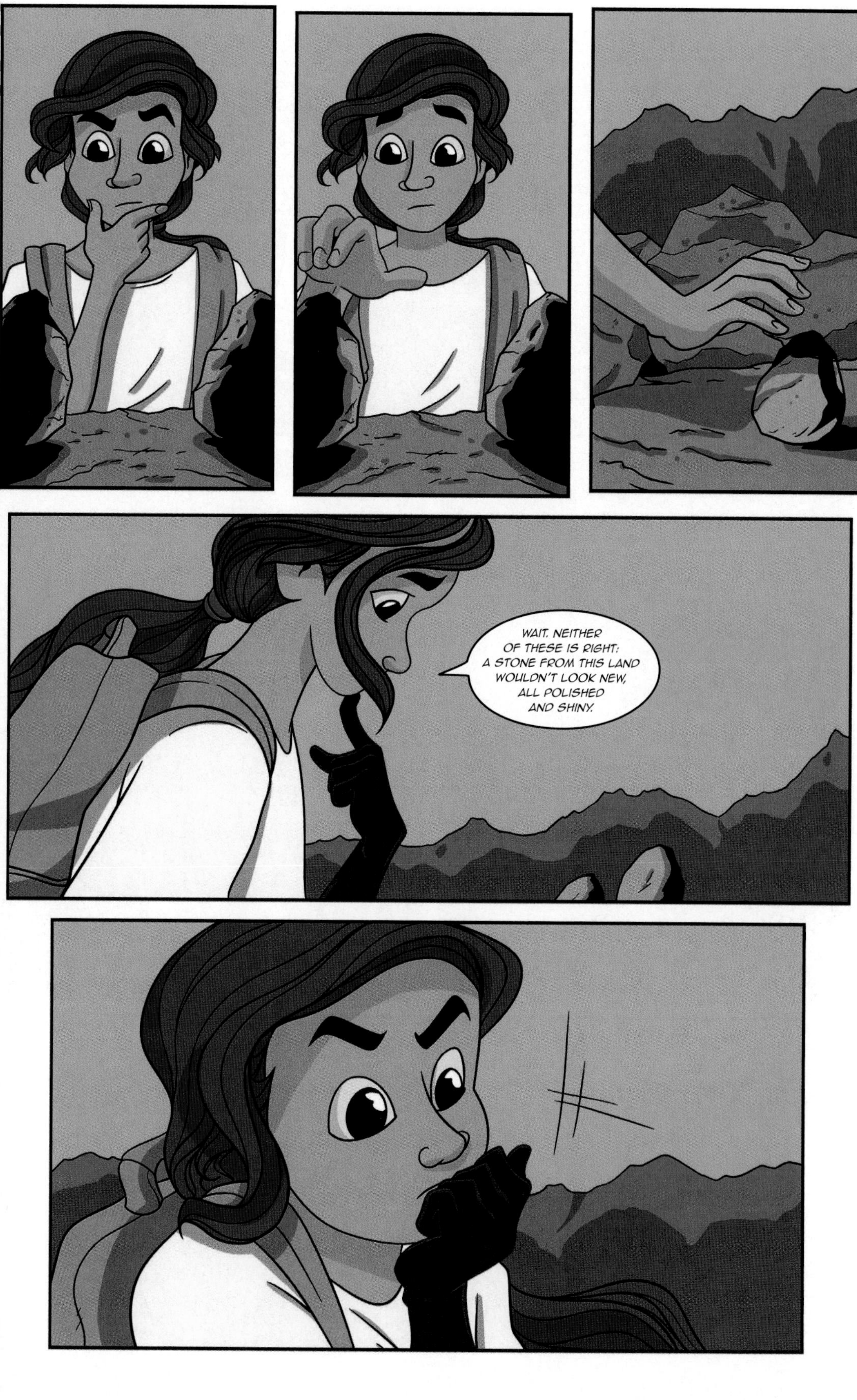
WAIT. NEITHER
OF THESE IS RIGHT:
A STONE FROM THIS LAND
WOULDN'T LOOK NEW,
ALL POLISHED
AND SHINY.

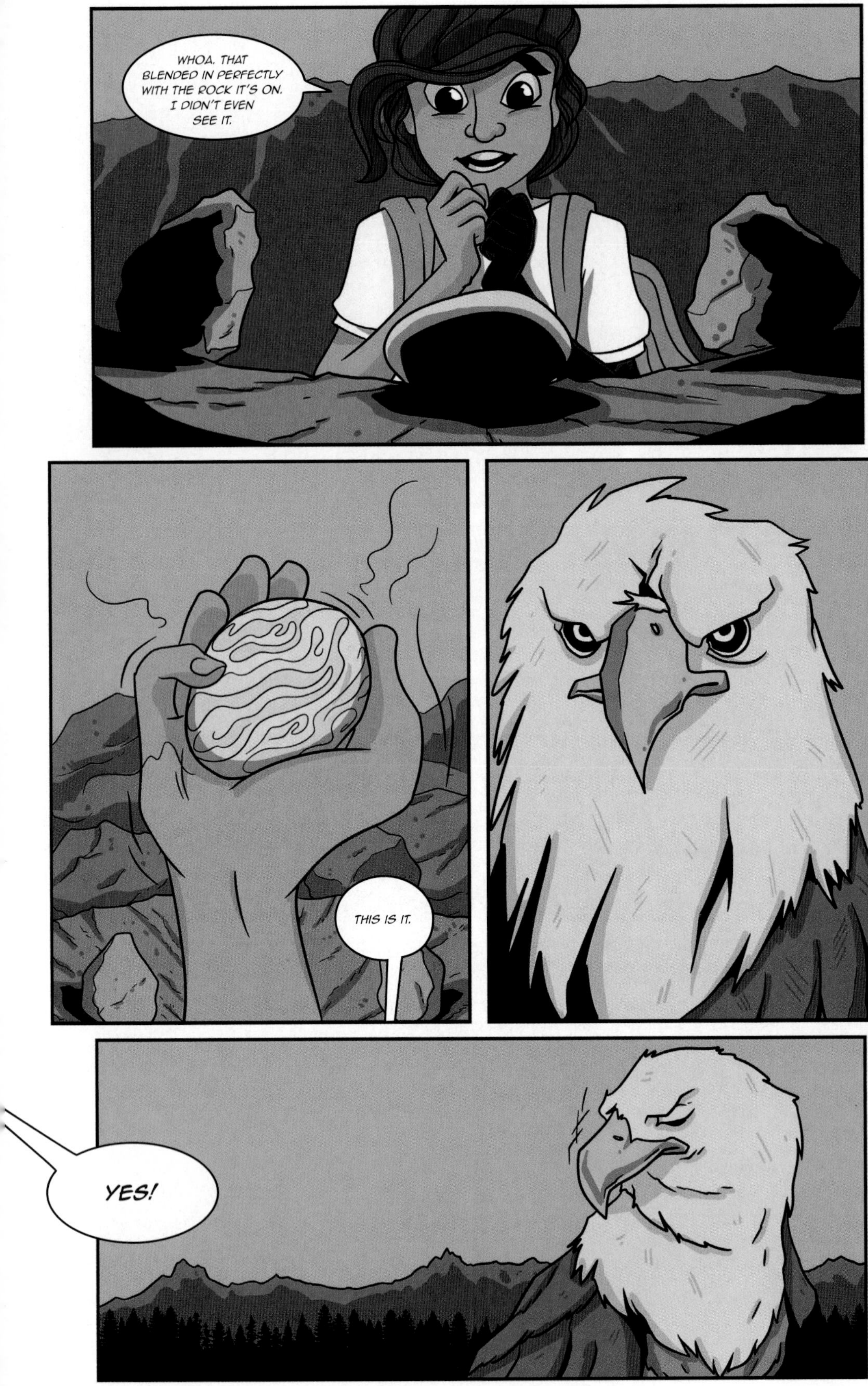
WHOA. THAT BLENDED IN PERFECTLY WITH THE ROCK IT'S ON. I DIDN'T EVEN SEE IT.
THIS IS IT.
YES!

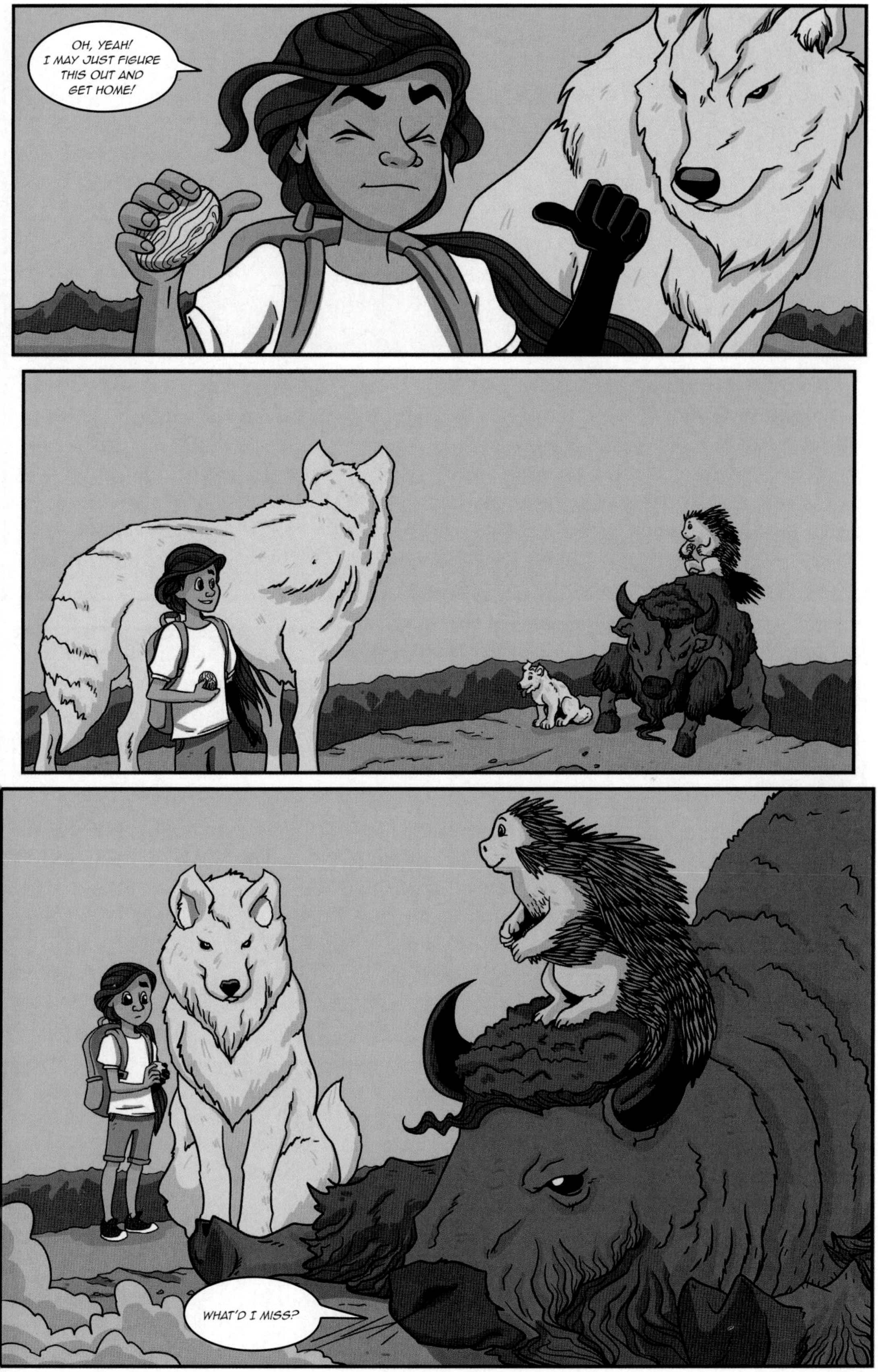
OH, YEAH! I MAY JUST FIGURE THIS OUT AND GET HOME!
WHAT'D I MISS?

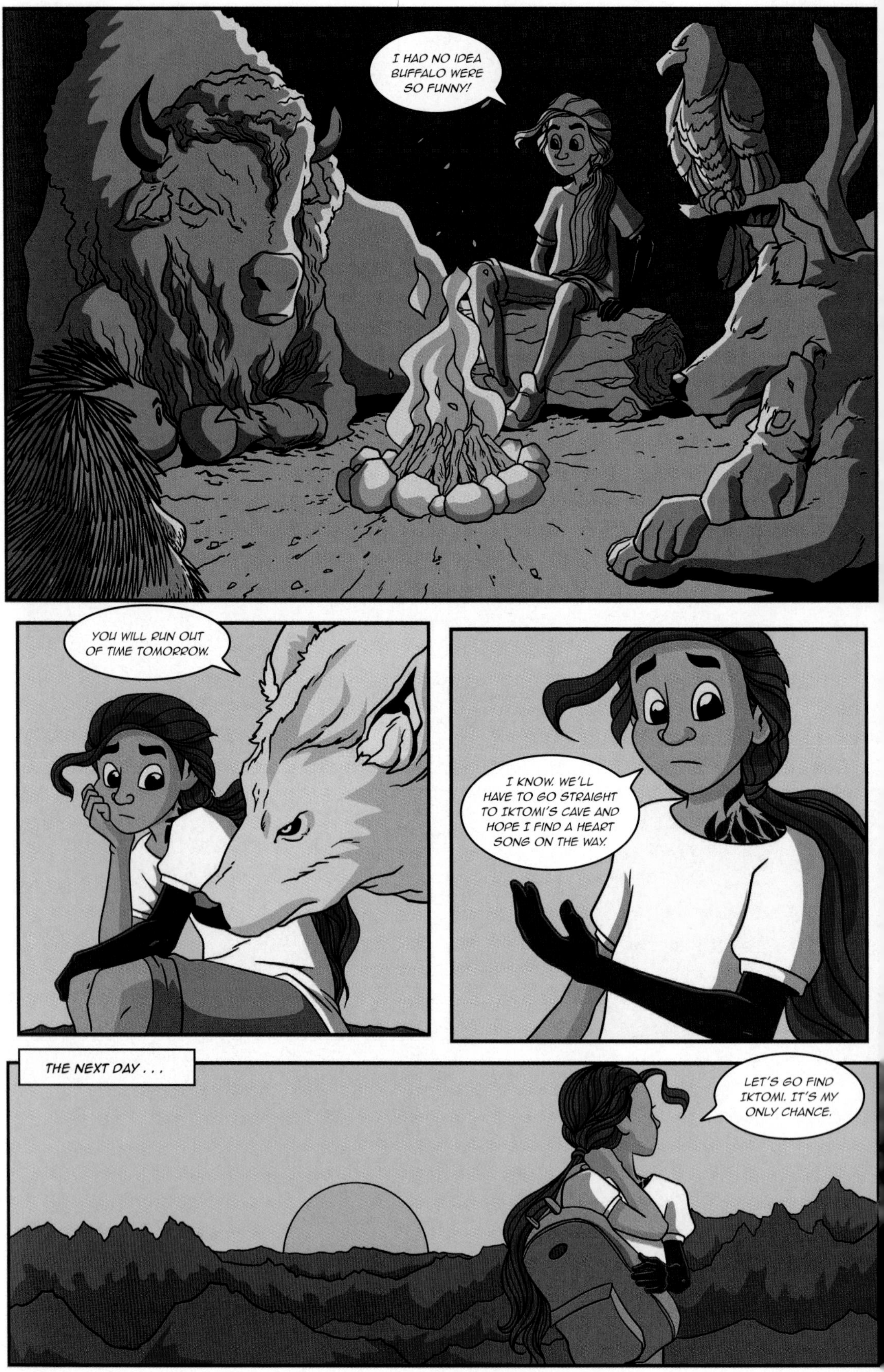
I HAD NO IDEA BUFFALO WERE SO FUNNY!
YOU WILL RUN OUT OF TIME TOMORROW.
I KNOW. WE'LL HAVE TO GO STRAIGHT TO IKTOMI'S CAVE AND HOPE I FIND A HEART SONG ON THE WAY.
THE NEXT DAY . . .
LET'S GO FIND IKTOMI. IT'S MY ONLY CHANCE.

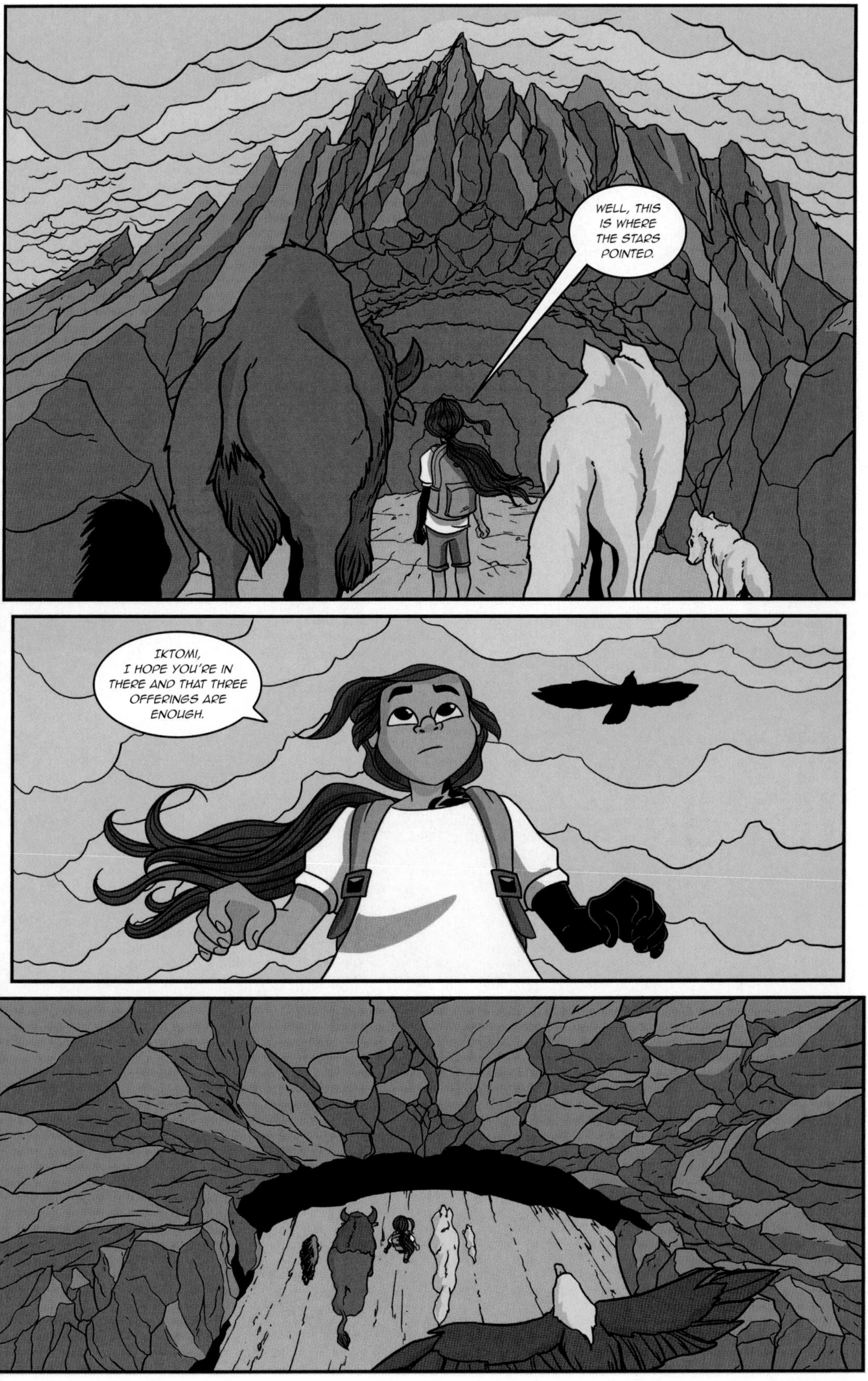
WELL, THIS IS WHERE THE STARS POINTED.
IKTOMI, I HOPE YOU'RE IN THERE AND THAT THREE OFFERINGS ARE ENOUGH.

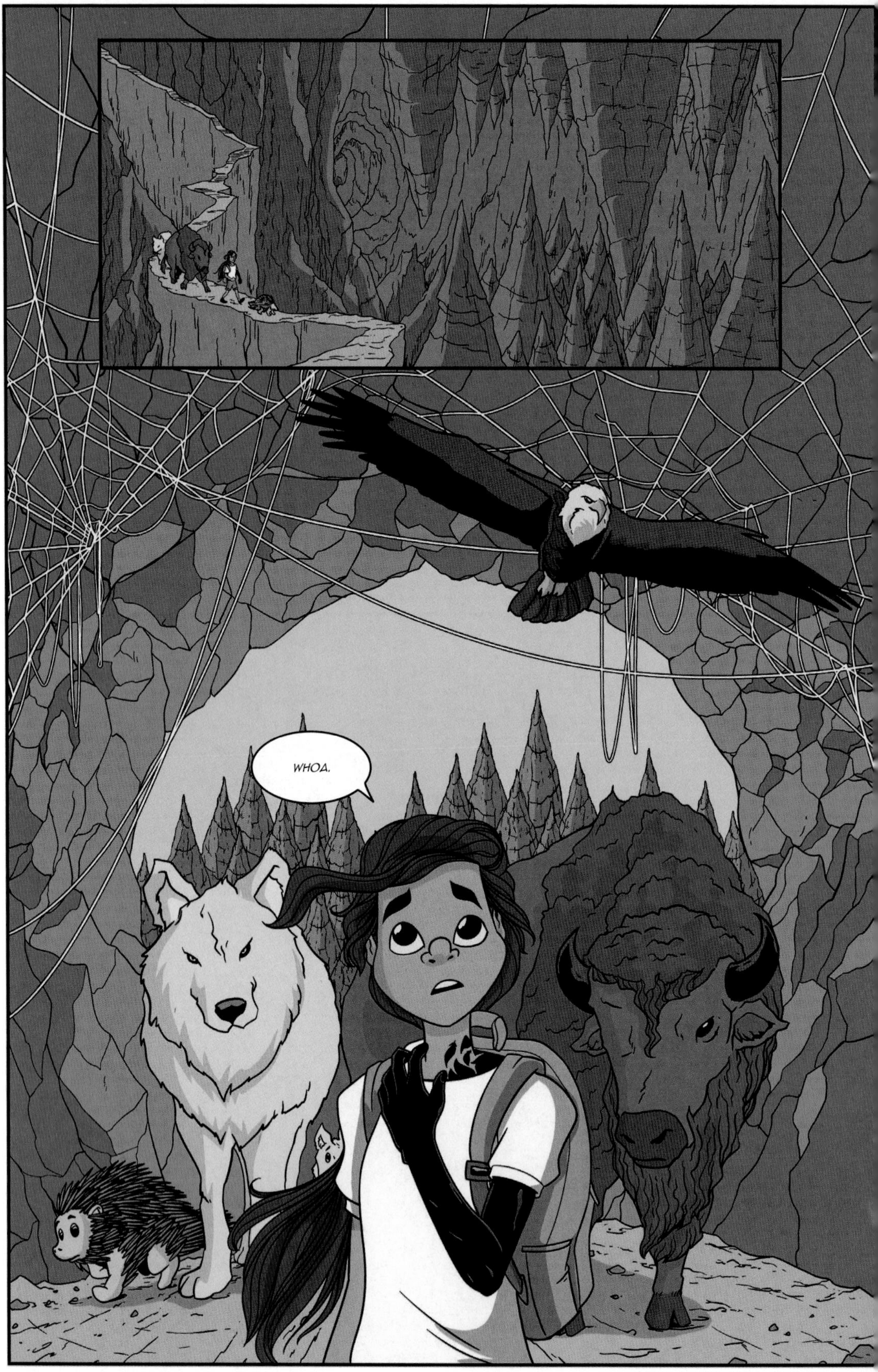
WHOA.

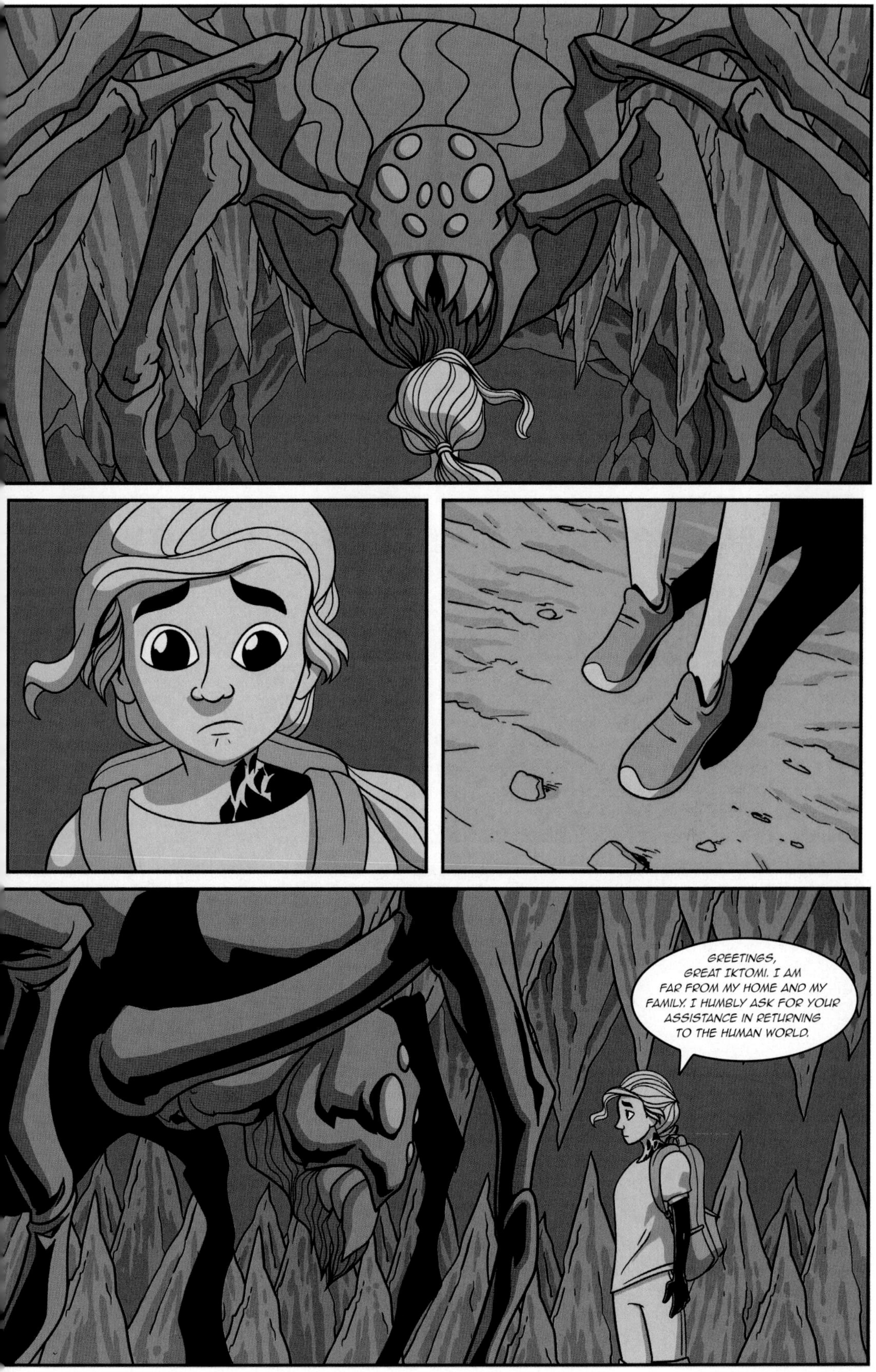
GREETINGS, GREAT IKTOMI. I AM FAR FROM MY HOME AND MY FAMILY. I HUMBLY ASK FOR YOUR ASSISTANCE IN RETURNING TO THE HUMAN WORLD.

I HAVE BROUGHT OFFERINGS.

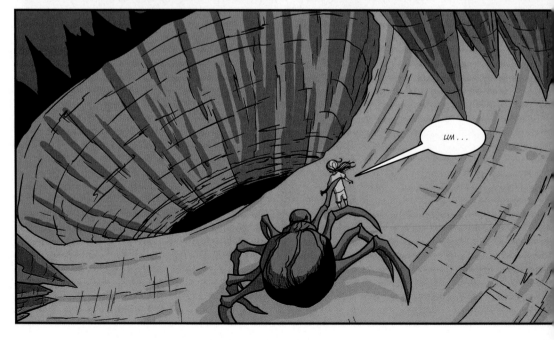

UM...

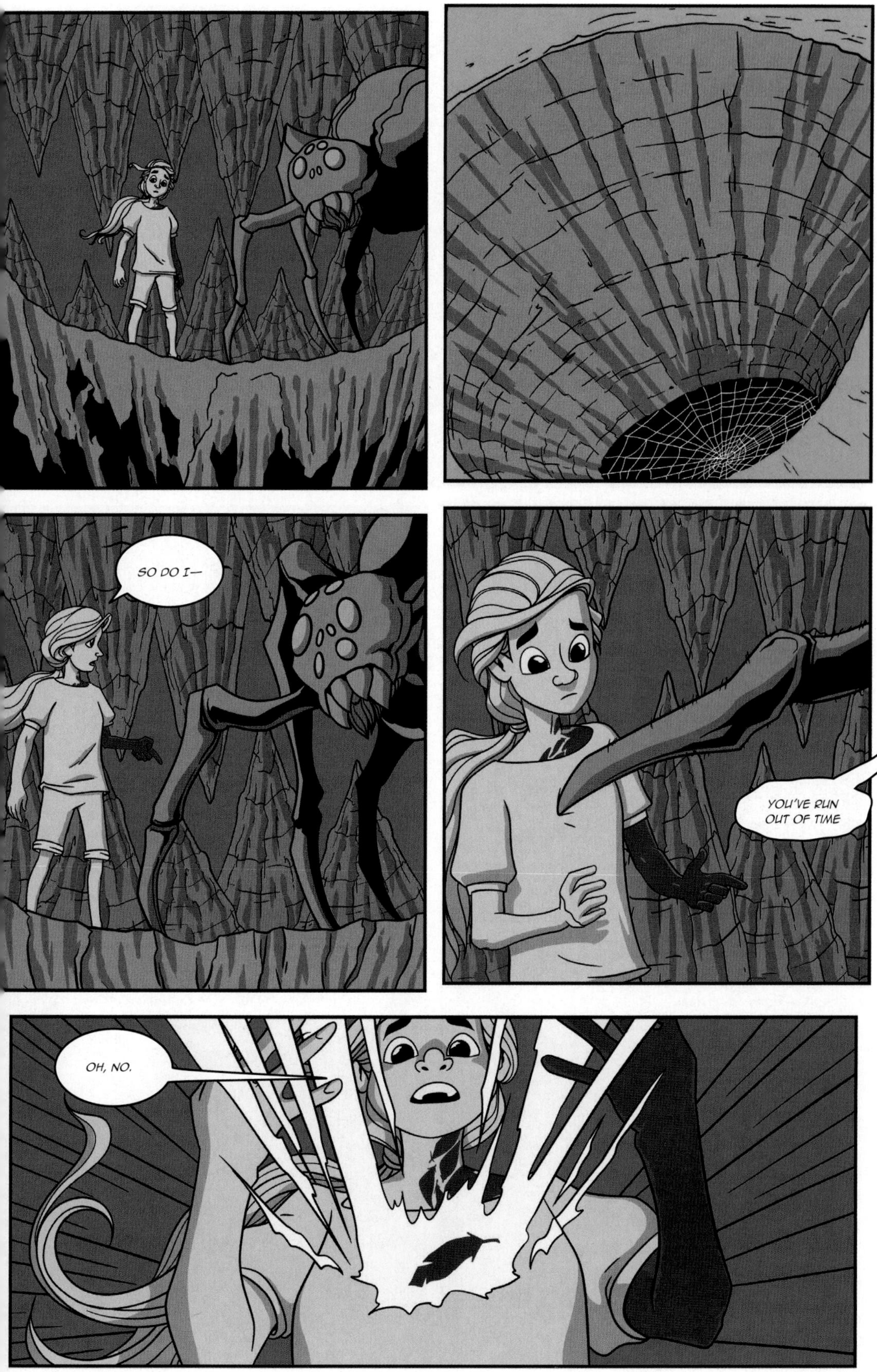
SO DO I—
YOU'VE RUN OUT OF TIME
OH, NO.

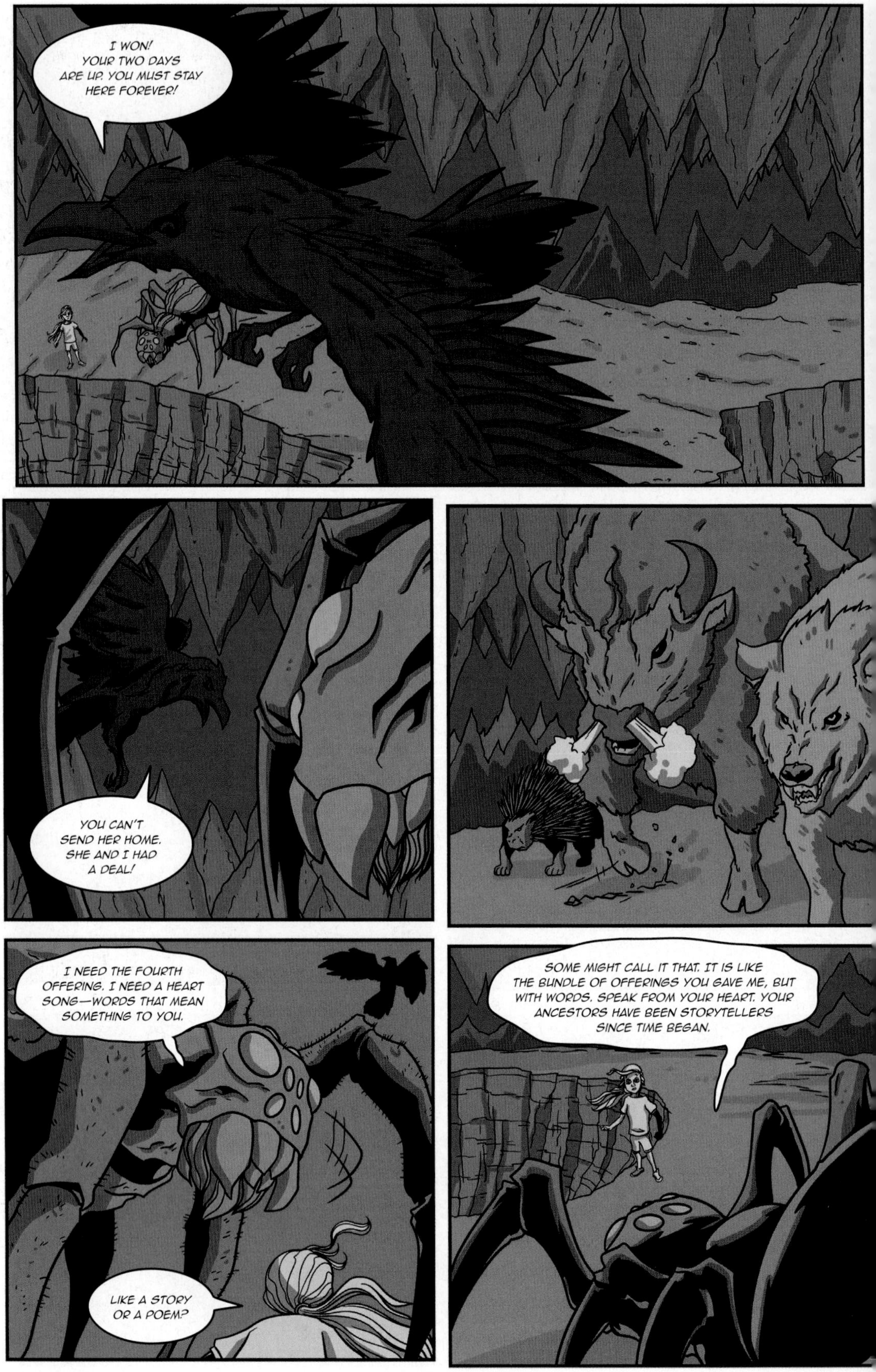
I WON! YOUR TWO DAYS ARE UP. YOU MUST STAY HERE FOREVER!
YOU CAN'T SEND HER HOME. SHE AND I HAD A DEAL!
I NEED THE FOURTH OFFERING. I NEED A HEART SONG—WORDS THAT MEAN SOMETHING TO YOU.
LIKE A STORY OR A POEM?
SOME MIGHT CALL IT THAT. IT IS LIKE THE BUNDLE OF OFFERINGS YOU GAVE ME, BUT WITH WORDS. SPEAK FROM YOUR HEART. YOUR ANCESTORS HAVE BEEN STORYTELLERS SINCE TIME BEGAN.

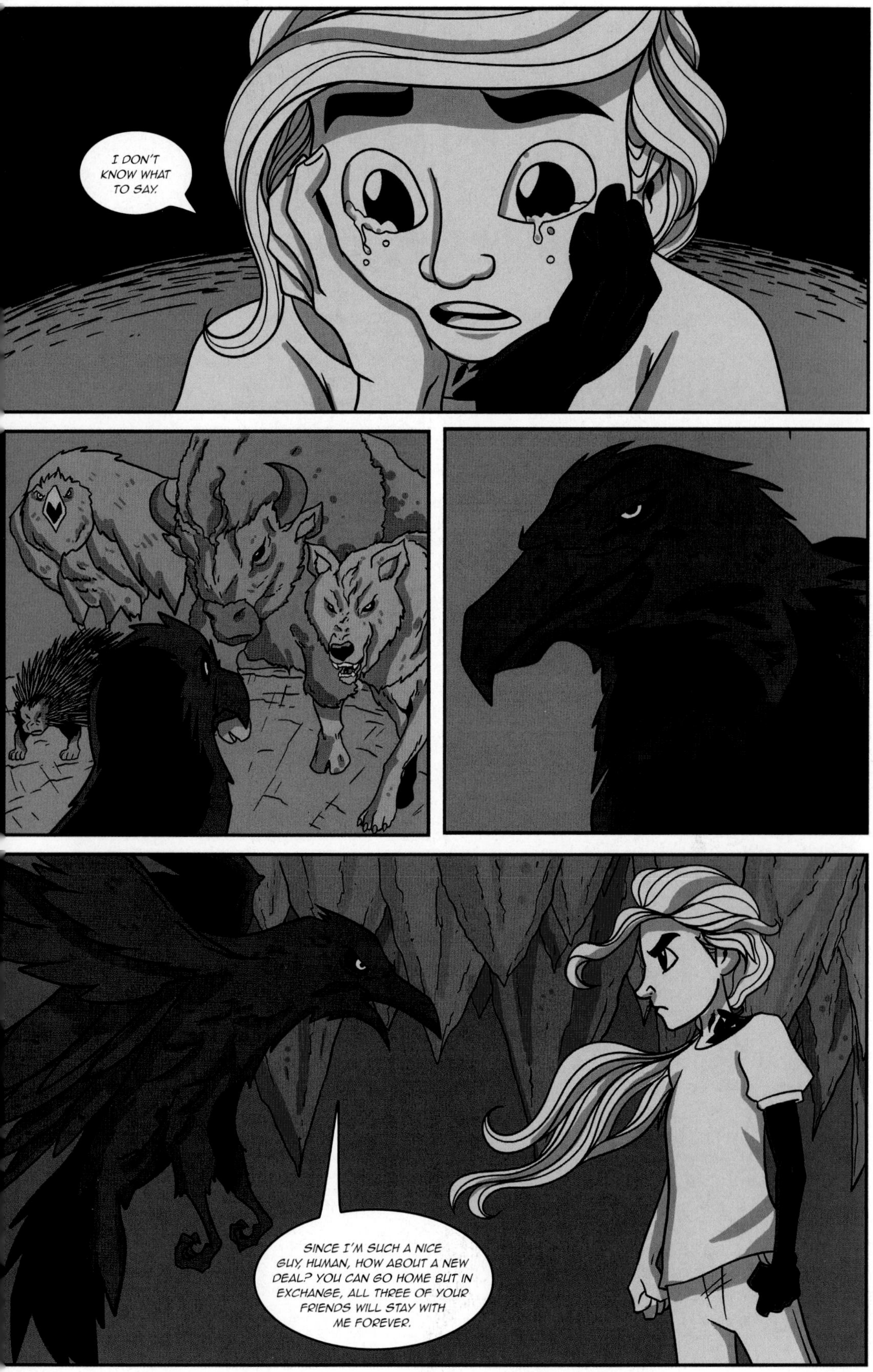
I DON'T KNOW WHAT TO SAY.
SINCE I'M SUCH A NICE GUY, HUMAN, HOW ABOUT A NEW DEAL? YOU CAN GO HOME BUT IN EXCHANGE, ALL THREE OF YOUR FRIENDS WILL STAY WITH ME FOREVER.

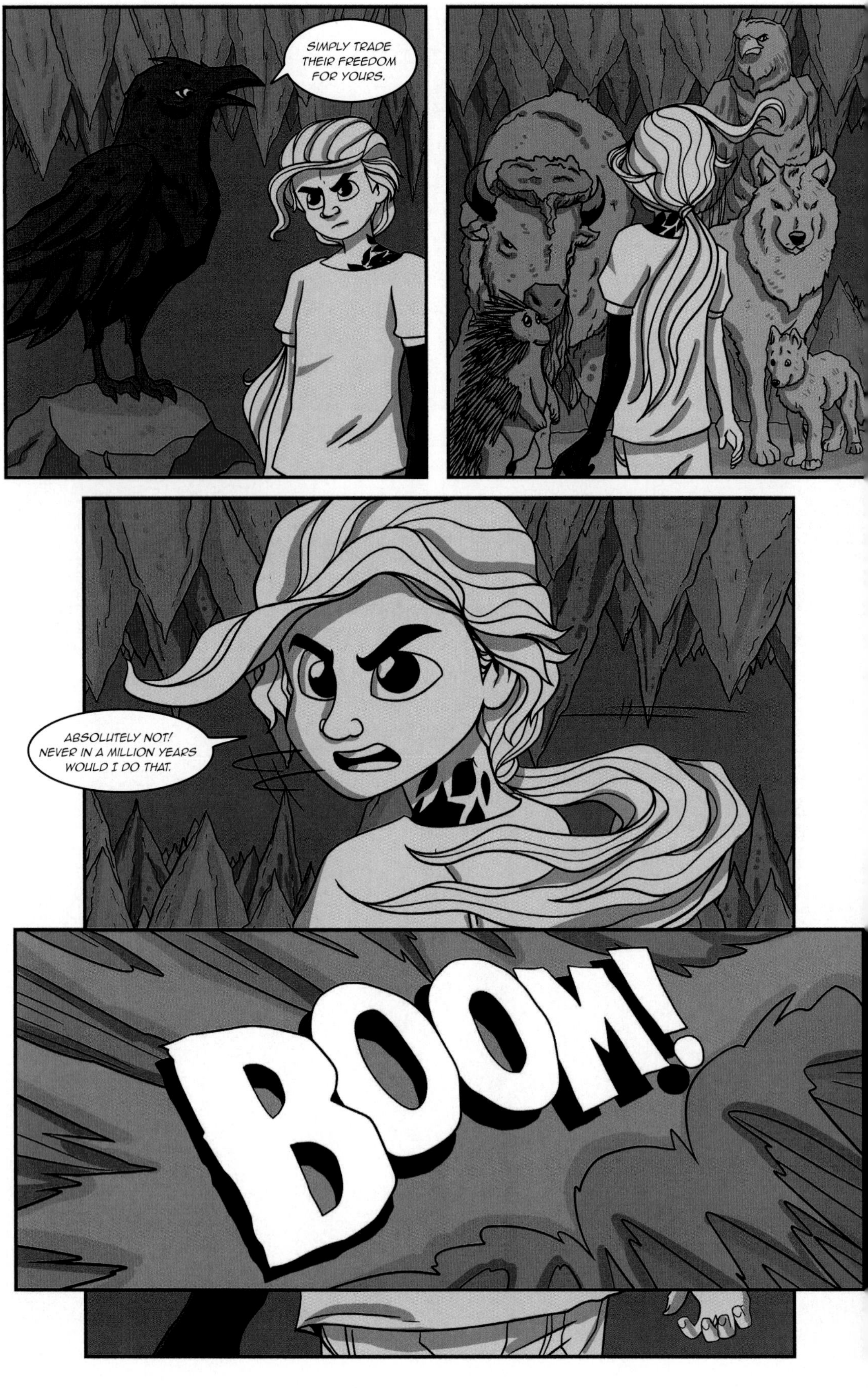
SIMPLY TRADE THEIR FREEDOM FOR YOURS.
ABSOLUTELY NOT! NEVER IN A MILLION YEARS WOULD I DO THAT.
BOOM!

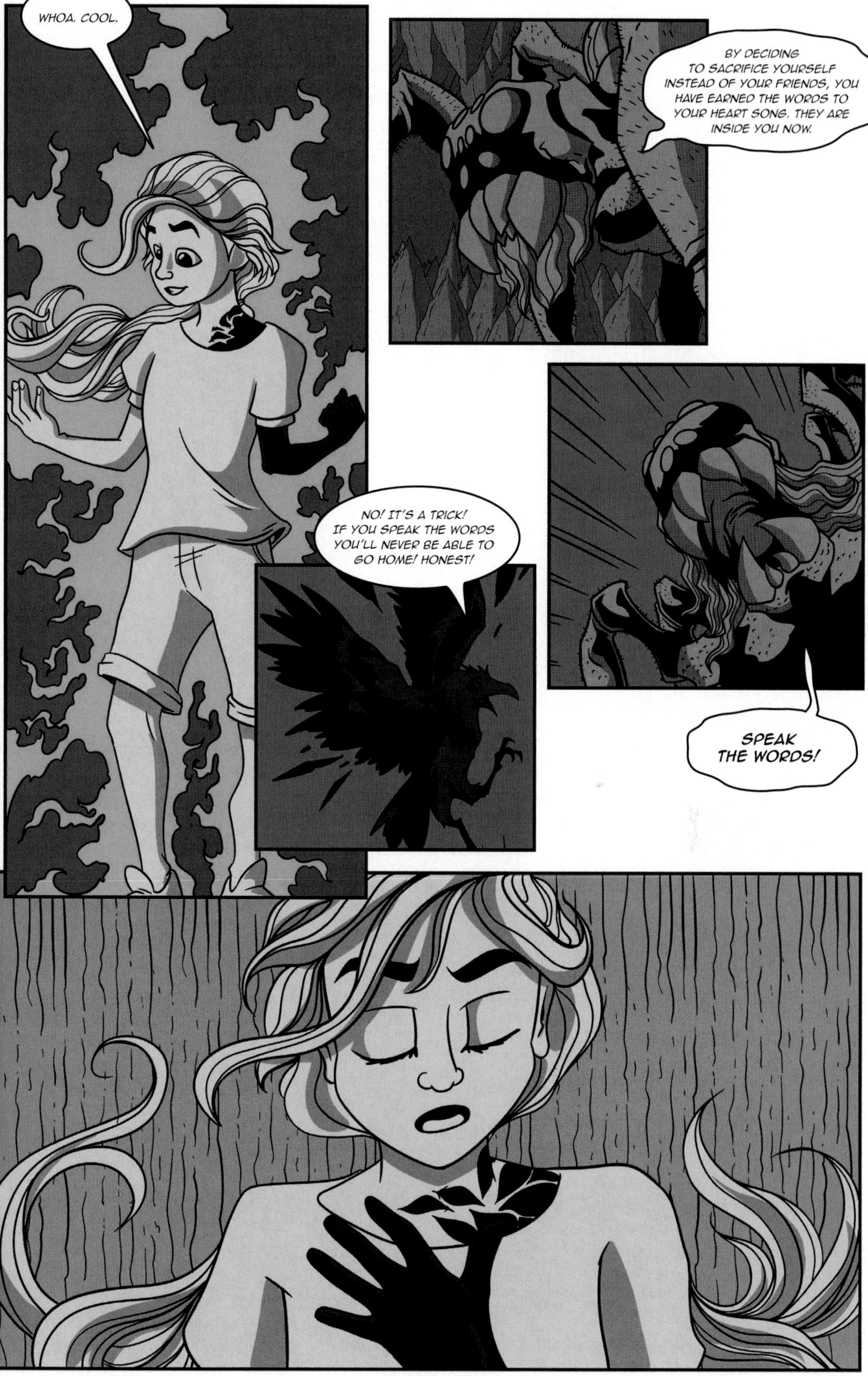
WHOA, COOL.
BY DECIDING TO SACRIFICE YOURSELF INSTEAD OF YOUR FRIENDS, YOU HAVE EARNED THE WORDS TO YOUR HEART SONG. THEY ARE INSIDE YOU NOW.
NO! IT'S A TRICK! IF YOU SPEAK THE WORDS YOU'LL NEVER BE ABLE TO GO HOME! HONEST!
SPEAK THE WORDS!

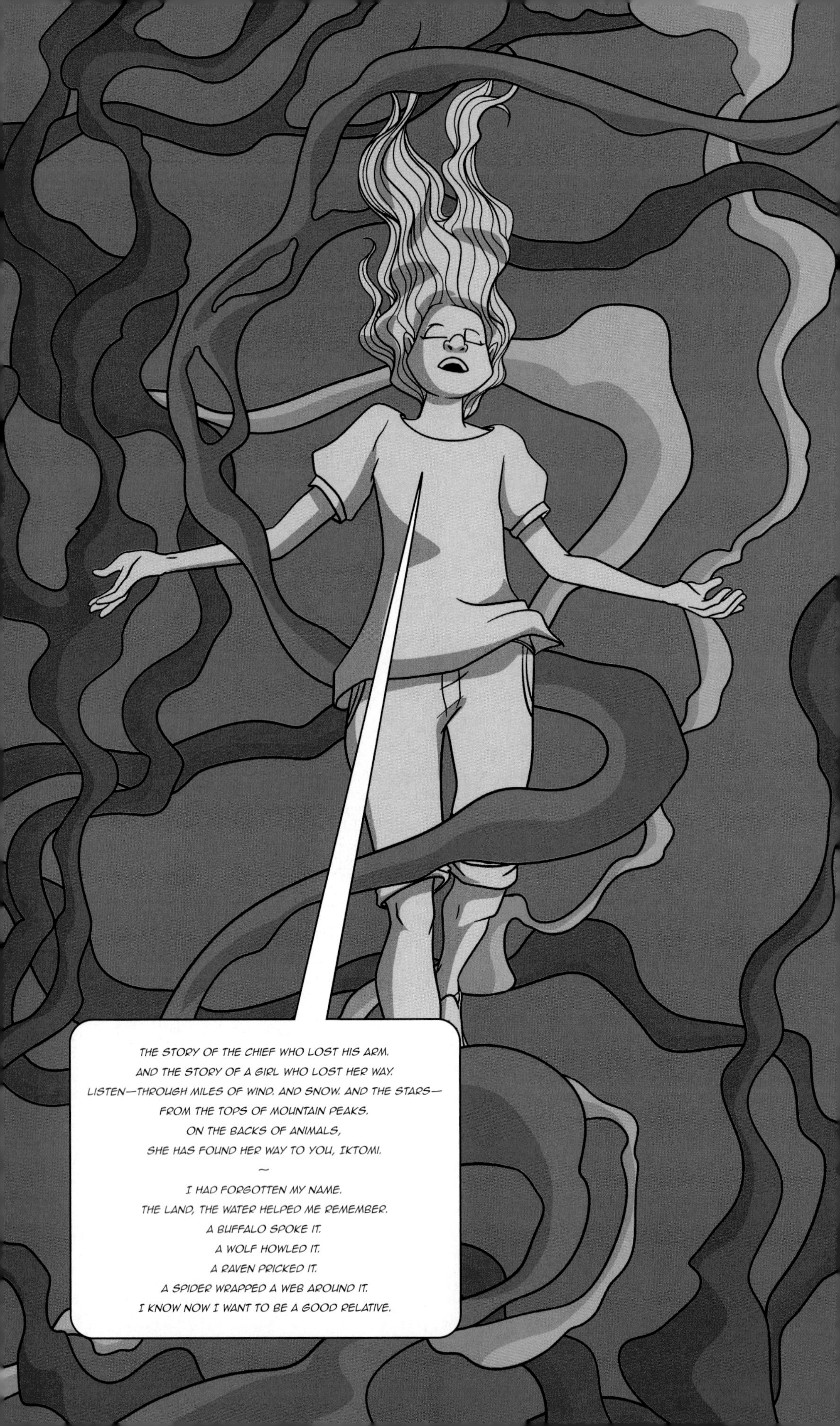
THE STORY OF THE CHIEF WHO LOST HIS ARM.
AND THE STORY OF A GIRL WHO LOST HER WAY.
LISTEN—THROUGH MILES OF WIND. AND SNOW. AND THE STARS—
FROM THE TOPS OF MOUNTAIN PEAKS.
ON THE BACKS OF ANIMALS,
SHE HAS FOUND HER WAY TO YOU, IKTOMI.
~
I HAD FORGOTTEN MY NAME.
THE LAND, THE WATER HELPED ME REMEMBER.
A BUFFALO SPOKE IT.
A WOLF HOWLED IT.
A RAVEN PRICKED IT.
A SPIDER WRAPPED A WEB AROUND IT.
I KNOW NOW I WANT TO BE A GOOD RELATIVE.

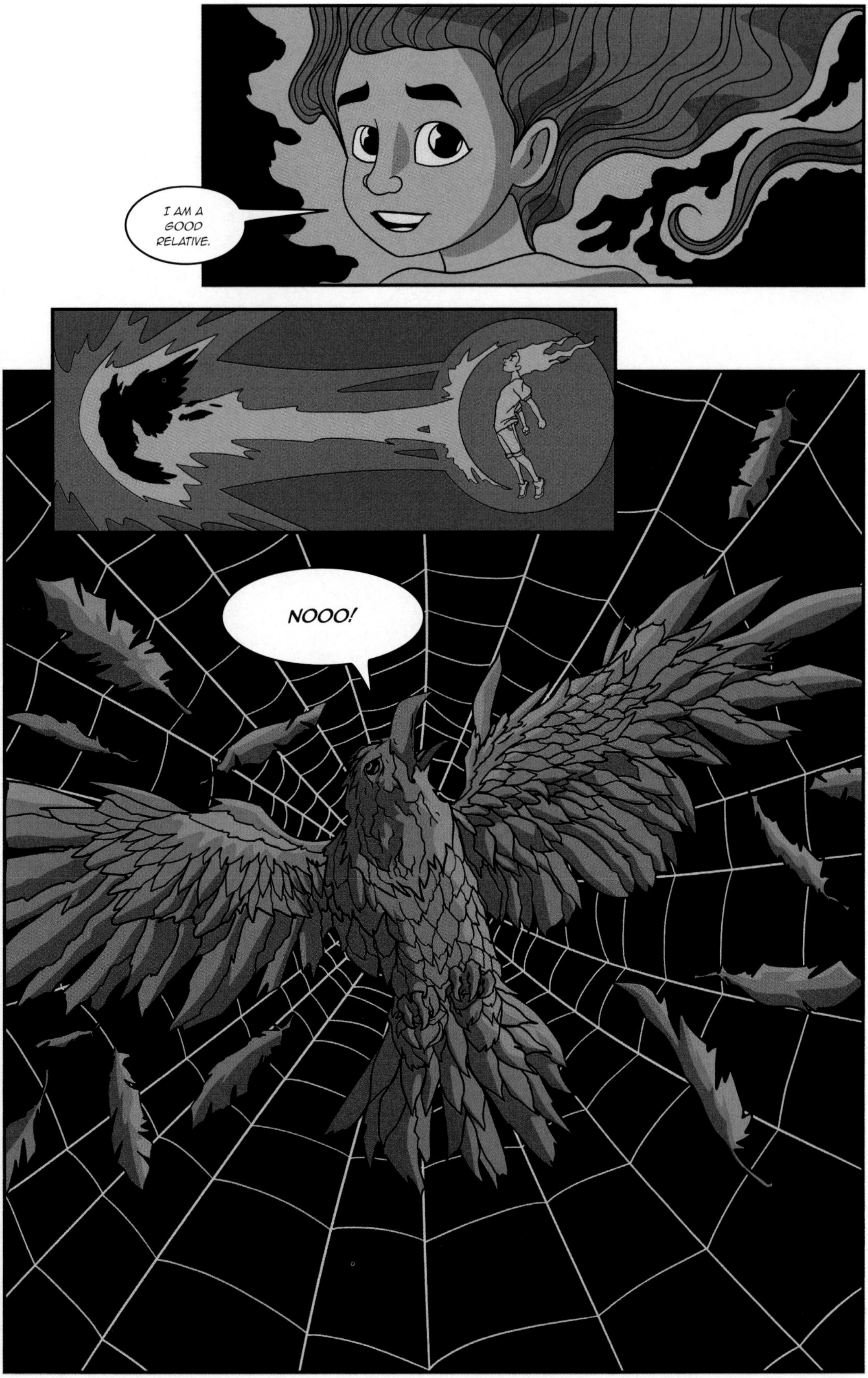
I AM A GOOD RELATIVE.
NOOO!

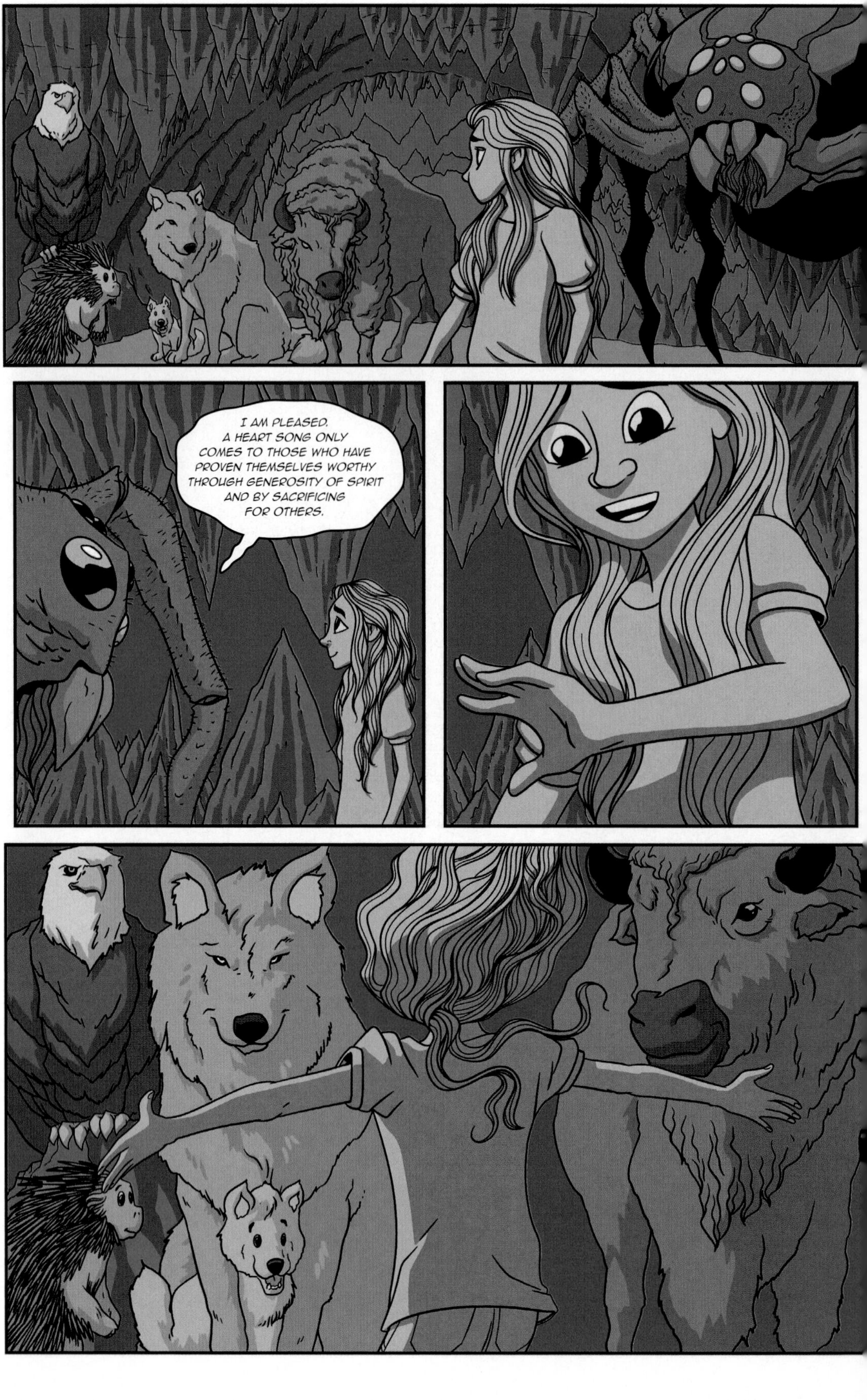
I AM PLEASED. A HEART SONG ONLY COMES TO THOSE WHO HAVE PROVEN THEMSELVES WORTHY THROUGH GENEROSITY OF SPIRIT AND BY SACRIFICING FOR OTHERS.

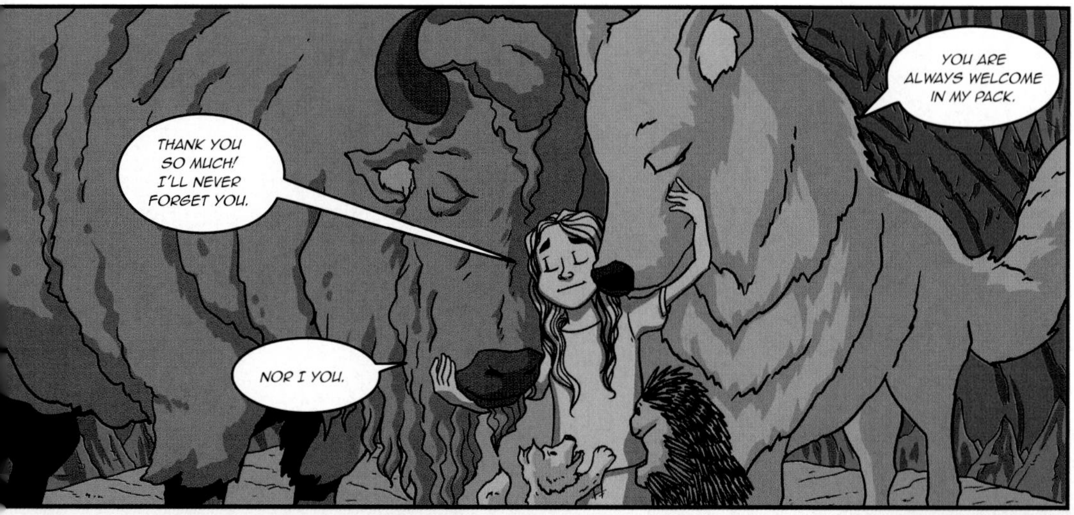
THANK YOU
SO MUCH!
I'LL NEVER
FORGET YOU.
YOU ARE
ALWAYS WELCOME
IN MY PACK.
NOR I YOU.

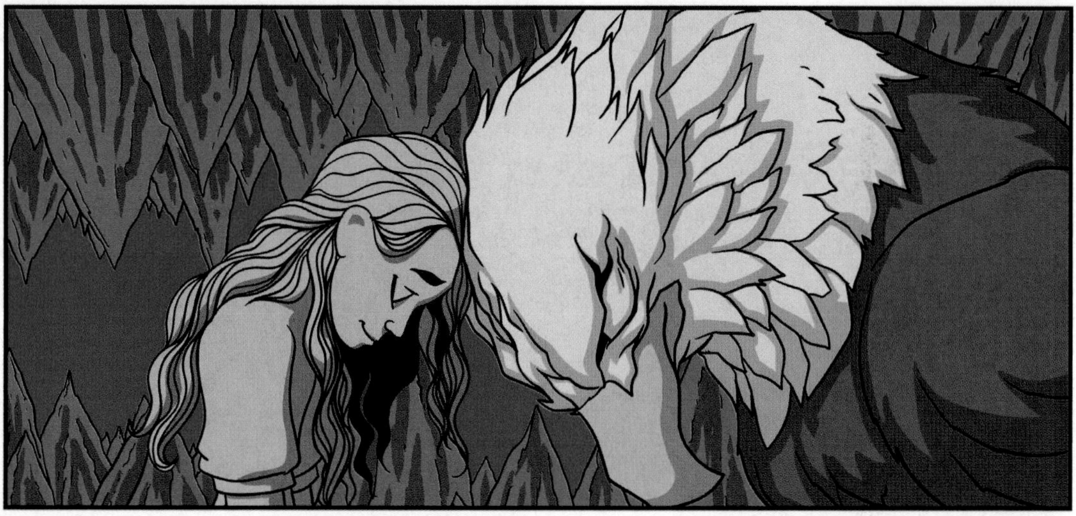

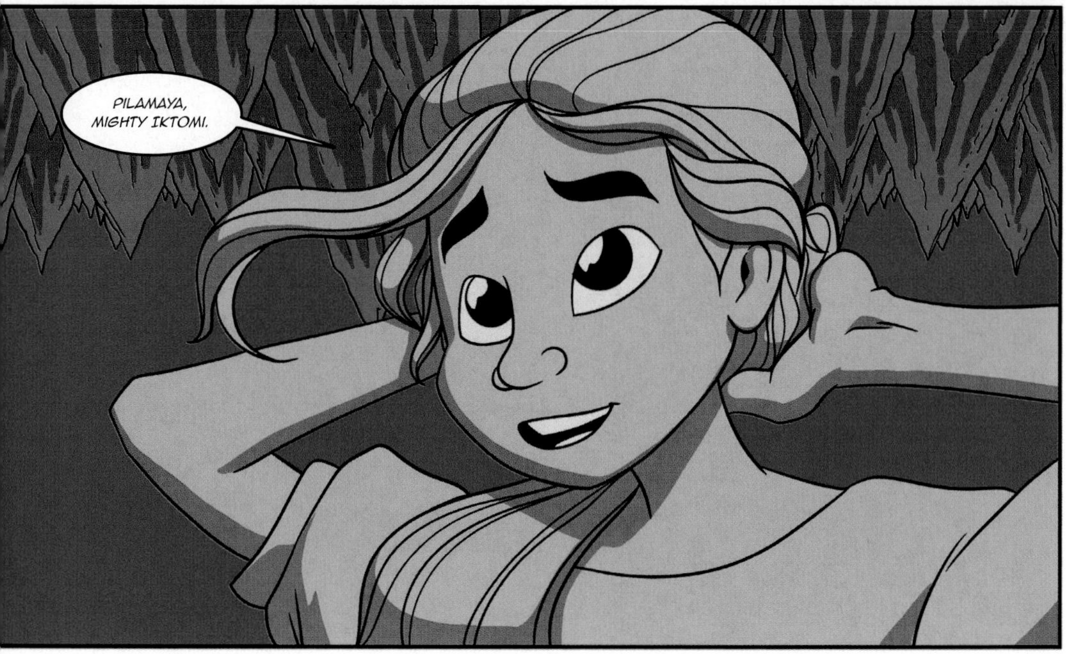
PILAMAYA,
MIGHTY IKTOMI.

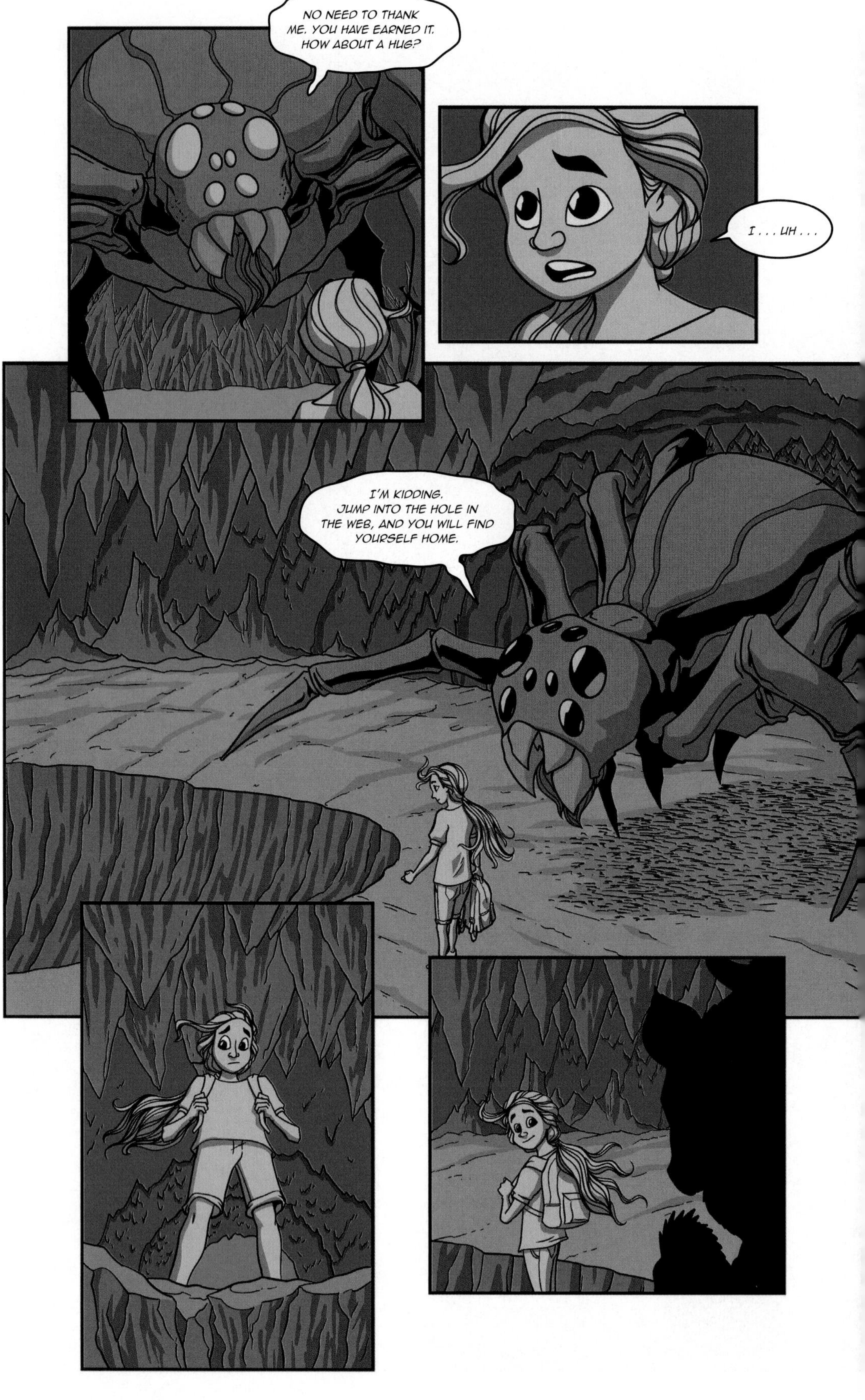
NO NEED TO THANK ME. YOU HAVE EARNED IT. HOW ABOUT A HUG?
I . . . UH . . .
I'M KIDDING. JUMP INTO THE HOLE IN THE WEB, AND YOU WILL FIND YOURSELF HOME.

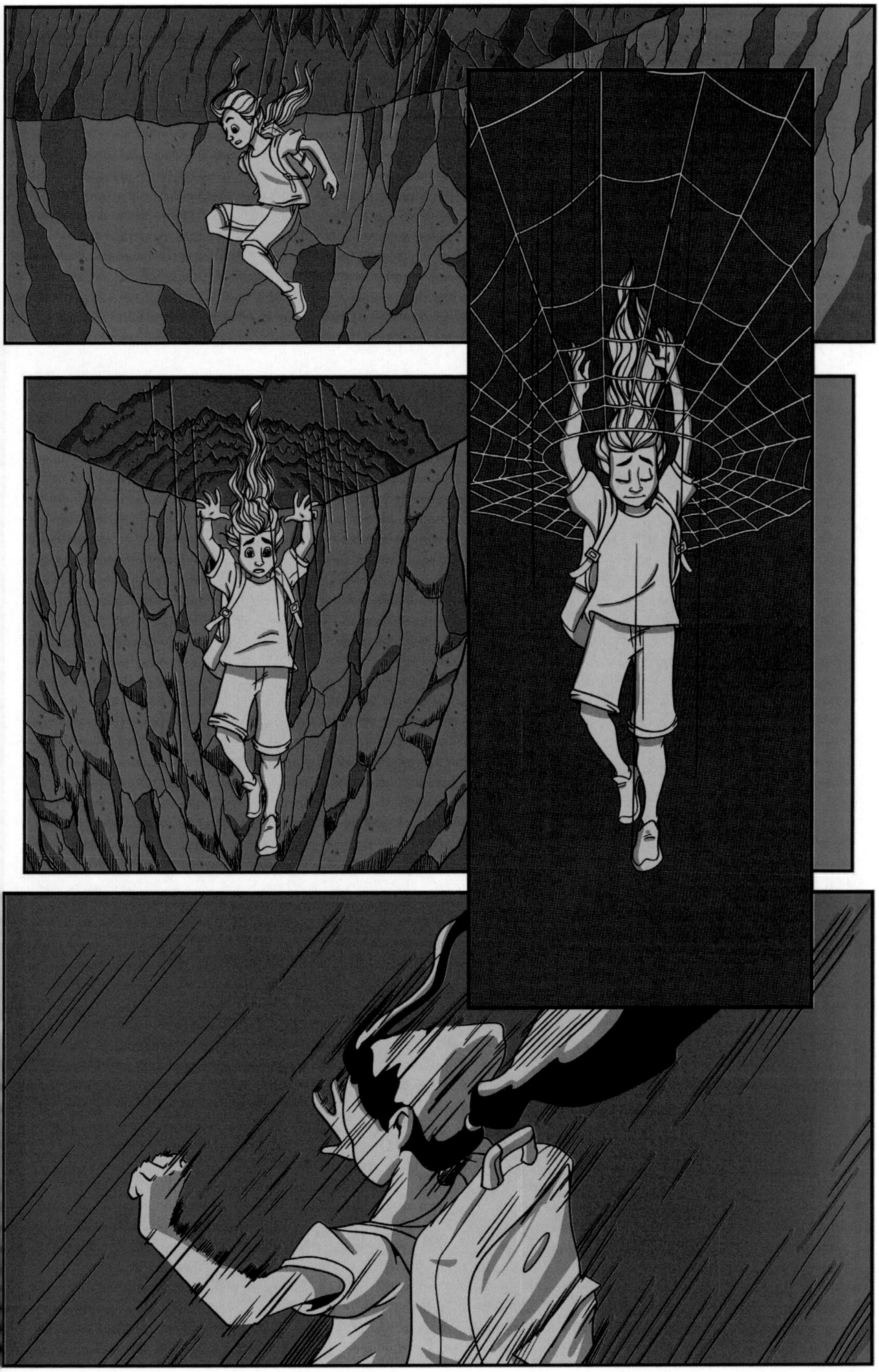

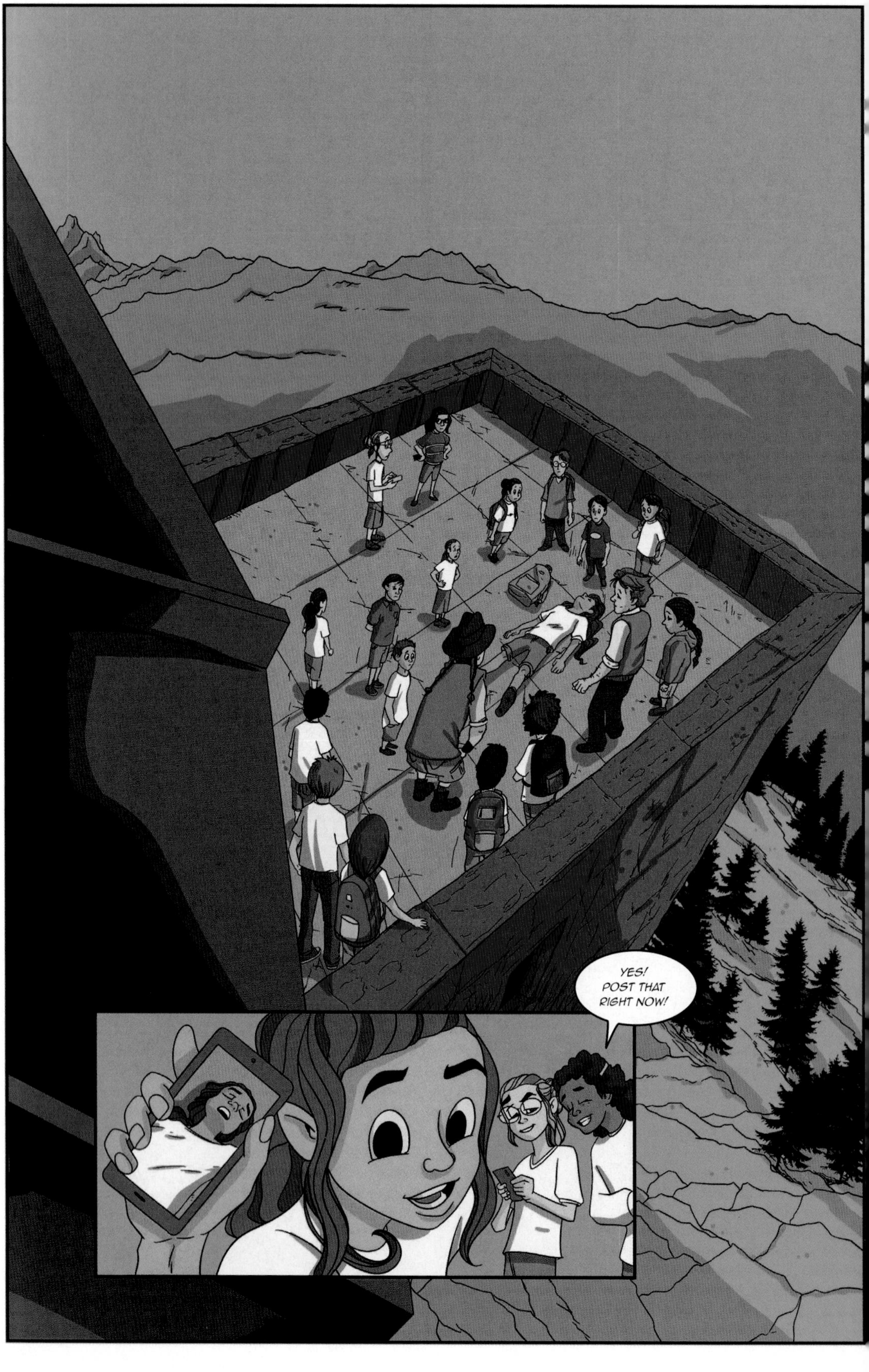
YES! POST THAT RIGHT NOW!

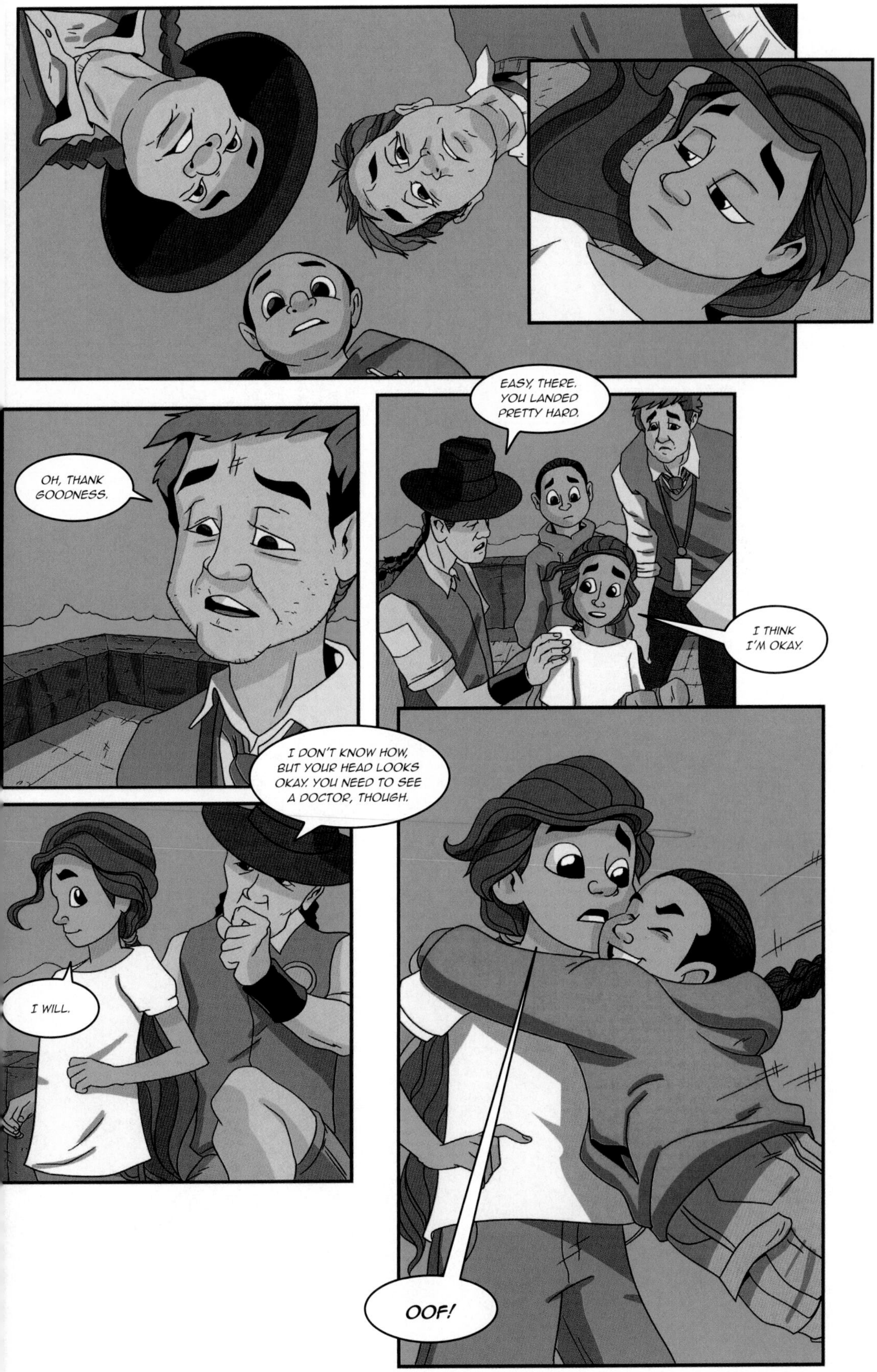
OH, THANK GOODNESS.
EASY, THERE. YOU LANDED PRETTY HARD.
I THINK I'M OKAY.
I DON'T KNOW HOW, BUT YOUR HEAD LOOKS OKAY. YOU NEED TO SEE A DOCTOR, THOUGH.
I WILL.
OOF!

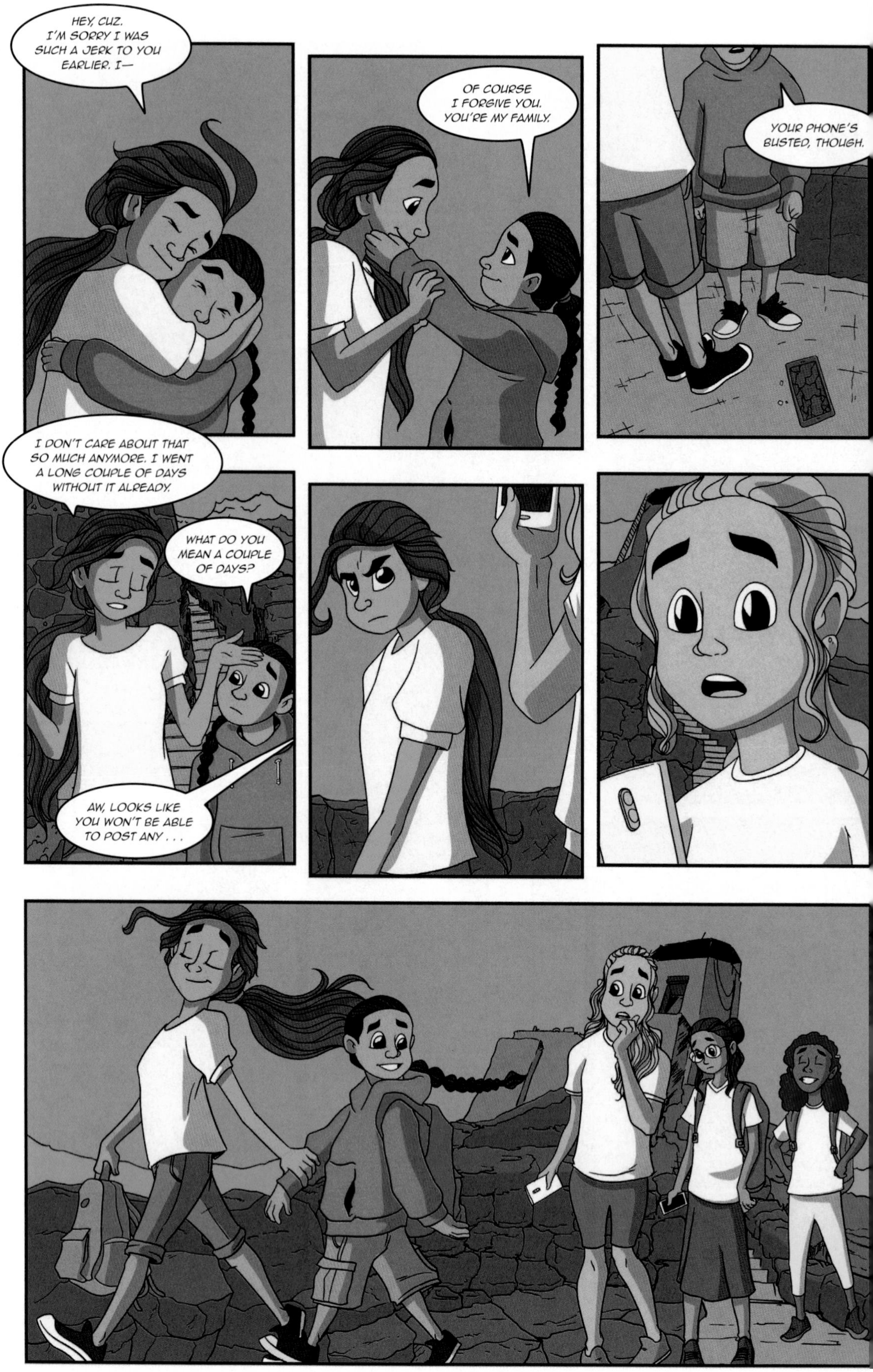
HEY, CUZ. I'M SORRY I WAS SUCH A JERK TO YOU EARLIER. I—
OF COURSE I FORGIVE YOU. YOU'RE MY FAMILY.
YOUR PHONE'S BUSTED, THOUGH.
I DON'T CARE ABOUT THAT SO MUCH ANYMORE. I WENT A LONG COUPLE OF DAYS WITHOUT IT ALREADY.
WHAT DO YOU MEAN A COUPLE OF DAYS?
AW, LOOKS LIKE YOU WON'T BE ABLE TO POST ANY . . .

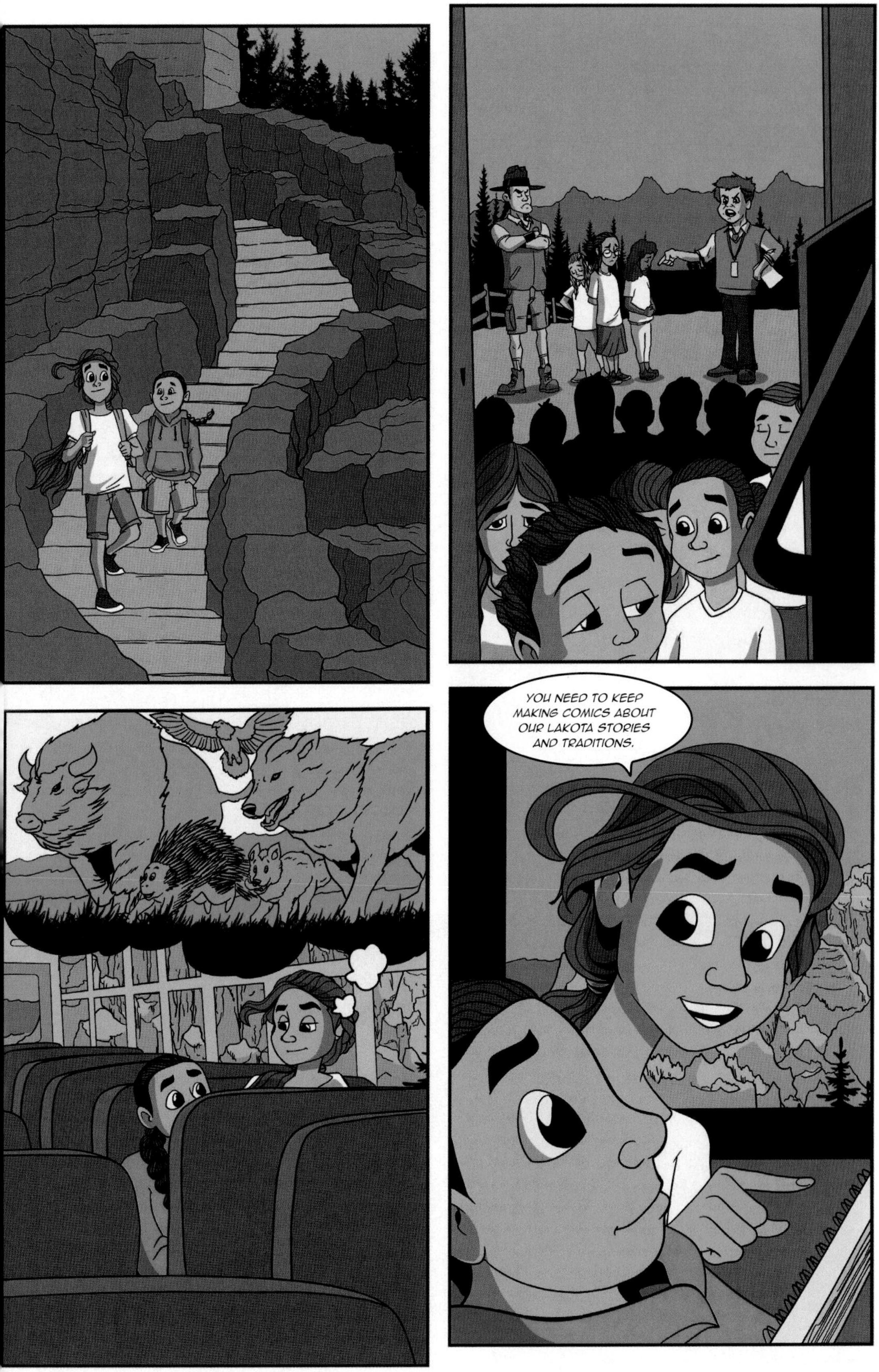
YOU NEED TO KEEP MAKING COMICS ABOUT OUR LAKOTA STORIES AND TRADITIONS.

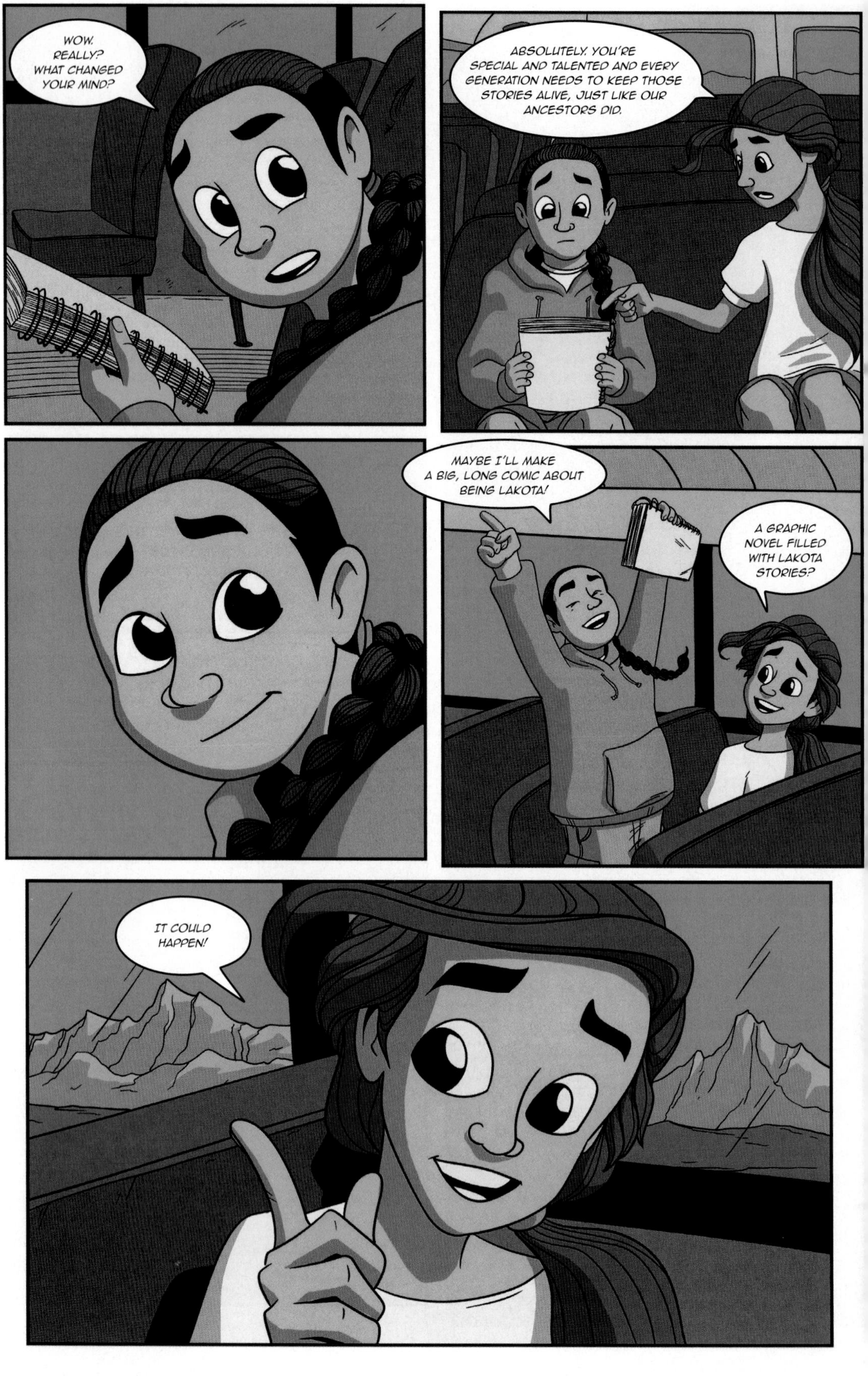
WOW. REALLY? WHAT CHANGED YOUR MIND?
ABSOLUTELY. YOU'RE SPECIAL AND TALENTED AND EVERY GENERATION NEEDS TO KEEP THOSE STORIES ALIVE, JUST LIKE OUR ANCESTORS DID.
MAYBE I'LL MAKE A BIG, LONG COMIC ABOUT BEING LAKOTA!
A GRAPHIC NOVEL FILLED WITH LAKOTA STORIES?
IT COULD HAPPEN!

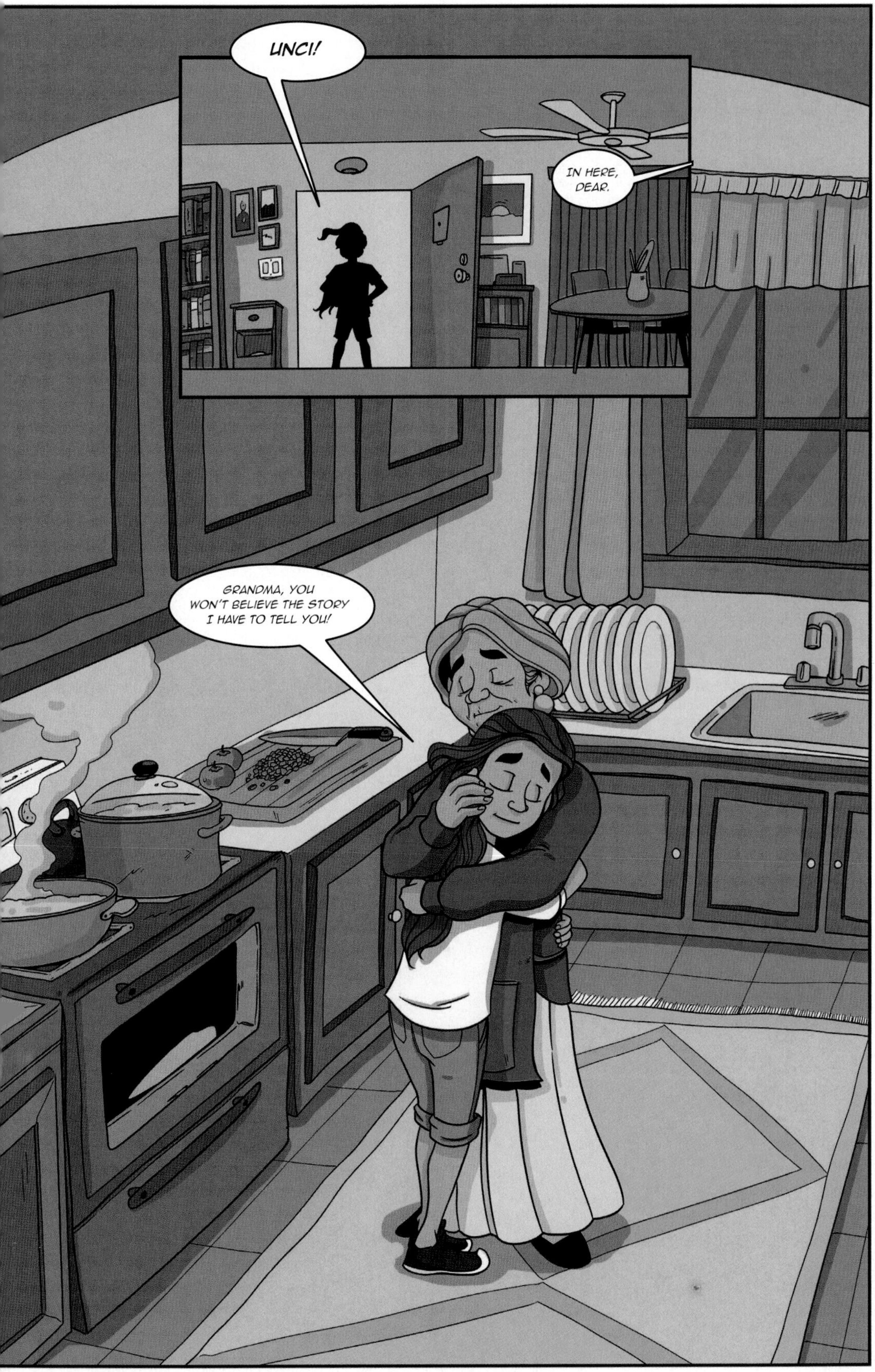
UNCI!
IN HERE, DEAR.
GRANDMA, YOU WON'T BELIEVE THE STORY I HAVE TO TELL YOU!

DEDICATION AND ACKNOWLEDGMENTS

For our children:
Dezmond, Erica, Adela, Magdalena and Daniel.

We would like to thank Mato Standing High
for his inspiration, support and thoughtful
considerations in bringing Aiyana's story to life.

Additionally, special thanks to Jeremy Red Eagle.